The Shape Of New Beginnings

DOELIZA

STARFISH CITY PUBLISHING

Starfish City Publishing

401 Pine St, St. Louis, MO 63102

starfishcitypublishing.com

Cover created by GetCovers

ISBNs: 9781732720312 (paperback), 9781732720329 (Kindle), 9781732720336 (ebook)

First Edition

Contents

Two Grandiose Parties

(OR AT LEAST ONE)

"You ready for this, baby?" I ask as I stand in my walk-in closet.

I turn on the spotlight and pose before it, producing a silhouette on my strawberry-colored curtains. I prefer curtains over doors. They're easier to open, and you can never get locked out or—even worse—locked in.

I slowly slide the curtains to the left, revealing the sexy new six-piece lingerie set I recently bought from the boutique down the street. The way the lace hugs me has me appreciating my new curves differently. Whenever I wear new underwear, I fall more in love with my shape.

I playfully bite my left index finger while my face tries its best to make the seductive vixen expression I see influencers make all the time on social media. I've grown to embrace my sexy side more.

I place my right hand on my thigh and watch as it slowly reaches my panties, tracing the random circular patterns in the lace. Then, across my stomach, my fingers dance on my navel ring. Finally, it makes its way to my breast, cupping and lightly squeezing each before sliding my bra straps gently off my shoulders.

I finally step out of my closet and do a little pose—you know, the one where both arms are folded above my head? The one where my head isn't facing head-on but pivoted to the right, my nose almost touching my armpit? Yes, that one!

I finish the look by squinting my eyes, tensing my face, and slightly opening my mouth.

I break my pose with a slight moan before walking seductively to my bed, slowly removing a piece of my lingerie with each strut. I get a glimpse of my long legs in the side mirror, halfway between my bed and my closet. My heels are in rhythm as they hit the wooden floor. Just before getting to the bed, I strike a pose, this time fiercer and absolutely no smiling.

With my hands on my hip, I ask, "Can you handle this, Apollo?"

On the bed sits an eight-inch vibrating dildo. Its brown head is throbbing so violently that I hope the concoction of belts and scarves I used to secure it can hold it steady while I enjoy it. The lube gives its thick shaft and realistic veins a gloss. Of all my toys, Apollo is my favorite.

I slide off my remaining piece of lingerie: my panties. A smirk comes across my face as I check out my handy trimming work—a perfectly shaped heart in my pubic hair.

I hop on the bed, burying my knees in my mattress, my pussy hovering over Apollo. I slowly descend, relaxing my body in preparation for the throbbing head.

"Destiny!" I hear Mama yell from downstairs. I faintly hear the front door close and the clicks from her heels.

I rush to throw on jogging pants and a T-shirt and shout, "Coming!"

"I got you something! I couldn't wait to show you. Get down here!"

I struggle to free the dildo from the belts and scarves. Ugh, I really need to invest in some kind of harness for this thing. Once free, I throw the toy in a drawer and rush to the bathroom to clean my hands of the slippery lubricant. I take a few seconds to check myself out in the mirror before heading down the stairs.

"Ma'am?"

Mama is sitting on the chair holding a Mochacours dust bag. "Guess what I got you!"

My eyes light up, and I curiously walk toward her. "What did you get me?"

"Look!" she says with a giant grin, her open hands framing the bag.

I rush to open the bag and reach inside. I pull out a cherry red backpack with a gold Mochacours emblem attached to the front. I jump up and down a few times before hugging her.

"Thank you so much!" I say.

"Now you can walk around your new college campus in style! I got it because of that Dollarstar song."

We start bobbing and rapping, "Look at you dating all those fours. My chick only wears Mochacours."

"Thank you, thank you, thank you! I have to call Erika!" I turn to run back upstairs to my room.

"Not so fast," Mama stops me. "You need to get ready. I just found out that Antoine's surprise party is tonight. We had to make your dinner party earlier to make it to his party on time. We're leaving in an hour."

"But I was going to go hang out with Erika today. I already—"

"No ifs, ands, or buts! There is no way you are missing your cousin's party," Mama interrupts.

"Yes, ma'am."

I head back up the stairs to prepare for my cousin's party. You would think that since I'm nineteen, I could decide where to go. But no. I call Erika to relay the bad news.

"Ahh, girl, that sucks!" Erika says, her voice dropping.

"Girl, I know, right? Shouldn't I, as an adult, be able to decide where I want to spend my time?"

"Exactly! I'm going through the same shit with my mama. She is so controlling," Erika growls.

"Girl, tell me about it, even in conversation. It's 'watch your tone' this. 'Your attitude' that. I can't even cuss, not in person, not online. It's always the radio version of shit too. Like no mama, it's 'my bitch only wears Mochacours,' not chick! There are no chickens here!"

"I actually prefer that they replace bitch. It is so disrespectful."

"That's not the point, and I do not feel like getting into a feminist discussion right now!" I say a little more aggressively than I mean.

"You're right. Let me stop derailing. But yeah, being an adult who still lives with their parents suck. That is exactly why I can't wait to leave for college. We'll be Qousa women and dorm room living in a bit, girl. Just hold out a little longer."

"Dorm room living at two different universities," I reply with a cracking voice. I press the speakerphone button and toss the phone on my bed. I look at potential outfits for the night out. "Why are you going to that hueless ass school anyway?"

"I don't know," she laughs. "I visited the school, and I just fit in, you know? I like the diversity!"

"Girl, black people make up seven percent of the student body! That ain't hardly diverse!"

"Well, going to a school where ninety percent of the population is black isn't diverse either. Besides, diversity is more than just race."

"Okay, if you say so, girl," I tell her as I look at the three dresses I've laid on my bed. All of the chosen dresses are summer styles with flower patterns but in different colors. "Video chat me real quick. I need your help picking a dress!"

I press the video button on my phone, and my friend's beautiful face pops up. I first notice her daffodil-painted eyelids, which she matches with a bronze blush and nude lips.

"Girl, your makeup is gorgeous," I say.

"Thanks, boo."

I flip the camera and slowly go over each of the dresses. "Which one?"

"You know red is my favorite color, but I'm feeling that pink halter one more. I think the pink dress fits more for the occasion. And you know DL in pink is a baddie! You might be able to pull one of Antoine's friends."

"Girl, stop! You know damn well that isn't the type of time I'm on."

"Don't judge. One of his friends could be a real winner."

"Eww. Never in a million years!"

"I'm just messing with ya, DL," she says affectionately.

"Girl, when are you going to stop with the DL? That was so long ago!" I say, rolling my eyes.

"Never in a million years," she mocks. "That will always be my nickname for you."

"Just wait 'til I come up with one for you. Just wait." I questionably hold up the pink dress. Erika's quip about my cousin's friends has me second-guessing wearing the dress for the evening. But she is right about two things: the dress is perfect for the occasion, and I am a Bad B in pink.

I tuck the other dresses away and pull out some shoes to match the dress. I flip my phone camera so she can see my face again.

"I'm still sad that we won't see each other for a whole year."

"At least we got to spend our gap year together," she says, trying to comfort me about our impending separation. The video breaks up, and we are back to voice chat only. "We'll still see each other during school breaks."

"Backpacking was dope," I say, smiling, reflecting on our year exploring Europe. "I just don't understand, girl. How are you going to find a man at that university? I mean—"

"Oh shit," she says. "My little brother's father is here to pick him up."

"Which one?"

"Girl, Aj's."

"He is a trip."

"Tell me about it. Complains about child support all day on social media and randomly shows up at the house every few months for a visit. And if we're not home when he does his pop-ups, he calls it a missed opportunity."

"A straight clown."

"Girl, he is walking away from the door already. He literally did two light knocks, waited 15 seconds, and then started walking back toward his grandma's car.

"Are you serious?"

"Yes, boo. We have a camera on our door recording whether you ring the doorbell or not. We have to collect those receipts. But I need to go chase him down because AJ likes spending time with him, even if his dad is just in it for the photo-op," she says, panting, suggesting she is already running to the front door to catch him before he's gone.

"Okay, girl, I'll call you tomorrow to let you know how everything went, and maybe we can reschedule!" I tell her while still considering potential footwear for the night. "Love ya."

"Girl, you love me?

"Girl, like cooked food."

"Cooked food!" we shout in unison while giggling.

I hang up the phone and jump in the shower.

Pretty, summery dress flowing and with carefully done makeup, I strut down the steps in my designer heels to find my dad, my little brother, and my baby sister sitting in the living room waiting for Mama.

"Hey, Dad. Hey, PJ." I wave, walking towards my baby sister. I pick her up. "Hey, Laila."

"Hi, Destiny," she says, smiling. Then she gives me the sweetest hug.

"I like your dress, princess. So beautiful," Dad says.

"Thanks, Dad."

"I was about to wear that same outfit, but you cop my style, so I had to switch it up," PJ says jokingly.

"Yeah, you would wear something like that," Dad replies sarcastically, "trying to be one of these lil gay rappers."

I shake my head and concentrate on Laila, avoiding eye contact with either male in the room. But I must not have turned away quick enough.

"What's the headshake for?" Dad asks in a stern, slightly raised voice.

I turn to look at him. My eyes meet his hard, cold ones, and my heart races. Should I lie and tell him I was shaking my head at Laila? Or should I tell him about his homophobia? I choose my next words carefully. "Nothing. I—"

A fist goes through the air and lands lightly on Dad's shoulder. It's PJ physically returning Dad's verbal jab. I am saved.

"It's not gay," PJ says, chuckling.

Dad playfully hits him back. One thing leads to another, and they are both on the ground wrestling. They alternate between putting each other in headlocks and saying, "I quit, I quit."

Mama enters the room in her lengthy, red designer dress and tan Mochacours purse. She sighs and taps her nails on her purse as she watches Dad and PJ wrestle. "Paul Sr. and Paul Jr., we do not have time for this! We need to go, or we will be late! Quit playing so damn much!"

"Damn, baby, we're going to make it in time," Dad tells her in a high-pitched tone.

I recognize the expression on his face. Awkile, I've nicknamed it. His eyes are slightly wide and not blinking. The fake smile plastered across his face is toothy, mouth slightly shut, top lip slightly turned up, with a stiff bottom lip. If the description sounds confusing, it is because it looks confusing. He is trying to cover the fact that Mama's words upset him. But the mouth and eyes tell the contradiction between the brain and the heart.

"Calm down," he projects but still high-pitched.

"Let's go!" Mama shouts, walking towards the door.

"Jesus," Dad says, following her.

I grab Laila, and we all file into the car and head to the restaurant for a dinner party in my honor.

The name of the restaurant is Stanton. Stanton is a beautiful upscale restaurant with a live jazz band. The outside isn't much to holler about, just a plain brick building with neon lights that flashes the name **STANTON**. But the inside has high ceilings with recessed lights that flood the place blue. Former possessions of the jazz greats line the wall: Billie Holiday's gardenia, Louis Armstrong's trumpet, Ella Fitzgerald's microphone, and so on.

"My name is Diana, and I have a five-thirty reservation," Mama tells the hostess.

You can probably guess that my mama was named after the legendary Diana Ross, and the way she dresses goes along with the name.

"Right this way, ma'am." The hostess leads us to our table.

As we follow the hostess to our table, I can't help but get into the groove. I lightly tap my thigh on the beat of the guitars. I would have never imagined liking jazz before. Don't get me wrong, I still like my trap music. But, in the future, I can throw in a little jazz occasionally. I open my menu, still on beat with the music.

"$35 for a salad?" I pivot my head toward Mama and narrow my eyes.

"Yes, honey, this is a special dinner! You deserve it for working so hard and getting a college scholarship," Mama says proudly. "Order anything you want!"

"Thanks, Mama. Thanks, Dad." I smile and order the most sumptuous dish I would probably ever have in my entire life.

Like clockwork, after my brother finishes ordering his meal, he pulls out his phone and looks at internet videos. I watch him swipe frantically as if he is playing a game and trying to get the highest amount of swipes in under thirty seconds. A huge grin appears on his face, and he wastes no time taking out his earbud and showing Mama what's on his screen.

"Boy, I don't want to see it," Mama says.

"Yeah, but this is the proof." PJ is adamant and is not moving the phone out of her face.

Mama sighs, "Let me see. Who is this? He looks like your cousin."

"That's AuthenticCap, a podcaster," PJ replies. He looks at Mama's face and sees the same thing I see: a woman who couldn't care less and doesn't want to look at that long-ass video. He clears his throat. "So, he is saying that the girl has to be lying because the video timestamp does not match her statement."

"What is your obsession with that case?" Mama asks.

"Cause," PJ says.

His order of French fries comes, and he steals a fry from the basket, tossing it in his mouth. He closes his eyes, savoring the flavor as if he is a recovering zombie who lived on a diet of human brains for far too long but, deep down, misses the taste of potato flesh.

"Why do you even care about those people?" Dad asks, stealing the opportunity while PJ is still in a food trance. "You don't even know them."

PJ opens his eyes and finishes his statement. "Cause if she is lying, that means he was in jeopardy of losing his football scholarship for no reason."

"But he is still playing football," I interject. "And still has his scholarship."

"Ugh," PJ exasperates, almost like a vocal fry. "That is not the point."

"What's the point?" Dad asks, genuinely confused.

"Never mind," PJ says, defeated. "Are we going to give her the cards now before the rest of the food comes?"

"Ah, shoot!" Mama pops back into her proper posture and opens her purse, pulling out three envelopes and extending them to me. "Here you are, sugar."

I collect them from her with a smile. I open up the first card, a cartoonish one from PJ. **Now, a hand-me-down I can actually appreciate: your allowance** is the punchline. Funny. Little does he know, I will still get an allowance in college. Besides, the amount he is getting now is something I could only dream of when I was his age.

The next card is from my parents. It is long and serious with phrases like, **We've guided you well. Now, it is time to make your own decisions.** Also, funny. Because what am I doing after my celebration dinner? Exactly!

The last one is from Laila, hand-drawn, and smells like my favorite oil from the boutique down the street from our house. Now I see it; she used oil drops in the place of eyes in her portrait of us. My creative little ball of kindness has so much talent already, and it can only get better from here. It reads, **When I grow up, I want to be just like my big sister Destiny**. Marksmanship is Mama's, of course.

I give them all hugs, and we linger a bit longer, discussing my future college career.

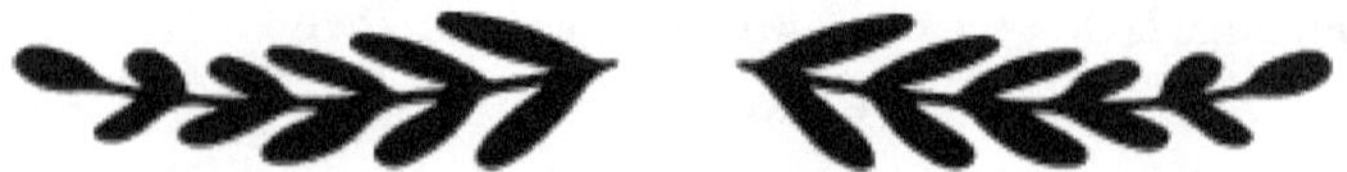

After leaving Stanton, we take the long, perilous trip to Aunt Fefe's house for my cousin's surprise party. I gaze out the window and observe the beautiful mini-mansions. I watch as the beautiful upper-middle-class homes slowly turn into small homes. Then to apartments. Then to abandoned houses, with every other building condemned. Unlike us, she lives in the hood. And not just any hood. She lives in one of the most dangerous neighborhoods in America. My parents are from the hood, but they worked hard and got lucky enough to raise my siblings and me in the suburbs. Aunt Fefe worked just as hard but wasn't as fortunate.

Aunt Fefe is my dad's aunt. So technically, she's my great aunt. She, along with my late great-grandmother, Mary, practically raised him. Dad's father, who is Mary's son and Fefe's brother, was somewhat of a player. I don't know how many children he had, but I've met around twenty-three.

When Dad talks about his childhood, one of the memories he brings up the most is his fun but chaotic weekends with his father. My grandfather would have all his baby mamas drop off his kids at Great-Grandmother Mary's house every other weekend so the kids could know and see each other. But he was rarely there because he was working all of the time. A man with many kids needs many jobs.

I have my own less chaotic memories of my great-grandmother's beautiful colonial home. The Lowry Estate used to be the envy of the neighborhood. I remember sleepovers with my cousins at her place, arguing about who gets which of the seven bedrooms. Each bedroom had connected full bathrooms, but only one had a jacuzzi tub. She would show us some recipes in the spacious kitchen, and we would devour the meal in the dinette or, if we were feeling fancy, in the dining room. That aroma of hot cocoa with a dash of cinnamon would fill the air as we cozy up next to the fireplace on cold winter nights. When it rained, we would stay inside and play one of the old arcade games she had in the basement. We would sit out on the porch during the spring and drink her special pink lemonade while admiring the garden, and she would tell us stories about our great-grandfather. *We had dreams of growing our own fruits and veggies and living off of the land*, she would say.

But now, since her passing, the house has gone downhill. Not to mention, the neighborhood has become progressively worse. My great-grandmother left the house to her daughter, Aunt Fefe, who has allowed a revolving door of randoms to destroy what my great-grandparents worked so hard to get and build. Not only are too many adults and children living in this house, but three bedrooms aren't livable as they've been dedicated to hoarding.

Dad always makes a point of family being first, so we visit our relatives often and regularly attend family gatherings. I especially like seeing my cousins as I always learn something new from them. Even though we come from different places, they've always understood me. And when I say cousins, I mean my female cousins. My male cousins are an entirely different story for another time.

Although it is supposed to be family first, my parents claim that my cousins negatively influence my siblings and me. My siblings and I aren't allowed to hang out with any of our cousins outside of family functions.

We do a traditional round of greetings and hugs upon arriving safe and sound. It feels like I have been hugging and greeting for hours because the house is full of people, and half of the guests haven't even arrived yet. And, of course, each hug and greeting comes with a standard set of statements and questions personalized just for me.

"College girl!" Dad's oldest step-brother, who is visiting from another state, exclaims.

"What are you majoring in?" asks one of Dad's older female cousins, who is considering returning to school.

"Whatcha gonna do with that major?" Dad's older half-brother asks as I repeatedly explain that general studies is my interim major.

"Tuh, good luck with that!" says Dad's youngest half-sister, who has recently dropped out of vocational school.

"Ya know college isn't everything?" says one of Dad's younger half-brothers, whose career consists of trying to get others to join one of his pyramid schemes.

"Just because you are educated doesn't mean you are knowledgeable. Nahmean?" says one of Dad's younger cousins while he taps his fingers on his temple.

But for the most part, I get a greeting personalized for my family.

"Who are these bougie people?" says a close family friend.

I follow my nose to the food. On my way, I pass a table filled with gifts for my cousin: leather shoes, jewelry, and even a brand-new phone. I nod at my Aunt Ruby, who is sitting at the gift table.

"Can't trust these negroes," she says to me. She always thinks somebody wants to steal her old-ass purse. I smile and hurry past the table before she can say another word. But I can still hear her mumbling, "Makes no sense why there's never any greens as these functions. Have we lost the recipes?"

I find the food, and it does not disappoint. Ham hock & black-eyed peas, wings, mac and cheese, corn, potato salad, cornbread, and, my favorite, peach cobbler sit deliciously on the table. I should have saved some room, I think to myself, looking down at my stomach. I grab a plate and add a bit of peach cobbler. But I am bound to get hungry sooner or later, and I will be back for those wings. And it will go down!

"Just want dessert, I see," I hear a soft, calm voice behind me. "No worries, I usually start with the best as well."

I turn to face a slim build, tall woman in her early thirties. She is wearing a white button-up blouse with tiny black squares tucked into black pants with six decorative buttons in the front. Black heels complete her look. No visible brands. She is tossing a Gala apple from one hand to the other. A playful grin comes across her face as I study to figure out who she is. My plate of cobbler almost drops with my jaw.

"Aunt Vanessa?"

"You look like you've seen a ghost." She gives a gentle laugh.

"I might as well. It's been years since I've seen you. What brings you here?"

"Isn't it obvious? I came to celebrate my nephew Antoine's newfound freedom." She takes a bite from the apple in her hand.

"Really?" I twist my lips. There is no way she expects me to believe she came all this way for Antoine. "Why are you really here? Did something happen?"

"I wasn't as convincing as I thought, huh?" She laughs and takes another bite of her apple. "No, I came to see you."

Me? I try to wipe the shock from my face. *She came to see me, but,* "Why?"

"I hear you're going to college soon, and I want to wish you the best."

"Yes, ma'am. I will start soon. Thanks." I fix my rounded shoulders and stand up straight. "I'm honored that you came to congratulate me. I don't have a major yet. Well, actually, I'm taking general studies to explore what I would like to do. I've always known that I wanted to work with the brain, but I don't know what career path to take. So I did a gap year in Europe to see if that would help clear things up, but it—"

"Yes. You've always been obsessed with the brain," she cuts me off. "I'm sure you'll do great in your studies.

"I know I will."

She comes closer to me. "There's that confidence I love to see. So you've been reading those books I've sent you over the years?"

"Yes, ma'am, and I've enjoyed every last one of them," I say.

"Good, and no need for the honorifics. It would be best if you didn't use it at all, even with family. It creates a hierarchy that is difficult to get away from," she tells me sternly.

"Yes, ma'am. I mean, yes. Yes." I clear my throat. "I particularly enjoy the self-help books you sent. The ones about childhood trauma are interesting."

"Great!" She edges closer and softens her voice even more. Finally, she whispers, "Has anything come up?"

I wrinkle my nose. "What do you mean? Do you think I have suffered childhood trauma?" I ask, my eyebrows furrowing.

She releases the tension in her face. "No, just wanted to make sure you're mentally healthy. That's all. It could be pretty hectic growing up here."

"Is that why you're rarely around," I ask.

"Partly. That and I have found my tribe. The people who are most like me. The people with whom I share similar ambitions, and goals, and passions, and—" She stops abruptly and stares at me. "Have you thought about joining a sorority?"

"Yes, I have. I spent my gap year collecting REC letters from alumnae of pretty much every sorority on campus." So, is this why she is here? Did she want me to join her sorority? I give her another once over, seeing if she is wearing any apparel that will hint at her newfound tribe. I see a thin gold bracelet with a small charm, but it is hard to make anything out. "What sorority did you join?"

"I don't want to influence you. You need to choose what you think is best for you," she says. "I'm just here to tell you to keep an open mind, follow your heart, and listen to your intuition."

"You know I will." I put my arms behind my back and interlock my fingers—the sweet position. I need to know what sorority she joined. "Any tips?"

She comes closer to me, placing her hands on my shoulders, our chests touching. She tilts her head, puts her lips next to my right ear, her warm breath sweeping my earlobe, and whispers, "Grab the white quartz."

She pulls back and nods. I'm confused, but I nod back anyway.

"I love you," she says, kissing me on the cheek. "Give my brother my best."

"I love you too, Aunt Vanessa," I reply.

"It was nice seeing you. I need to get out of here." She waves her hands around. "This isn't really my ideal environment. But I hope to see you soon. Bisous!" She air-kisses and walks past me.

Still trying to piece together what a mineral has to do with a sorority, I rewind our conversation. I usually start with the best as well. Was that a hint? Peach cobbler? Peach *cobbler!* I turn around to ask one more question. But by the time I turn, she's already gone. There is no visible sign of her anywhere, just the sweet smell of bergamot and vanilla lingering from her perfume.

I find my cousins in what used to be the dining room but has now become an improvised bedroom that houses a couple of futons. Great-grandmother Mary's expensive China is nowhere to be found.

I eye a spot next to one of my favorite cousins, Acari, but decide to plop down next to my least favorite cousin, Sheila, to get a better view of everyone. Sheila didn't do anything to me; I just have sensitive ears, and her scratchy voice, paired with her talk-too-much syndrome, is irritating.

They are updating each other, and I eagerly join the conversation. We talk about everything; school, new boos, clothes, makeup, what we did during the summer, hair, our latest phones, work, reality television, music, romance novels, and our dreams for the future.

Our conversation is full of compliments and brags. And it ends like it always does. We tell each other how much fun this is. We tell each other that we should all go out sometime. We tell each other that we need to talk to each other more often. Most of it is directed towards me because they always talk to and see each other.

I tell them we need to meet up before I go away—something that would never happen because I'm not allowed to hang with them alone. But they don't know that. Or maybe they have a slight clue. Or perhaps they are fully aware, and I'm unaware of their awareness. Regardless, I always see pictures of their outings on our socials and wish I could have been there.

A familiar beat starts playing as we are rounding out our conversation. We stop our discussion and look at our aunts and older cousins, who are now strutting toward the makeshift dance floor in the living room. Shouts of "Y'all than did it now!" and "Oooooh, this my song!" ride the soundwaves to my ear.

My cousins and I join them, and we all get in position as Juvenile does his introduction on his popular song, Back That Azz Up.

We drop simultaneously and do our best bouncing and twerking as if our life depends on it. After the song ends, we all laugh and hug each other. We brag about our moves. I love every bit of this fun, joyous moment. Then Aunt Fefe comes running in.

"Everyone hide!" Aunt Fefe shouts as she runs towards the light switch. "Antoine is here."

Everyone hides behind the furniture, staying silent. Aunt Fefe flips off the lights and whispers, "Everyone knows what to say?"

I imagine most people nod as it is darker than a zebra's stripes, and I can't see anything.

The room is uncomfortably void of human noises. Only human, though, as I can still hear scurrying animals in the walls, maybe giant roaches or small rats. That makes me kind of regret eating that peach cobbler earlier.

Footsteps approach the front door, and two bulky shadows cast on the window. The roaring laughs of the men outside tell us that the man of the hour is here as the door begins to unlock. The door swings open, and I hear them feel around for the light switch. A few seconds later, the light finally flicks on, and we all jump up and yell, "Welcome home, Antoine!"

Antoine smiles and says, "What's happenin', family?"

He then proceeds to thank everyone. The first thing I notice is his jail tattoos covering his face and neck.

It's Quite Normal

With more family members arriving, there is barely enough room to turn around. I squeeze my way through the crowd, giving nods while I pass. Some I'm happy to see. Others, not so much. Some I have never seen in my entire life, but they claim to know me.

Mama is heading towards me with a tall, slender man. He looks about the same age as Mama. I glimpse a gold tooth every time he opens his mouth. He talks broadly with his hands, and they are laughing hysterically while in a deep, nostalgic conversation. I try to read their lips but can only make out "remember" and "when."

When they finally approach, Mama points to me and says, "This is her."

"Oh, she has grown so much. And she is so damn beautiful!" the man says as he admires me. He tilts his head dramatically to one side, as if his neck muscles have suddenly deteriorated, and stares at me before finally asking, "Remember me?"

"Um," is all I manage to get out. I never know what to say when a relative or family friend asks me this. "Uhhh…"

"I haven't seen you since you were"—he lowers his hand a couple of feet from the floor—"this high."

"Wow," I say, thinking about how the hell am I supposed to remember this man when I was so young. "That was a long time ago."

"I used to babysit you when you were five. I picked you up sometimes from school when your parents had to work late."

"Boy, no, you didn't!" Mama laughs. "Your sister used to babysit her. You might have kept her 1 or 2 times when your sister was busy, but you definitely weren't the prime babysitter for my babies."

"Aw, okay," I say awkwardly, not knowing what to say next. "Are you Mama's friend?"

"Your mama and I go way back!" He then pulls out his cell phone and proceeds to show me a picture on his phone.

I try to keep from laughing. This man took a picture of a printed photo instead of just scanning it. Two kids dressed like Michael Jackson are in the image, their outfits complete with a white, sequined glove.

He then says, "We were about fourteen in this picture. I had just moved into the neighborhood, and your mama was one of the first people I met."

"Ah, okay," I say as if suddenly remembering who he is. I remember seeing pictures of my parents when they were younger. This picture looks so familiar.

"I met your dad in my sophomore year of high school. We used to all hang out together. I stayed at your daddy's house often. Your daddy is like a brother to me."

He shows me more pictures on his phone. A wave of déjà vu comes over me as he shows me the photos—like I did this before.

"My name is Jason, by the way," he says while simultaneously holding out his hand.

I hold out my hand to meet his, "Destiny. I was wondering if—"

"You fast-ass little girl!" I hear a woman shout nearby. We all whip our heads toward the loud wails coming from a corner of the room.

"Sex!" I watch Aunt Teressa, Aunt Fefe's youngest sister, place her hand on her hip as she shouts from the top of her lungs. "You're out here having sex? Not in my house, nu-uh!"

My aunt is holding my little cousin's cell phone, shaking her head as she swipes on the phone. "Who is this lil boy, Rachel?"

My 14-year-old cousin stays silent as she gazes down at the floor, her body motionless. A single tear falls from her right eye.

"Rachel, look at me, little girl." She holds up the phone and points to the screen. "Who is this lil boy?"

"Ron," Rachel answers quietly.

"Who the hell is Ron?"

"He lives down the street."

"Ron from down the street! Are you talking about the Johnsons' boy?"

"Yes, ma'am. He always talks to me when I'm walking home from school."

"Twenty-three-year-old Ron!"

"Yes," Rachel quivers.

Uncle Charles, Teressa's younger brother, jumps in. "She out here messing with a twenty-three-year-old man. She hot, ain't she?"

"You got this man sending you pictures of his privates?" Aunt Teressa continues.

"I didn't ask him to send them to me. He just sent them." Rachel looks down at her shoes.

"What is he even doing with your number?" Aunt Teressa's nose is flaring.

"I told you already! He always talks to me when I—"

Slap!

We all saw it coming. More tears are running down Rachel's face, her hand caressing the cheek that my aunt just struck. I look at my parents uncomfortably, but they are just shaking their heads along with the rest of the family.

"Don't you get smart with me, lil girl." Aunt Teressa starts reaching for a belt. "You about to get your lil ass whoop. I ain't raising no more children. I have four more years until I am childfree, and I will be damn if you out here thottin' around, fucking up my plans."

"Let me get her after you," Uncle Charles says while taking off his belt.

Rachel darts to the door, but a bunch of family members apprehend her. They hold her as Aunt Teressa wildly swings the belt on her.

I look around the room and notice some family members recording the punishment. Some are live streaming, so others can voluntarily witness it.

Memories of my childhood fill my head as I watch, each lash bringing up more and more memories. I am numb. I stare blankly, covering my ears, trying to drown out all of Rachel's screams. After about eight lashes, Uncle Charles gets into position to begin his turn. Rachel tries to run, but my uncle grabs her by her micro-braids and starts swinging his belt. He has a smirk but quickly veils it by stiffening his jaw and narrowing his eyes. With each lash, my cousin's screams get louder and more perceptible to me.

I can't take it anymore. I slowly make my way to the kitchen, hands shaking and heart racing. I try to find a cup to drink some water. I can still hear my uncle's lecturing her between his hits.

"This will slow your fast ass down!"

Whip!

"You want to act grown?"

Whip!

"You want to wear low-cut shirts that show your titties?"

Whip, whip, whip!

"You want to be hot in the ass?"

Whip!

"You want to mess with grown-ass men?"

Whip!

"You want to wear tight-ass coochie cutters?"

Whip!

"And don't think that I didn't see you twerking earlier!"

Whip, whip, whip!

I feel a tap on my shoulder. I turn around to see one of my cousins, Ciera, who I was dancing with earlier. She takes my arm and leads me to one of the back rooms in the house, away from all the commotion in the front. The backroom is filled with a few of my female cousins and alcohol. A lot of alcohol. I pour vodka and soda into my cup and discuss what's happening to Rachel.

About thirty minutes later, we all emerge from the room, a little tipsy but nothing noticeable. We try to find Rachel to talk to her, but she and her mama have already left.

I spot Uncle Charles playing pool with some family members. I want to avoid him for the rest of the night.

We grab some food and sit at an empty table. I told you I was coming back for those wings, even if it meant pushing out the memories of those rats scratching to escape the wall. Or were those roaches? Who knows.

We observe an ongoing game of spades on the table next to us. Dad is one of the players, and Mama is sitting behind him, watching while holding Laila. Laila is playing with one of her dolls. Jason is teamed up with my dad. They seem to be in the lead so far. Uncle Tan, my dad's eldest full-brother, and Lisa, Uncle Tan's ex-girlfriend turned family friend, are on the opposing team. As I eat, I can overhear their conversation.

Uncle Tan throws down a card and says, "That was something."

"You know, we used to get it way worse when we were younger," Dad says, slurring some of his words. "My granny used to make us pick out our own switch from the backyard for whoopings."

"Paul, man, that's old school," Jason says as he lays down his card. "There are better ways to handle your children nowadays."

Lisa lets out a sigh and lays down her card. She moves her lips, but nothing comes out.

"Like what? Time out? See, this is why these kids today are so disrespectful. They're not being punished like we were growing up. And now they have it where you can't even hit your kids, or you'll get locked up!" Dad lays down a card.

"Yeah, man, that's called abuse!" Jason swoops up the pile of cards in front of him, putting them with the other hands that he and Dad won in this round. "You can't treat kids like that. They have rights, too."

"Yeah, okay," Dad says, laughing. "See, this is what I'm talking about. You're treating these kids like they are adults. Like they're your friends. You need to be and act like the parent and treat your kids as the kids. Plain and simple."

"You can treat your kids like kids without violating them. Remember, I'm a part of an organization that helps abused kids," Jason says, putting down an ace of spade.

Lisa throws out a low spade and says, "I love that you are standing up for these children."

"You're still a part of that organization?" Dad asks, ignoring Lisa and playing another card. "I remember you volunteering there when we were in high school. You're probably the president now."

"Naw, still a volunteer. I'm a child advocate, and what just happened wasn't right. There are better ways."

"See, man, look at my kids. You see them out here acting all wild. No. That's because I didn't treat them like they were my friends growing up. They were treated like the children they were. They say I'm mean."

"Mean. Really?" Uncle Tan asks while throwing out a low spade.

I look at my plate, but I can feel their eyes peering at me. I nervously shift in my chair and try to eat my wings as if I didn't hear anything.

"Yep, they say I'm mean. Can you believe that?"

"Not you, Paul. You're one of the nicest people I know," Uncle Tan validates. "You may be a bad card player, but you are not a bad father."

Dad laughs, "Man, you tried to slide that in there. I'm one of the top card players on this planet." He gathers and stacks the cards next to his and Jason's other winnings. "See that? The best."

"That was Jason's ace of spade, not yours," Uncle Tan says while patting Dad's shoulder.

Dad laughs again, "But for real, I tell my kids all the time I'm not mean; y'all are just spoiled."

"Ain't that the truth," Uncle Tan agrees. "Kids these days are spoiled rotten. They don't suffer the way we did back in the day."

"Fefe didn't whoop Antoine, and you see how he turned out," Dad continues. "We're now at his getting-out-of-jail party!"

"Okay, Paul!" Jason laughs. "Let's just agree to disagree. Ay, why was Antoine in jail anyway?"

"Aw man, no one told you what he did?"

"Nope."

Dad starts to laugh, "Aw, man."

"What did he do, Paul?" Mama asks impatiently. Her leg is bouncing, so I know she has been waiting for this gossip all night.

Dad lets out a short laugh and lays his cards face down so that his hands are free to gesture while he tells the story. He begins, "Y'all know how racist they are on the west side, right? Well, this fool started messing around with a lil white girl who lives there. They went to a club there, and when they left, these two white men followed them. They didn't like that he was with a white girl and started calling him the N-word. He yelled back at them until one threw a banana at him. He then beat both of their asses."

"Shit, that's all he did?" Uncle Tan asks. "They locked him up that long for beating up a couple of racists?"

"Nah, man, it didn't end there," Dad says, waving his hands. "He walked over and picked up the banana. He pulled his pants down and started lubricating himself with the banana. And then he raped them!" Dad lets out a vicious snicker.

"And that didn't hurt him?" Lisa asks. "He should've hurt himself more than anything!"

"Nah," Dad answers. "And his girl was scared as hell. She the one who called the cops."

"My goodness! I never knew that," Mama says, shaking her head.

"When the police came, he was still raping them," Dad says, laughing joyously. "There was no way he could've gotten away with that. But they shouldn't have locked him up for that long for what he did. It's not like he killed somebody."

They each lay down a card, and Jason swoops them up, adding another win to the stack.

"Yeah, they shouldn't have given him that long," Uncle Tan agrees. "If he were white, he wouldn't even have gotten six months. They gave Murky a shorter time than Antoine, and he stabbed someone."

"Aw, how is lil Murky? I haven't seen him in a while. I heard he was in that new Dollarstar biopic acting like a crackhead," Dad says.

"Shit, he is a crackhead," Uncle Tan replies. "He stay on dem streets, can't get him off."

"Damn, that's all bad," they all say in unison.

"Damn, you sure it was him?" Dad asks.

"Yeah, man, you know I had to see it twice, and it was definitely him," Uncle Tan responds.

"It was that good, huh? We're going next weekend to see it."

"Nah, you know they both wanted to go see it," Uncle Tan says, looking around.

Bewilder flushes the faces at the table except Lisa's.

Lisa twists her lips and says, "See, this is why we ain't together now."

Everyone at the table glares at Lisa, then, one by one, understands what Uncle Tan means.

"Aw," Dad laughs.

"That's what happens when you sneak around," Lisa says. "You spend more money than you have to."

"You know, he has two girlfriends, and that's alright," says Mama while scooting Laila off her lap. Laila sits on the floor beside her and continues playing with her dolls. "Plenty of men have multiple girlfriends. And since he's single and unmarried, he can do whatever he wants."

"But they don't know about each other," Lisa says. "That's wrong."

"Aw, stop hating," Uncle Tan responds.

"But," Mama starts, "who are you to judge? I feel like that's no one's business but his."

"You're right, Diana," Lisa says, giving Mama a glassy stare. Mama smiles, not picking up on Lisa's sarcasm. I'm sure Lisa wants to say more, knowing that the family most likely knew about his infidelities while they were together but smiling in her face.

Everyone throws out their last card, and Lisa sweeps them in a neat stack.

"Looks like we're tied now. And boy, no one's hating on you. It ain't nothing to hate on," Lisa says.

"Yeah, whatever," Uncle Tan says while gathering the cards to shuffle.

Lisa rolls her eyes, then closes them and rubs her stomach.

"When is the baby due?" Mama asks Lisa.

"Girl, in two months. It feels like I've been pregnant for years, though. Ugh, just two more months, and you're out!" She says while pointing to her belly.

"Right, it feels like you've been pregnant forever. Do you know what you're having?"

"Yep, a boy. Jasmine is going to have a little brother."

"A half-brother," Uncle Tan interjects. "That's what happens when you out here cougaring. These young men want a child of their own. You told me you were done when I wanted another one."

"Oh, stop it, Tan," Mama says. "Family is family."

"Thank you," Lisa says, looking at Mama endearingly.

"And you said a boy? Oh, you're going to have fun raising this one. Boys are so much different. You can do more things with them. Girls are boring." Mama stretches and walks off to grab more drinks.

Ciera taps on my shoulder, breaking my gaze. It looks like she has been trying to get my attention for a while now.

"You want to go back to the living room and dance?" she asks. "They're playing old-school funk music."

"Cool."

I toss my plate and follow Ciera to the living room before seeing the panic on Mama's face. Laila is no longer by her side. I look around and spot her playing dolls with Uncle Pat. Growing up, nearly all of my female relatives told me to never follow him into a room. Actually, to never follow him anywhere and make sure that I am never alone with him. I point Laila out to Mama and mouth to her that I will get her.

Ciera and I walk up to Laila and Uncle Pat.

"Hi, Uncle Pat," we say simultaneously.

"How you all doing?" his rusty voice musters.

"Good," I say quickly. "We were just going to take Laila and show her some old dance moves."

I grab Laila's hand and lead her to the living room, making a mental note to keep an eye on her all night.

As we dash away, I hear him mumble, "Boy, that girl is getting thick."

At the end of the evening, we all crowd into the living room. In what now seems to be a family ritual, Aunt FeFe grabs a CD case covered in welcome home decor. She pops out the CD, which contains only one song: a song made by one of my want-to-be rapper cousins about being freed from jail.

In my family, there are two CDs like this. One that we use at family reunions with multiple recordings of "Lift Every Voice and Sing." And this one. The one we use when we celebrate loved ones coming back home from jail. We always play this song before most people begin to leave.

Antoine is enjoying his time in the spotlight. "I was locked up, but now I'm out!" he sings while dancing.

He does a few old-school dance moves while singing proudly to the song. PJ shows him some new dance moves he missed while in jail. As the song ends, Antoine sings the song's last line loudly while the rest of the family joins him.

"Thanks, fam," Antoine starts. "This was fun! The food was the bomb. I haven't had anything that tasted that good in years. I appreciate all of the gifts, shit, the shoes, the jewelry, I even got a TV. We did it big, didn't we? This is going to help me out big time. Thanks again, fam, and y'all are always welcome to visit me at the telly. Ma got the address."

I follow my parents' lead, making my way around the house and saying my goodbyes, which takes about half an hour. We all have to get our final conversations in and, of course, plate some leftovers.

We pack in the car to begin the journey home. It is now late at night, a time when most criminal activities happen, which is nerve-racking for me. I gaze out the window, my nervousness slowly drifting away as the abandoned buildings turn into mini-mansions.

Laila drifts off to sleep as soon as the door closes. She looks so precious, with her tiny mouth slightly ajar, little whistles escaping as she exhales. I am going to miss her the most when I go away to college. I mean, who will be here to keep an eye on her? Who is going to nurture her beautiful spirit? I will need to send her loads of books, just like Aunt Vanessa did for me. Aunt Vanessa...

"I saw Aunt Vanessa at the party," I say quickly, looking at Dad in the driver's seat. "She told me to give you her best."

Dad shifts in his seat and clenches his jaw. He taps his fingers on the steering wheel. He finally says, "What does that even mean?"

I shrug my shoulders. "I think it just means that she wishes you well."

"Okay, why couldn't she just say something simple?" Dad says, slightly slurred. "Or better yet, come over and say hi to me?"

I shrug again. "I think she had to be somewhere. I only spoke with her briefly before she rushed out."

"See, and that is what I'm talking about with my bougie ass sister," says Dad emphatically. He looks at Mama. "Wasn't we just talking about that?"

"Yes, honey, we were," Mama says with a yawn. "People change as soon as they get money."

My eyes meet my dad's bloodshot ones in the rear-view mirror. His droopy eyelids make me question why he thought he was fit to drive and why he didn't surrender his keys to Mama when she asked for them.

"Except for us," he continues. "We didn't change at all when we got money. Same family, same friends, same morals and values. We just live in a different area."

"People forget where they came from," Mama affirms.

"Exactly. Vanessa pops up every few years, acting brand new. She knows not to come around family with that fake mess. That's probably why she dipped so quickly. What did she talk to you about?"

"Nothing much," I say, carefully thinking about my words to avoid offending him. "She congratulated me for getting accepted to college and asked about my major."

"That's what changed her: college. She came back acting like she was better than everyone and accused everyone of abuse."

"She didn't seem all that different," I say.

"Of course, you didn't notice a difference. You didn't know her twenty years ago. She switched up," Dad says so loud, I'm pretty sure the people in the cars around us heard every single word. "Everything from her style, to what she eats, to who she be around, to her beliefs. She did a complete 180."

"Oh," I respond as if I've had an epiphany, "I had no clue."

"Well, you know now," Dad says, a little less slurred. "And you just make sure you don't let going away to college get to your head like it got to hers. She went—"

I look up to see why he stopped and notice his eyes are closed.

"Dad, are you up!" I panic and shake his shoulder.

"Why wouldn't I be up? I'm driving," Dad says sternly while moving his shoulder to encourage me to let go.

I get a second look at his eyes and notice that they are open, just squinted. His upper and lower eyelids are so close that they may as well be closed—a drunken eye squint.

"Look at that car," Dad says, pointing. I follow his finger to a small car in front of us. PJ and Mama look up from their mobile devices. Dad laughs nervously, "Someone's drunk."

The irony.

The front passenger door keeps opening and closing. The car is driving under the speed limit, swerving in and out of the lane.

"Somebody's trying to get out," PJ says.

The swerving stops, and the car speeds up a little. I raise as far out of my seat as my seatbelt allows me to in order to get a good look. The car is dark red and a little beaten up. I can't really tell the brand, but it is very boxy. There's a hole in the back window, the cracked glass around it making it look like a giant spider in its web. As far as I can tell, there's no one in the back seat. No license plate. The car slows down again and swerves to the left as the passenger door opens slightly before being yanked closed. It slows almost to a complete stop, engaging its brake lights.

Dad speeds up to pass the car, slowing down a little when next to it. Being nosy, we all try to get a good look at what's happening inside. There is a man in the driver's seat, one hand on the wheel, the other tangled up in the woman's hair in the passenger seat. Grimace fills her face. Mascara tears run down her cheeks, snot fills her nostrils, and the dark magenta lipstick on her heart-shaped lips is smeared.

The woman tries to open the passenger door again, but the man pulls her dyed lime-green hair. The car veers and nearly hits us when he takes his hand off the steering wheel to close the door. The man darts his deep brown eyes at us.

He then focuses his eyes on me as if we're in a staring contest, not blinking and not caring about the road ahead. His sideburns are thick, black, and curly, like the hair on his head.

"Should we call the police?" I ask, breaking his eye contact and already dialing.

"Nah, we don't get into that mess," Dad answers.

I pause.

"She's a grown woman," Mama adds. "She makes her own decisions. It is none of our business."

Dad speeds up, leaving the little red car in the dust. I look behind me to see it pull off to the side of the road. I watch, hoping to see if either person gets out, until we go over a hill, and I can no longer see the car. I turn back around in my seat. I glance back every few minutes to see if they are back on the road, but no luck. They've probably turned on a side street by now. I give up once we turn on our street and pull up the driveway.

I get ready for bed, but my thoughts return to the black couple in the strange car. I think about how nonchalant my parents were. I think about how old the man looked. And how young the woman looked. She looked as if she was my age.

First Day Away

Adrenaline fills my body as we pull up to what will be my home for the next four years. I think of everything I can do now that I am away from my parent's house. No more going to places that I don't want to go. No more sneaking around. I am now free to do whatever I want to do. I am a grown woman who can make her own rules.

I look out the window to observe some students walking around and exploring the campus. I can't help but notice how many white students there are. If I didn't know any better, I would've thought this was a PWI.

"Looks like we're here," Dad says as we approach the women's dormitory. I step out of the car and observe the architecture of the residence hall. Faces of revolutionary women are carved into the building. I recognize a few of them: Harriet Tubman, Rosa Parks, and Maya Angelou. I glance over the incredible carvings but stop when I get to a woman named Audre Lorde. Aunt Vanessa sent me some of her books. My face beams at the thought of all the women I would learn about here.

I enter the building, and there's a short line of students with their parents. Overhead is a huge sign painted with elegant handwriting that reads, **WELCOME, ASHFORD WOMEN!** Yep, we're in the right place.

The campus has many women-only dormitories. I just so happened to pick Ashford as my first choice and got in. This residence hall is named after Evelyn

Ashford, an Olympic gold medalist. "Go for Gold" is the motto that this hall lives by, and it provides so many resources to help us obtain our goals, two of the many reasons I chose to live in this dorm my first year.

I get in line, and again, I can't help but notice some non-black students waiting in line with me to receive room assignments. I knew Erika's ninety-percent statistic was over-exaggerated, but still, I expected a mostly black campus.

After a short wait, it's finally my turn. This year, I will be living in room B38. I receive my key, an Ashford lanyard, an Ashford t-shirt, a planner with the University logo, and a custom Ashford tea cup. There's a rumor that we have Sunday tea parties that serve as dorm meetings.

As my parents and I make our way up to the room, I notice more black historical women drawn on the walls, with quotes that tell nothing but the truth.

I finally get to my medal-adorned door. Destiny, one of the medal-shaped door decs reads, with shooting stars underneath it.

I look at my roommate's dec, similar to mine, but with rabbits underneath it. Trixie, it reads. I wonder how her parents got that name. I remember having one of those toys, a Ty Beanie Babies, tagged with the name Trixie.

I texted Trixie over the summer. She seems like a cool girl. She doesn't believe in social media, so we've just been emailing back and forth, mostly talking about how to decorate our room and what to bring. She won't be here for a few days, therefore missing most of the freshmen welcome week, but I will catch her up when she finally gets here. After all, we will be spending a lot of time together.

My parents and siblings help me bring up my stuff: four suitcases, three duffle bags, and a Mochacours backpack. I am going to dread unpacking.

As I stare at all my stuff, I notice how quiet my family is. It's about that time. Mama puts her arms around me and squeezes me as if I'm an orange she's trying to juice. Tears are running down her face as she pulls away.

Dad hugs me. "Okay, princess, we will be back to pick you up during your break. It won't be that long."

PJ tries to play it cool. "Keep ya head up in these streets!" he says to me, trying to keep a straight face. We both laugh and hug.

Laila covers her face with her hands, but I can still see her trembling chin. Her puffy eyes reveal when she moves her hands. She goes to her backpack and pulls out a colorful drawing. She hands me a picture that she drew. Two stick figures, one short and one tall, are on the page with the words **LAILA AND DESTINY FOREVER** written underneath. I hug her tightly, and she hugs me back. My vision begins to blur as I think about never letting go. I never imagined saying goodbye would be this hard.

I walk my family down to the car and repeat our goodbyes. I wave as they pull off. I watch as the car gets smaller and smaller as it drives farther away. I realize I am alone now, and my chest becomes tight.

I turn around to return to my dorm to finish unpacking, but something catches my eye in the distance. A large group of students is heading toward the center of campus, holding signs. I check out what's going on, procrastinating unpacking even further.

I make out some of the students' signs as I approach the crowd.

STOP KILLING US!

AMERICA, LAND OF THE NOT ACTUALLY FREE, HOME OF THE... I FEARED FOR MY LIFE!

ONLY CERTAIN PEOPLE ARE FREE IN AMERICA!

END POLICE BRUTALITY!

POLICE UPHOLD WHITE SUPREMACY!

BLACK PEOPLE CAN'T RUN NOW?

I hear them chant, "We're not quittin' til there's justice for Quintin!"

I then see a young man's picture in a graduation cap and gown on one of the posters: Quintin James.

I remember seeing Quintin James on the news several days ago. Witnesses say that a group of young men tried to jump him, and he ran from them, attempting to escape. He made the deadly mistake of running past police officers sitting in their car, prompting them to follow him with their sirens on. They hopped out of the car and tackled him when they got close enough. Quintin James then struggled with the officers and pushed one of them off, which eventually led to the officers shooting and killing him. So far, the officers have not been charged.

I join the protest and begin chanting with them, "We're not quittin' til there's justice for Quintin! We're not quittin' til there's justice for Quintin!"

Our chant becomes louder as more students join our protest.

"We're not quittin' til there's justice for Quintin!"

As I chant, I steal a glance at the protesters, noting that these will be the women I will be bonding with over the next few years. I peek at the non-black people holding their anti-police brutality signs and am grateful that they have decided to join the protest. Hopefully, they'll use their privilege when the time comes.

We finally make it to our destination, and the march halts. We stand silently for about a minute, watching a man climb the steps to the stage while holding a bullhorn. He turns around when he reaches the peak, and my heart skips a beat.

He has beautiful brown skin with matching big brown eyes. His eyebrows can bring out the green monster in anyone as they are naturally shaped, thick, and black. His coarse, curly black hair shines as if drenched with oil sheen. Chiseled? How often do you see a chiseled face in real life? Shit, his entire body looks as if Michelangelo sculpted it. His biceps are muscular but not bulky, more like a slim athletic build. I fix my slack jaw as he begins to speak.

"We are gathered here today to fight for justice," he says in a baritone voice. "We are here to fight against police brutality. We are here to fight for our lives! Our lives matter just as much as any other life! Too many times have America allowed cops to shoot innocent black people! Too many times do these cops get away with murder! And we are damn sick of it! Let us bow our heads in silence for all the brothas who have lost their lives this year."

We all close our eyes and lower our heads.

"Quinton James," he says. "Bernard Henshaw, Robert Williams, Mike Robinson..."

He names each of the men killed so far by police this year, with a short pause afterward to give way for reactions. This man knows what he's doing. His professionalism attracts me, and I fall deeper in love with each syllable he utters.

"Let us raise our heads," he says while walking across the stage. He turns on a projector, and various logos line the screen. "These are the brands and companies who don't think that our lives matter. At this very moment, brothas on college campuses nationwide are holding this same march."

The permanent fraternity symbol on his arm catches my eye, and I try to remember the mark. I'll figure out later what fraternity he's in.

"We've all agreed that we must hit these companies where it hurts. We must hit them in the pockets!" He pulls out a stack of bills and waves it at the crowd. "We will boycott until they agree that we are worthy of life. If it's on the list, we must resist and spend our money at black-owned businesses."

He grabs a stack of papers. "I have flyers for everyone. Hang them wherever it's permitted. We must let people know that these companies believe we deserve to die. Everyone come and get a stack, and let's spread the word! If anyone has any questions about the brands on this list, do not hesitate to come and ask me."

Must my brain turn to mush in times like this? My eyes study each logo as I try to find something to ask him. Anything. I make my way up to the stage, hoping that I don't sound like an idiot when I ask this silly question I just came up with. Other college women surround him. I guess I wasn't the only one who liked what I saw. I join the crowd of women, waiting for my chance to talk to him. The women are spouting question after question, and he's easily answering each one. My impatience grows, and I finally push to the front and stand before him. He looks at me and smiles.

"What's your question?" he asks.

I point to one of the logos on the flyer. I flash my pearly whites and ask, "Why are we boycotting this company? I didn't hear anything in the news about them being racist or anything."

"Well, that is the parent company. We don't think it's very effective if we only boycott one product. We need to boycott the entire company and all of the products it makes. Our boycott will have a bigger impact. If we apply pressure to the parent company, they will turn around and talk with the companies and products they own, hopefully changing their ways. And maybe even give donations to a few of our organizations. It's all about strategy."

"I see," I tell him, still smiling. "I will spread the word to my family and friends. How do we know if a company is black-owned?"

"We have an app," he says, gesturing to his phone. "Let me see your phone, and I'll download it for you."

I hand him my phone. I stare at him as he swipes, getting lost in his movements. My imagination starts to run wild. I imagine what our life would be like: the dates, the romance, the sex. Is he all I dream him up to be, or am I doing that thing that Erika always says I do? I can hear her voice: *Girl, stop placing your expectations on a stranger.*

He says something that breaks my daydream. "I'm sorry, what?"

"I said all downloaded," he says. "And I also put my phone number in there, just in case."

My cheekbones rise, but I quickly suppress the involuntary action. I don't want to seem too eager. I clear my throat, "What did you put it under?"

"Marcel," he says. "Marcel Moore."

"Okay." I open my contacts and send him a text. "I just texted you my name, not our fate."

"Destiny," he says while peeking at his phone. He then reaches out his hand, and I meet it for a shake. "I think you texted both because we were destined to meet. What's your last name?"

I giggle at his line. Literally, every guy I've met has said that to me. I will let it slide just this once. "I guess so. Lowry."

"Well, Ms. Lowry, you look like a freshman. Let me show you around campus."

"Okay," I say, gushing.

He grabs my hand again and leads me toward the campus buildings.

He spends the next couple of hours with me on campus. He shows me how to get to my classes and gives me a heads-up about certain professors. We eat at his favorite places on campus, where I learn that we enjoy some of the same foods. He tells me everything I need to know to survive on campus, but on top of that, we talk. We talk about movies, music, love, life.

After about eight flights of steps, I bend over and take off my heels. I would have worn flats if I knew we would be walking up so many steps. But then again, I only had a few minutes to change after Marcel's private campus tour. How can he have a surprise for me already, and we just met?

"Are we there yet?" I ask.

"Almost," he says sweetly.

"Isn't there an elevator or something in this building?"

"There is, but it's too fast. I want more time to talk to you." He picks me up and cradles me in his arms. I wrap my arms around his neck for better balance. "I'll carry you the rest of the way."

This validates all of the feelings that I had when I first met him. He is everything that I thought he was.

"Okay, we're here," he says as he slowly puts me down.

"What's behind the door?"

"You'll see."

He pulls the door open, and my mouth drops. I stroll forward, taking everything in. I stop and shiver as a gush of wind hits me, but in perfect gentlemanly fashion, he saunters behind me and sneaks his jacket on my shoulders.

My eyes don't know what to look at first: the clear constellations in the sky above or the sprawling, lightly lit campus below. I take out my phone to capture what would, in the future, be one of the memories I choose to embarrass my children with when telling the story of how I met their daddy.

"I can take a picture for you if you want," he offers. I hand him my phone and do my signature pose. He smiles, "Nice one."

"Thanks," I say, swaying.

"This is the highest point on campus. You can see everything."

"Thank you for bringing me up here. This view is just breathtakingly beautiful!"

"I got us a few things," he says.

He removes his backpack and empties it: half sandwiches, chips, grapes, and a bottle of wine.

"I know it's not fancy, but it's what I could snatch up at the cafeteria without you noticing. Oh, and the bottle of wine from the corner store."

I smile. The romantic that I've been searching for my entire life. My first day on campus, and I've already found him. Oh, I can't wait to tell Erika that the MASH games we used to play really predict the future.

He pulls out a big blanket, laying it neatly on the ground beside the food.

"Shit, I forgot the cups," he says.

"It's okay," I tell him, "we can drink out of the bottle."

"You're going to drink after me?" he teases, lightly stroking my jaw.

"Yup."

"Is that right?"

He pulls me in gently with his hand, tilting his head to go in for a kiss. I close my eyes and meet his lips, feeling the heat coming from his mouth. His tongue gently parts my lips and then thrusts roughly in my mouth. I try my best to match the speed of his tongue. I rub the back of his head while he rubs on my booty. He takes his tongue out of my mouth, giving me a quick peck on the lips.

He backs up a bit while holding my hand, his other hand reaching for his pocket. When his fingers emerge, a familiar small, square wrapper comes with them—a condom. Cheap wine isn't the only thing he got from the corner store.

"You want to?"

"Yes," I say softly.

I follow him to the blanket. He throws the condom on the blanket and lifts me, my legs naturally wrapping around his waist. We stare into each other's eyes as we slowly fall onto the blanket.

We start with closed-mouth kisses, then alternate between light pecks and powerful, full-pressure kisses. I stroke the back of his head as he rubs my lower back. I open my eyes as the kisses slow down, meeting his pupils. I wonder how long his eyes have been open. Still staring deep into his eyes, I playfully lift up and lick the tip of his nose.

He wiggles his nose and bites his lip. I giggle.

"Oh, so you want it like that," he says while lowering my back onto the blanket and positioning himself comfortably on top of me.

He finds my lips again and brushes his tongue against them. His tongue gently moves across my upper lip, the bottom, and back to the upper.

My ticklish lips quiver as I wait for him to part my lips as he did the first time. Impatiently, I extend my tongue to meet his. He pulls back and does a quick lick on my tongue. We both giggle.

He pushes me further down until the back of my head touches the blanket and inserts his tongue into my mouth. I slide my tongue along his. Our tongues slowly stroke back and forth, gradually picking up pace. Heavy panting comes from both of our mouths as we slow down to a stop. He stares deep into my soul again as he rubs my right arm. I love this man's eye contact. He breaks our gaze with quick pecks on my lips, nose tip, and forehead.

Sitting up, he removes his shirt to reveal his sculpted abs, and my eyes widen. My favorite part of his body. I sit up to meet him. He starts kissing me again, this time on my clothed breast. He delicately places his hands on my stomach underneath my blouse as if I'm fragile glass he's trying not to break. His hands slowly reach further and further up my shirt until he can finally fondle my titties. His big hands go around my back to undo my bra while kissing my chest.

I raise my shirt a bit, revealing my pierced navel, which he kisses. Rubbing the jewel on the barbell, he looks up at me, lust in his eyes, waiting for me to reveal more. He helps me lift the blouse over my head, and I feel my strapless bra slide down my torso.

No longer blinded by my shirt, I notice his eyes looking longingly at my breast. His lips are slightly parted.

I smile and fold my arms across my stomach, my hands grabbing the opposite elbow. I force my shoulders up, which results in my tits being pushed together. Another pose that I've practiced countless times in my bedroom.

He licks his lips and finally says, "They're beautiful."

He gently pushes me until I feel the blanket on my bare back. For a moment, I swear I can see a shooting star in the sky right before his head pops up, and his lips land a kiss on my forehead. I gaze into his eyes, feeling his weight on me, until I see something moving behind him. Yep, a shooting star. I close my eyes, keep the shooting star's image in mind, and make a wish. His soft lips meet mine one last time as I open my eyes before he starts scooting down. From the looks of it, my wish may be granted soon.

His thumb traces the tiny bumps on my areola, arousing me even more. By the time his thumb makes it to my nipple, it is already erect and waiting to feel the grooves of his thumbprint.

I push out my chest as his lips meet my right nipple. Then, the left one. And then back to the right one. I can feel his hardness—his abs and dick—as he vacillates between my nipples, sucking each as if they were his favorite flavor of freeze pops.

"I can stay on these all night," he whispers.

I smile. "I wouldn't mind."

He gives me slow, soft kisses down my belly, then onto my clothed pussy. "Do you mind if I taste you?"

I raise my head a little to see him facing my crotch and let out a breathy, "Please do."

He starts by rubbing the tip of his nose up and down between my clothed lips. After a few seconds of nose action, he plants hard kisses on my bikini-style panties, the pressure causing my clit to pulse. Moisture soaks my panties as he continues to kiss.

A tickling sensation suddenly arises as he pulls down my underwear. I sometimes forget how my body reacts to the crevices on my pelvis being touched. Though it is just a light touch, it is enough to make my body jerk.

Placing his head between my thighs, his tongue begins to stroke the inside of my outer lips. He does this for a few minutes, his tongue brushing my clit every few seconds. His fingers spread my lips apart as he continues to lick me. Sections of the blanket scrunch in my hands as pleasure builds up in my body.

When his tongue starts to thrust in and out of me, I find my fingers going through his curly black hair.

In and out.

In and out.

His thumb, now my favorite body part of his, gently rubs my clit as his tongue reaches deeper into me with each thrust.

In and out.

In and out.

My body begins to jolt as I get closer and closer to—

He stops? I'm almost there, and... *he stops?*

He comes up and kisses me. Reluctantly, I kiss back but twist my lips to let him know what he did isn't cool.

"There's more where that came from, sweetie," he says, reading my mood. He plants another kiss on my lips before sitting up straight.

"I was about to cum."

"I know, doll, I"—he tears the condom wrapper open with his teeth—"thought that we can cum together. That's all."

He reaches into his boxers but pauses when he notices the unwavering dissatisfaction on my face. He bends over to face me.

"Destiny, look," he starts.

I look him dead in the eye, keeping my expression firm. "I'm looking."

"We are a team. I've always believed that the man and the woman work together to achieve their common goal in a relationship. We work together in each aspect of the relationship, including sex. Right?"

"Mmhmm," I concur. He starts rubbing my clit again, keeping me wet.

"So, if we have the same goal to receive pleasure, then both of us will work towards it and achieve it together. That's what I want in our relationship. For us to be a team."

I purse my lips. "So we're in a relationship?"

"We're dating," he says matter-of-factly.

"How are we dating if we haven't been on a date?"

"You with the technicalities." He laughs. "So FWBs, I guess?"

"We can go with talking," I respond, "since I expect us to be more than just friends."

"Bet." He stops rubbing me. He kisses my lips, and I enthusiastically kiss back. He then kisses my other set of lips before freeing the condom of its bind. The wind carries the wrapper across the other end of the roof. "You're still nice and wet. Just the way I like."

"Mmm," I moan.

He reaches his hand back into his boxers and pulls out his dick. Before he starts dressing it with the condom, I take a peek. His member is the spitting image of Apollo, with prominent veins along a thick shaft. The only difference is the length; Marcel is a little shorter than Apollo, but all is well, as I could never take the entire length of Apollo anyway. Which just means that my new man might fit me perfectly.

"You still want it, baby?" he asks. To make the deal even sweeter, he points to his dick and says, "It has veins for her pleasure."

We burst out laughing. Warmth overcomes me as I think about how comfortable I am with this man. How I'm free to express my feelings, positive or negative, with him. When my laughter subsides, I let out a breathy, "Yes."

"I'll take it slow," he says, licking his lips.

"Okay."

Butterflies fill my stomach as he spreads my thighs. He places his left hand lightly on my stomach and uses his right to guide his dick to my opening. He pushes forward, and I can feel his girth against my walls. He goes deeper and deeper, slowly, until I can feel his weight pressed against me. He gently thrusts in and out of me.

In and out.

In and out.

Our panting coordinates while pleasure builds down south.

In and out.

In and out.

He picks up speed and whispers in my ear, "Does it feel good, baby?"

"Yes," I whimper. "Faster, please."

Pacing faster, he cums after about a minute. A light breeze brushes across my naked body. I shiver, and he covers me with his warmth while I lay comfortably in the nook of his neck. I can feel his chest against me as it fills with air and then slowly exhales. Warm breath touches my ear, and with it, a snore incompatible with my light sleeper self.

After a long night on the roof of the communications building, I am now walking back to the dorms, hand in hand with Marcel. He wants to stay with me but has things to do with his friends this morning. No worries, I need to go back to my dorm and get the sleep I didn't get last night.

Recognizing the faces carved in the building, I realize we are back at my dorm already. I am not ready to part ways with him. "So this is it," I say, turning towards him.

"Yeah," he says to me. "I'll call you when I'm done meeting with my brothers. We're getting everything ready for the Activities Fair. You should come."

"When is it?" I ask.

"It's tomorrow," he says while digging in his backpack. He hands me a flyer with many organizations on it. **Activities Fair** is typed at the top. "I'll come by tomorrow and pick you up, and then we can head there together. I don't know what time yet, but we can discuss more later this evening."

"Sounds good."

While holding hands, we give each other small pecks on the lips. We step apart, still holding hands, and stare deeply into each other's eyes. Realizing I do not want him to leave, he kisses my hands and tells me, "We'll see each other in a little bit."

"Okay," I murmur.

We kiss each other one last time, and I turn around to head up to my room. I begin ascending the stairs to my room. I stop at a window between the stairwells just in time to see Marcel turning the corner to head to his meeting. Those two seconds of seeing him ignite a fire throughout my body.

The door is slightly open when I get to my room. I must've forgotten to close and lock it before I left. I cross my fingers and aggressively push the door, hoping all my things are still there.

"Hello!" shouts a tiny white girl sitting on the bed opposite mine. She tosses her straight blonde hair over her shoulder. "You must be Destiny. Nice to meet you!" She holds out her hand, still sitting on the bed, expecting a handshake.

I meet her hand. "Are you Trixie?"

"The one and only." She poses by framing her face with her hands and looking at the ceiling. She breaks her pose and points to her pile of shit in the corner. "Sorry about all my stuff. Also, I didn't know if you had chosen a desk or closet, so I just picked one. Hope that's okay?"

"Oh yeah, it's fine. I brought a lot of stuff, too. I got a little distracted yesterday and wasn't able to unpack."

"Haha, what distracted you?"

"There was a protest going on yesterday for Quintin James. I joined them, and the day just went on from there. There's another protest happening soon if you want to join."

"Oh, I'm not into that kind of stuff. I kind of just stay out of politics." She smiles. "I got some potato salad in the fridge if you want some. No raisins, I promise!"

"No, thanks." I wait for her to turn to roll my eyes. Japanese anime posters fill the wall on her side of the room. Her bookshelf is full of manga. Her pens even have anime characters on them. "So you're really into anime, huh?"

"Yes, I love anime. I am an art major, and I have a Japanese minor. I hope to create a manga someday," she says with excitement in her eyes. "What's your major? I never got to ask you over the summer."

"I am doing general studies. I wanted to become a doctor, but I don't know if I want to go that route. Our dorm is holding a career placement test next week. I'm going to take it and see if anything else interests me."

"Good idea."

I walk over to my luggage, undisturbed from where my family placed it yesterday, except for the bag I got my current outfit out of. I start unpacking my things, stealing glances at my roommate. I watch as she pushes her big, dull glasses up the bridge of her nose and twirls a strand of her stringy blonde hair.

"Are you going to the Activities Fair tomorrow?" she asks.

I tussle at my suitcase to seem like I wasn't just staring at her. "Yes, I am, are you?"

"Yes, I can't wait. There are so many amazing clubs here!"

"What clubs are you planning on joining?"

"Well, I'm definitely joining the Japanese club. Hopefully, they include lots of anime and manga. I think I want to rush a sorority as well, you know, become a Qousa girl. Their outfits are so fly!"

"Oh, wow, Qousa? I was thinking about rushing the same sorority!" I say.

"Yay! We can both be queens of the USA! I can't wait to wear one of those cool African outfits."

"Their Egyptian attire. God yes. They dress like queens every day!"

"Yes, girl! We're going to be Egyptian queens!"

"Yes, I can't wait! And their parties look like so much fun. And the men there are so fine."

"Those are Kousa men, and they are so fine! I need to get me one of those! This morning, I saw a few of them with their attire decked out in the Kousa symbols." She shows me a picture on her phone that she took of some of the Kousa men.

"That's their symbol?" I ask her, realizing it's the same symbol on Marcel's arm. An abstract illustration of an African crown with a flower, a more masculine version of the Qousa logo.

"Yes, and every last one of them is fine as hell," she says, clapping after each word.

"I think I'm talking to one right now. He has this tattooed on his arm. I forgot to ask him about his fraternity."

"Ohh girl, you lucky! Those men stay on fleek!" she forces out.

I laugh at her attempt to seem cooler by using AAVE. Maybe it won't be so bad after all.

Life on Campus

"How about this one?" I ask my roommate for the 12th time. I've tried on nearly everything in my closet to find an outfit for my date with Marcel tonight.

"Again, I like the pink one better," she says. "Pink looks great on you."

"Thanks!" I take off the silky green dress and put back on the pink one. It does look better. I check myself out in the mirror, spinning around to get a look from each angle before deciding that this is the dress I'll wear tonight.

Marcel wants to take me to a nice restaurant outside of campus after his meeting. I'm so glad that I packed some lovely evening gowns.

I turn to Trixie, "My best friend, Erika, always says that pink is my color."

"I'm going to have to agree with Erika," Trixie says, looking up from her phone. "Your friend has—"

A loud screeching sound pierces the air. Our heads turn to investigate. I look at my phone on my desk to see that Marcel is calling me.

"Girl, why do you have that ringtone?" Trixie asks. Her hand is over her heart.

"Sorry. I want something unique to know when Marcel is calling." I grab my phone. "I want something that will give me a jolt when he calls."

"Well, that is too much of a jolt," she says, "more like a heart attack."

"I'm going to change it. It's just temporary. I need to find the right sound," I say before answering the phone.

"Hey, you ready?" Marcel asks. "I'm just pulling up to your dorm."

"Yes, I'm heading down now. See you in a little bit."

I hang up, a big smile on my face. No one has ever made me feel this way before. I touch up my makeup a little before heading out.

"Ohh, girl, you look so beautiful!" Trixie says.

"Thanks! I have to look beautiful for my handsome man!"

"Yeah, he has to be hot! All of the Kousa men are."

"He is fine! He is sculpted and has this beautiful face with great hair!" I end, realizing I'm bragging. "You should come to meet him."

"I'm down with that."

We make our way downstairs. I can see his red car through the windows of the staircase. I try my best to have a sexy face instead of my regular smiley, goofy one. We finally make it to the bottom, and I open the door. Trixie and I walk toward his car, and, like a gentleman, he gets out of the car and opens the passenger door for me. I greet him with a kiss.

"I miss you," I tell him, giving him another peck. "Oh, and by the way, this is Trixie. My roomie." I gesture toward my enthusiastic roommate. "Trixie, this is Marcel."

They shake hands and greet each other. "Nice to meet you," they say in unison.

"So, I see they roomed you with a snow bunny," he says, winking at her before turning to me.

"Yeah, but she's totally cool. We're even rushing the same sorority," I tell him.

"Yeah, we're going to become Qousa women!" Trixie chips in.

"Oh, that's great," Marcel says. "You know I'm a Kousa man myself. I can give both of you the ins and outs of this life."

"That would be great!" Trixie says, ecstatic. She looks at me with a gigantic smile, "Can't wait to become a queen with you!"

"Girl, I can't wait either!" I hug her and tell her that I will see her soon. Who knew I would become so close to someone this soon? College life is great already!

I get in the car. I admire his face and aura as he closes my door and goes to the driver's seat. I couldn't have asked for anyone better suited for me. He finally gets in the car and gives me another peck, this one landing on my cheek.

"How have we never talked about rushing before? Or even about my fraternity? I talk about them all the time," Marcel says.

"I must have distracted you," I say. I lick my lips and wink at him. He kisses me again.

"What kind of music do you like?" he asks.

"R&B," I reply.

"I can get that for ya. Do you like old R&B or the new stuff?"

"Either is fine with me."

"Cool." He grabs his cell phone and streams an R&B station. "So I hope you like seafood."

"Yes, I love seafood. Is that where you're taking me?"

"Yep, I was praying and hoping that you weren't allergic or one of them vegans or something. Or I will have to go to plan b."

"Haha, what was plan b?"

"Subway."

"You lying," I say, laughing.

He smirks.

"But, wow, seafood on the first date? You must really like me, huh."

"Yep, yep. Doing my best to impress you. I've never dated a brown-skinned sista, but when I saw you, I was just amazed. You took my breath away. I just knew I had to have you. You really are something special."

"You're so sweet!" My face lights up, and I turn away from him to avoid the embarrassment I'd have if he ever saw my face like this. Keep your face sexy, I think to myself. Keep it sexy. "I think you're kind of special, too."

"Oh, yeah?"

"Well, not as special as me," I tease. "No, but for real, I think that you're unique. I like your intelligence. I like how we can talk about nearly everything and not just gossip about what everyone else is doing. I like your activism. And you're handsome. You really are special."

"We really can talk about everything. I do enjoy talking to you and looking at you. I think we look good together. Can I ask you something?"

"Of course. What is it?"

"Will you be my girlfriend? I know our first date just started, but I don't want to spend another minute without you being my girlfriend. I know deep in my heart that we are meant to be together. I felt it when we first met."

"Yes, I would love to, and I feel the exact same way."

And just like that, we are boyfriend and girlfriend. He reaches for my hand, pulling it close to him. He gently kisses my knuckles and holds my hand for the rest of the drive. I am screaming with excitement on the inside.

Trixie jumps up as soon as I open the door to our room.

"So, how did it go?" she asks. "I take that it went very well, yeah?" She sits up on her bed, her eyes connecting with mine. "You have to tell me the deets!"

"It was amazing. The best date of my life." I kick off my heels and lay on my bed. "He has been all I wanted all of my life!"

"Where did he take you?"

"He took me to a seafood restaurant. We ate steak and lobster tails dipped in the delicious butter sauce. Shit, even the broccoli was good. We had salad, apple pie, and a bread and cheese plate. One of those five-course meals, ya know. And he paid for everything! I didn't even see the bill, but it had to cost three hundred dollars."

"Wow, he has money!"

"Yeah, girl. He got money, and I didn't even know!"

"He's a good one. And on the first date, wow! What did you guys do after?"

"He took me stargazing. We drove up a hill, sat on the hood of his car, watched the stars go by, and just talked." I get up and walk over to my vanity to remove my makeup. "And he asked me to be his girlfriend before we even went on the date."

"That's great. He's not one of those commitment-phobes."

"Yeah, I think I'm in love!"

"Ohh, girl, I see you. I need to get like you. I can't wait to meet some of the Kousa men tomorrow. It's gonna be lit!"

I walk out to the bathroom, wash my face, shower quickly, and moisturize my body. I can't help but think about Marcel and our future.

I'm waking up early today for the on-campus job I applied for. This is my first job ever, disregarding babysitting my little cousins. Today is one of the mandatory pre-training days. Fortunately, the training will only last two hours because of the Activities Fair. As noted on our work contracts, our other training days will last approximately four hours. I will receive my uniform after I finish training. In the meantime, I must come to work in non-slip shoes, black pants, and a plain white shirt.

I grudgingly make my way over to the building. I arrive about five minutes early, still tired from the night before, and open the door to a lively crowd. Excited morning people greet me, and I am excited to meet them all but so confused about how they can be so functional this early in the morning. I can barely keep my eyes open. Despite my fatigue, I try to be as social as possible, making good first impressions and getting to know my future co-workers.

A loud thud comes from the entry. The room gets quiet as our heads spin to see what's up. A woman is pulling down the security gates and placing locks on them. She isn't security, or at least she isn't dressed like them. She is wearing black shoes, pants, and a white shirt adorned with our university logo. Short, curly, beautifully styled hair sits on her squarish head, her bangs brushing across her dark-rimmed glasses. Her light brown, blemish-free skin is glowing. She turns around and makes her way over to us.

"Can anyone tell me when the work contract said you were supposed to be in this building?" she asks.

"Six A.M," someone says.

"That's right. Six. Not ten after six. Not even one after six. You're supposed to be here at six o'clock on the dot. Can anyone tell me what time it is right now?"

"My watch says one after six," another person replies.

A group returning from a smoke break knocks and bangs on the door.

"Uh, some people are knocking on the doors. They're one of us. They were here earlier. They just went out to smoke cigs," the student next to me says nervously.

"They're no longer with us. They are late. The gates are now closed, and it's time to move on. They are now one of them." She comes closer to us, holds up a finger, and smiles. "Rule number one of the zombie apocalypse: *always be on time!*"

We all nod our heads. She walks calmly in front of us.

"My name is Jeanette Pierce. I am the safety and training manager and will conduct all your training. I am also the person you will see if you violate any safety procedures. Does everyone understand?"

We all nod our heads once again.

"Good. Let's get down to business!"

We follow Jeanette down the hall as she explains some job details. "You are what we call front-of-the-house workers. You will not be preparing food, just serving it. Sounds easy, right?"

We nod.

"Well, it isn't as easy as you think. There are a lot of safety issues that go along with front-of-the-house work, as you will learn today."

We walk to the end of a hallway, standing silently before a big, heavy red door.

"I have nicknamed the following place the Safe House. Rule number two: *only employees are allowed and can get inside.* Please do not bring outsiders into this room with you. You will all obtain a badge embedded with a security chip for clearance by the end of your second training day." Jeanette holds her badge up, modeling the front and back before swiping it across a scanner attached to the door. The red door makes an unlocking sound and cracks open.

"You will use this badge to clock in and out and open the door. Since none of you have badges yet, we will have to clock in the old-fashioned way today." She whips out a few clipboards from her bag. "Everyone, sign your name on one of the sheets. Ensure it's legible so I won't count you missing."

We all line up to sign our names on the sheets. I don't know what to expect from my first job, but I can now add intense to my list. The room is still, so quiet that you can hear the sound of chewing gum, but that soon stops as people grow aware that they are drawing attention to themselves. The loud, warm environment I initially walked into has become a quiet, cold one.

A group of people walks in, dressed similarly to Jeanette. They look older than us, and their faces are stiff.

"These are your shift managers," Jeanette says while holding up three fingers. "Rule number three: *always listen to your managers!* They've been working here for quite a while now, and they know the ins and outs of serving. These leaders were very generous to offer their time to help with training today." She turns and smirks at them, "Although, I'm sure they're here just to get paid that triple time."

The managers chuckle, breaking the tension enough for us to join in.

One by one, the managers show us the equipment in the Safe House. They review dietary restrictions, allergies, gluten-containing foods, contamination, and numerous other safety guidelines. Who knew that food, something that we need to survive, could be so dangerous? We can all tell that they take this job very seriously.

After repeating the many safety guidelines and learning about rule 4, *practice makes perfect*, they hand us a booklet.

Jeanette puts 5 fingers in the air and says, "Rule 5: *study this booklet*. In order to survive and become a server, you must pass the exam. You only get two tries."

I glance at the other students, observing the bewilderment on their faces. I guess I will have to be the brave soul to ask what everyone else wants to ask. I raise my hand.

"Do you have a question, young lady?" Jeanette asks me.

"Yes. I thought that we were already hired. When I applied online, I took a short test that said I passed."

"So, young lady, all that means is that you passed that questionnaire for hiring," she says in a sweet yet boisterous tone. She looks around at all of the students. "You all will need to pass the actual safety exam. We cannot have you working without passing. You'll just be a safety hazard."

"Oh, I see."

"Does anyone else have any questions?" She looks around the room once more. "No? Then let's proceed to the practice room for the remaining thirty minutes."

The practice room is two doors down from the big red door. Looking around, it definitely could have been a playroom or some sort of daycare. Children's drawings line the wall, and the smell of Play-Doh fills the room. Jeanette is carrying a big plastic container overflowing with various fake food items. She puts us in groups, each group led by a manager. In this exercise, we are supposed to practice dietary restrictions.

My group is led by an older white woman, perhaps in her late 50s or 60s. Her fiery red hair blends with her overly-tanned skin. Within ten minutes, I know everything about her children, her four ex-husbands, her current younger boyfriend, her battle with skin cancer, why she still tans, the current college courses she's taking, and why she's deciding to change careers at this point in her life. Her name is Linda.

Accompanying her is a young black man. He has a statuesque, husky build. He is a student who has been a server for two years. He isn't a manager, but he knows his way around, perhaps better than most of the managers, especially regarding technology. When one of the managers needs help with the tablets we are using, they go straight to him. His name is Gary.

"Hey, Gary, how do I get this to rotate?" Linda asks, fingers twirling in her red hair.

"Yes, ma'am. To rotate the PDF, click one of the little buttons down here that says rotate. In this case, you click rotate to the right."

"Perfect! I don't know how you know all of this stuff. Thanks again."

"Anytime, ma'am."

"You are so nice and respectful, Gary." Linda clears her throat. "Okay, if everyone can gather around the tablet," she says while waving people over. "I made a document, with the help of Gary, of course, pertaining to the various dietary restrictions we have to know."

Our small group huddles around the tablet. The document contains a table listing the restrictions and what they cannot eat.

"I will email you this document so that all of you will have this sheet," she says, holding up a piece of paper. "If everyone can write their emails here, that will be great. You will be one step ahead of all the other groups."

"Actually," Gary interjects, "it will be much easier if they put their emails directly into the list we created for them."

"What list?" Linda asks with her face scrunched up.

"The list that we are going to put their emails in. I thought it would be easier if they just put their emails in the list directly instead of writing it down on paper and then uploading it later."

"That doesn't sound very efficient."

"Well, it solves us trying to decipher their various handwritings and accidentally spelling the names in their email addresses wrong."

"Yeah, I don't think we have the time to do all that. Plus, I want a written record of the email addresses."

"Yes, ma'am. Understood."

We line up to write down our emails on the sheet. Gary is looking down at the floor, his hands gripping his elbows. After writing down my email address, I introduce myself to him.

"Hi, I'm Destiny."

Gary fiddles with his shirt sleeve and makes eye contact with me for a few seconds before gazing at the floor. "Nice to meet you, Destiny," he stutters. "I'm Gary."

"Are you okay?"

Gary looks up, and a smile slowly forms on his face. "Yeah, I will be. I don't even know why I bothered."

"Yeah, she doesn't seem very good with technology. I don't think she understood what you were trying to do," I suggest.

"This isn't the first time this has happened. I just need to learn to only do what they ask me to do instead of trying to make things more efficient."

"Yeah, I learned a lot from your exchange. I know what not to do now."

We both chuckle.

"So, Gary, what's your major?" I ask.

"Computer engineering. I take a lot of math and computer science courses. I thoroughly enjoy it."

"That sounds about right. It looks like you help a lot with the technology around here."

"Yep, this job, surprisingly, is very technology-based. I even developed an app for them."

"Wow, that's incredible. How much did they pay you?"

He lets out a sigh. "Zip. They said they couldn't pay me because it wasn't in my job description. But I got credit and experience. Another thing to add to my resume. But getting paid for all of those hours would have been nice."

"Yes, credit and experience are good. But getting paid would have been better."

"They are some cheap MFs."

Linda pops up out of nowhere and observes our conversation.

"What's your major?" Gary asks quickly, shifting his eyes.

"I am doing general studies at the moment. I wanted to become a doctor, but now I'm unsure. I know I want to do something that deals with the brain."

"Oh, really now," Gary says. "Looks like I might have a fellow STEM major with me if you go the biology route."

"Well, I'm not as confident about biology as you are about computer engineering. But it will definitely be STEM because I'm obsessed with the brain. Whatever I do will have to be brain-related."

"Wow, what's with your obsession?"

"I don't know," I say, laughing. "Ever since I was little, I just liked learning about the brain. I had books about the brain, science kits, and I even started a brain club at my high school."

Linda inches closer, occupying the space that was once between Gary and me. I can tell she is interested in the subject by how big her smile and eyes are. "Well, look at you, brain girl!" she says.

"Haha, thanks," I reply.

"You know, we learned a lot about the brain back in my day. Did you know that we only use ten percent of our brain?"

"That's actually a common myth. We use our entire brain to function every day."

"Oh, really?" she says. She rapidly blinks and rubs her chin. "That's not what I learned."

"That myth is widespread. Modern-day brain scans show that the entire brain is pretty active. It is interesting to see which parts are active when doing certain activities. I can send you a video if you'd like. I know I am obsessed with them, but you will not regret watching the video. It's so mind-blowing."

Linda shakes her head. "Yeah, I don't think so. I remember in middle school, we were shown a film that dealt with the brain, and the scientist in the film said that we only use ten percent. You should have read some articles about it, but that will probably be one of the first things you'll learn during your studies. I can't remember the name of the video, but I'll ask my teacher. She and I still stay in touch."

I can't do anything but stand there and look at that lady. I've just explained to this lady how much experience I have with this subject matter. How obsessed I am with it that I started a club to teach others about the brain. I regularly watch videos and read scientific articles about the brain as new discoveries emerge. This lady is seriously trying to discredit my knowledge because she watched a video about the brain over forty years ago!

"Okay," I say, no longer wanting to engage with her.

"Alright, everyone, listen up!" Linda shouts while turning around. "Follow me to get some chairs, and let's sit in a circle to discuss these restrictions!"

I follow the others while walking alongside Gary.

"How dare she?" I whisper to Gary. "How can she think she knows more than me about a subject I've studied my entire life because of a single video she watched? Has it ever occurred to her that recent scientific discoveries have proved that we use more than ten percent of the brain? Or that maybe she misremembered the video, as it was such a long ass time ago? Can you believe this lady?"

Gary pats my back softly. "They are conditioned to speak over us even with less knowledge about the subject. I thought you said that you learned from the exchange earlier?"

Everything will be okay, sweetie," Marcel says as he sweeps my hair from my face and plants a kiss on my forehead. We are on our way to the Activities Fair, and I'm telling him what happened with Linda at work. "She probably didn't mean it like that. I don't think it was because of your race. Honestly, it sounds like she was trying to find something in common with you. I think it was more because she knew you haven't started classes yet."

"I hope that's why because I can't be dealing with this on a daily basis. Hopefully, I don't have to work with her as much," I reply.

"It just sounds like you two started on the wrong foot. Next time you work together, y'all will probably become best friends."

"Unlikely."

Marcel brings me closer to him and puts his arm around my waist as we walk to the field holding the Activities Fair. My body relaxes at his touch. Walking next to us in her Sailor Moon-inspired outfit is Trixie. She can't contain her excitement about meeting her future sorors at the fair. I catch her walking with a joyous gallop every now and then. Marcel can't walk around with us because he will be on table duty with a few other Kousa men, but he wants to introduce them to us. As we make our way to his table, he takes it upon himself to tell us about the many clubs we pass and their reputations.

"You'll probably be interested in this club over here,' he says, pointing to a group of students wearing doctor coats in front of a computer table.

My hands tremble as I try to force words out of my mouth. "Is that a neurology club?"

"It sure is."

"Oh my god. I—I have to get a brochure or something from them," I say, beelining for their table.

"Hey, not so fast. I want you to meet my brothers first," Marcel says, grabbing my arm.

"But I need to be a part of this club. I need to get information about how I can join them."

"They'll be here all day. You can come back. Meeting the Kousa men will just take 5 minutes. And I want you to meet them since you want to be a Qousa woman."

"You're right. I'll come back later."

I quickly take out the map the organizers handed me before the event and place a star on the club. I take out my map and mark it regularly as we pass many clubs that interest me. How am I supposed to pick between all of these clubs? They all look so good to me.

"Cel, baby!" I hear a young woman shout. "Come over and show some love!"

"Here I come," Marcel shouts back. He grabs my hand, as well as Trixie's, and walks to the young lady. "Now I know you know who they are."

"O. M. G! The Qousa women?" Trixie exclaims.

"Yep," he says.

"They are all so beautiful!" I say. "And wow, their fashion sense is amazing!"

"Yep, they are all of that," Marcel says, "and you fit right in."

Both Trixie and I squeal.

"Ladies, how are you this afternoon," Marcel says to the group of women when we're about five feet away from them.

"We are good," they say collectively.

"Out here trying to recruit," says the one who called Marcel over.

"Well, I have two ladies here who've been looking forward to meeting you."

Marcel introduces us to each and every one of them. They are all so different. I only talk to each of them briefly, but I already feel a connection to them. I hope that the rest of their sorority is like this. Unlike the girls at my high school, they are very friendly and don't seem like drama. College is about to be an exciting, stress-free experience for sure.

"I know you're excited to talk to them more," Marcel tells the women, "But I have to introduce them to my brothers real quick. But they will be right back, I promise."

Trixie and I walk away, following Marcel. I have jitters throughout my body, and I'm sure Trixie also has them.

"How amazing was that?" Trixie says to me.

"I know, right!" I say, matching her excitement. "They are even more beautiful in person!"

"And they are so nice and friendly."

"Yes, they aren't stuck up at all. They are humble even though they are a part of this amazing group."

"I can't believe—" Trixie pauses. We almost run into Marcel, who has stopped walking.

"Bae, what's up?" I ask.

"Aye, you see those females over there?" Marcel points to a group of women surrounding a table labeled **THE GODDESSES**. They, like the Qousa women, are dressed to the nines. They are sporting casual chic styles and rocking their natural hair.

"Wow, they are so beautiful," I say to Marcel. "Are they another sorority? Like the Qousa women?"

"They are another sorority," Marcel starts, "but we don't fuck with them. They aren't really for black people, and they refuse to attend our marches. They like to think they are on the same level as the Qousa women, but they live for the white gaze."

"But they look so authentic," I say, staring in awe at the women.

"Well, they present as Afrocentric, but it's all talk. They are not in community with us. And when they take off all that makeup, you'll probably be questioning their beauty too."

"What happened between you and them? Maybe you got off on the wrong foot? Like Linda and me."

"This is completely different. I've had so many run-ins with them, and they all end the same." He finally takes his eyes off of them and looks at me. "There's something up with them. They are pretty new but have chapters springing up all over the place. It is very cult-like. They believe that most black men belong in jail."

"Oh, I see."

"There's another sorority called The Grosses or something like that. I've seen their other chapters; They are not fully black, nor would I consider them a sorority. There are men in some of their other chapters."

"Okay. Stay away from them,"—I point to the table of the expensive-dressed fashionistas—"and The Grosses. Who even calls themselves that?"

"They are self-aware."

I laugh. "Got it."

"Good."

Trixie turns her head in disgust. "I hate fake people."

"Let's go, y'all." Marcel puts his arms around our waists and leads us towards the Kousa men, just a couple of tables down. Trixie is right; every last one of them is fine.

"Did you have a great time, baby?" Marcel asks me as he kisses me on the lips.

Trixie and I haven't seen him since we dropped him off at his fraternity table at the beginning of the event. Given the expansive student field, it's amazing that we even found our way back to the Kousa table. We walk past the club tables that spill into the parking lot. I grab Marcel's hand and smile.

"An incredible time. I collected so many pamphlets," I tell him.

"Same," Trixie says, fumbling with the informational pamphlets in her arms. She was glued to my hip for almost the entirety of the fair, but we broke off to observe other groups, which was nice. She makes a final attempt to catch her pamphlets before giving up and letting them fall around her.

I bend over to help her pick up the sheets, observing the clubs that piqued her interest. Three clubs—Club Japan, Anime Watchers, and Cosplay—were a given; they were right up her alley. But she also grabbed sheets from the clubs I'm interested in, like SSN—Students Stimulated by Neurology. I hand her the sheets.

"Thanks," Trixie says. She cradles the papers in her left arm while using her right hand to organize them from largest to smallest. Marcel hands her the sheets that fell next to him.

I spot one more sheet behind her left foot and grab it. It's her map, and it has her chicken scratch writing all over it. I chuckle at the anime characters she drew in the top right-hand corner. My eyes lock onto a list of names in the bottom left-hand corner: BOB, Queen, Lawrence, Mare, Mike, Jenn. I believe Mike is one of the Kousa men, and I am unsure about the others. There's a line between Lawrence and Mare, separating the names into two groups. Bob is the only name in all caps with a star next to it.

"I see someone's been a social butterfly," I say to Trixie while handing her back her map.

"You know it," she says, grabbing the map, eyes still focused on organizing her pages.

"You know what, I should keep my map too." I turn to Marcel. "I'm going to go back to get my map."

"Why?" he asks. "The event is finished. You no longer need it."

"I know, but I want to keep it as a souvenir," I say, trying not to sound corny. I shrug my shoulders. "I only have one first Activities Fair."

"I get it. I'll head back with you to help you find it."

"No, no"—I wave my hand in protest—"I know exactly where I left it. I won't be long. I'll meet you and Trixie at the Student Canteen."

"If you insist." He smiles and grabs my hand. "I'll order your favorite, so it'll be ready by the time you make it back to us."

"Sounds good."

He kisses my hand before we part. I turn around and go against the rushing traffic of students. Loud stomach growls indicate they haven't found a work-school-life balance, just like me. I squeeze through the crowd, an involuntary sorry coming out every time I invade the personal space of a new person. When I finally get to the student yard, I spin around, searching for the booth where I left my map. I finally spot SSN packing up their supplies. Tanner is smirking at me.

I walk over, and before I can say anything, Tanner utters, "Third time's a charm."

I fiddle with the charms on my bracelet. "I must seem really eager to join." I let out a small laugh, and he does the same.

"You know you don't have to audition to be in the club," he teases.

A slight smile creeps across my face. The first time I came was to learn about the club and give them my contact information. The second time, I wanted to tell them bye before leaving the fair. I spot my map underneath the colorful brain model at the table's edge. I point to it. "Actually, I came for that."

"A map for the Activities Fair?" he asks.

"My annotated map to the Activities Fair," I correct him.

"And you came all the way back here for this?"

"I'll need it when I make my first year of college scrapbook."

He lifts the brain model and grabs my map. His green eyes meet mine right before he inspects my notes. "Um-hum. I can see why you would want this back. It has all of the nostalgic capabilities."

I lift my hand, thinking he will return it, but he continues speaking.

"Let's see. We have some stars here, next to SSN and one of the chemistry clubs. That would make for a good origin story when you become a mad scientist."

I cover my mouth and giggle. "You're such a nerd." I reach out again to grab my map, but he continues.

"You also have stars next to three different sororities. How fun." He hands me back my map, his chestnut-brown hair bouncing as he reaches forward.

"Thanks," I say. "Are you in any other clubs?"

"I'm actually in one of the chemistry clubs. It's not the one you have aster-isked on your map, but another one called Experiments with Student Chemists. We call it ESC. We go around the city teaching children about chemistry, doing experiments, and loads of other stuff. You should check it out. It's a fun escape."

"I will keep it in mind."

"Hope to see you at our first SSN meeting."

"I'll be there."

I turn around and start walking away. I glance at my map. Three sororities. I know for sure that I want to rush Qousa. They are my top pick. Another sorority, The Goddesses, stood out when I snuck to talk to them. Marcel doesn't like them at all, but I need to meet with them more. The last sorority I haven't even had a conversation with. The GROX. I passed their table but didn't talk to them as they seemed super busy. Marcel doesn't care too much for them, but I want to give them a shot. Ah, the pull of the forbidden fruits.

Just then, I bump my thigh against a table. I sit my map down and assess the damage to my thigh.

"Need an ice pack?" a sweet voice comes from nearby.

Without looking up and still rubbing the area where my thigh was struck, I respond, "Yes, that will be great."

Once I have the ice pack on my thigh, I look up and connect my eyes with a tall, gorgeous, medium-brown woman sporting a curly updo. "Thanks," I say.

"No problem." She places a fallen curl behind her ear and clears her throat. "Are you a freshman?"

"Yeah, this is my third day on campus, and it has been overwhelming."

"I remember the horrors of my first month on campus. Getting lost. Trying to balance work and school and still have a social life." She lets out a giggle and extends her hand. "I'm Deidra, by the way. I'm a sophomore here."

My hand reaches hers, and I say, "I'm Destiny."

"What a pretty name." She thumbs through the papers on the table and hands me a sheet. "Have you ever thought about joining a sorority?"

I take a deep breath as my eyes fixate on each letter that heads the page: **GROX.** I notice the women seated at the table where I placed my map and the downed sorority banner beside it. Most of the women are leaning forward, waiting for my reply. "Yes, I have. That is one of my goals for this year. To join my ideal sorority."

"Nice! I hope you will consider joining us," Deidra says, voice still soft and sweet. She points to the paper in my hand. "That'll tell you a little about our values as a group. You'll learn a lot more about us during rush."

"Is it gross?" I ask.

She laughs. "No, GROX rhymes with fox. It's an acronym for 'Get Rid of X,' with the X standing for anything you want to leave in the past. But we just call ourselves Grox."

"I was just thinking that I need to leave distracted walking in the past," I joke, laughing and pointing at my thigh. "I can't be walking around campus with bruised thighs."

One of the other women chips in, "That's a good start. But then you wouldn't have met us." She stands up to greet me. "Hi, I'm Lucinda. I'm the president of this chapter."

"Nice to meet you, Lucinda," I say as I grip her hand for a shake.

"We actually have a dare for you."

I look at her face to see if she is serious. Her sultry, dark brown eyes stare back at me, unwinking. Her cherry-colored lips, a perfect match for her golden black skin, form a grin. I look at Deidra, who is now standing behind her.

"A dare?" I utter.

"It's a first impression dare," Lucinda and Deidra say in unison.

Deidra grabs another sheet from their sorority table, glancing at it. Talking to herself.

"Okay," Deidra lets out. "It looks like you have to request from one of us to go skinny dipping with you." She hands me the paper. "You can confirm the dare if you like."

I look over the sheet. The title confirms that the sheet is for first impressions, so it isn't something that they just made up on the spot.

I think aloud, "Voice... slow and soft... request... okay. I agree with that. Eye color... brown... GROX sister. That looks good as well. Style... let's see... skinny dipping... matches with n—hey!"

First Impression Dare

1-Voice

Fast and Loud= Write   Fast and Soft= Draw   Slow and Loud= Tell   Slow and Soft= Request

Sign= Act

2- Eye Color

Brown= GROH Sister   Blue= Best Friend   Heterochromatic= Statue   Hazel= Roommate

Gray= Bird   Green= Crush   Amber= Confession Forum   Other= Stranger

3- Style

Classic= Best Childhood Memory   Streetwear= A Perfect Sunday

Artsy= Unpopular Opinion   Naked= Skinny Dipping   Elegant= Prank

Vibrant= Proudest Moment   Vintage= Cheesy Pick-Up Line

Casual= Summon Rain   Boho= Funniest Joke   Chic= Favorite Smell

Cosplay= Favorite Catch Phrase   Rocker= Favorite Book

Loungewear= Fake Cry   Trendy= Best Advice   Sexy= Secret Talent

Modest= Novels or Movies   Minimalist=Toilet Paper: Over or Under

Preppy= Bucket List   Gothic= Perfect Vacation   Other= Pineapple on Pizza

I turn to them, and they all laugh. My gasp turns into shaky laughter. Deidra approaches me and says, "We joke around a lot here. But it is always hilarious to see the faces of PNMs when trying to confirm the dare."

"PNMs?"

"Potential new members," she responds.

"Seriously, has anyone ever done the skinny dipping dare? I can't imagine showing up anywhere completely naked, let alone at an Activities Fair."

Deidra shrugs and utters, "The sixties and seventies were of a different time." She takes the sheet back. "It looks like you're in casual wear, so you must request one of us to summon rain."

I give all the women a once-over, but my eyes wander back to Lucinda. "How about the president?"

Lucinda undoes the cyan hair tie wrapped around her high afro puff without hesitation. Her 4c hair bounces satisfyingly just above her shoulders. She takes off her sandals and removes her cyan sorority top in a J.Lo 'Love Don't Cost A Thing' fashion, revealing a sports bra adorned with the logo of their sorority: a star. Blades of grass fold beneath her feet as she saunters across the field behind the sorority table. Once she finds a spot she likes, she sits on the grass, her legs crisscrossed, and before she closes her eyes, she says, "Take notes."

Stillness overtakes her body. The only part moving is her chest, which slowly raises up and down as she takes deep breaths. My breath matches hers as she meditates, and calmness rushes over me. After about a minute, she positions her hands under her chin, and the fingers of her right hand meet the palm of her left in two small, brisk claps.

Clap. Clap.

She moves her hands to the left side of her head.

Clap. Clap.

In a circular motion, her hands stop above her head.

Clap. Clap.

The fingers on her left hand slide down her right palm as she positions her hands to the right of her head.

Clap. Clap.

She then moves her hands counterclockwise until they are above her head once again.

Clap. Clap.

She unfolds her legs and slowly rises with both arms straight above her head, palms together. She stops when she gets on her tippy-toes, poses for about 3 seconds, and then breaks into dance. Her lithe figure compliments the ballet moves throughout her dance. Legs with perfect, pointed toes twirl around in the open space. The chest isolations in her Hip-Hop moves are proof of her control over her body. Her rawness in her modern movements and her power when she throws her arms to the sky prove her control over the environment. She pulls down in a squat, arms still extended and head still to the sky. She balls her hands and repeatedly pulls down as if there are ropes wrapped around each individual star, and she's forcing them down to earth. She shows off her flexibility by doing a backbend into a Chakrasana, the ending pose of her dance.

Applause comes from behind me as I realize the performance drew a crowd. Phones are in almost everyone's hands as they narrate what happened to their social media audience. I walk with the GROX women to join Lucinda in the grass.

"That was awesome," I tell Lucinda.

She winks at me. "Expect rain tonight."

Deidra grabs my attention, handing me the information sheet for their sorority. "We're going to finish packing up. It was lovely meeting you, and we hope to see you during rush."

"You definitely will." I tuck away the informational sheet and return to the table to grab my map.

I glance at my map. Three different sororities, and I think one just took over my top pick. I put my map away and begin the journey to the Student Canteen. I think about the pros and cons of my top three sororities.

The Goddesses are elite. They seem poise and just a tad bit snobbish. However, they have an extensive network and know people who know people. That could be a great advantage after I graduate. I'll already have connections when I am job hunting. But Marcel hates them.

The Qousa women are classy, with a little bit of ratchetness, just the way I like. They are relatable and easy to talk to. Plus, Marcel is a part of the Kousa men, making being a Qousa woman even sweeter. If my roommate gets in, I'll already have a close friend in the group.

The Grox women have a wonderful sense of humor and are unique. I love how easygoing they are, and I will love it if some of the confidence they all emit rubs off on me. But Marcel has issues with them.

I spot Marcel and Trixie through the glass walls of the Student Canteen. Trixie pinpoints me, then presents an empty chair next to her, my favorite sandwich and a milkshake already there waiting for me to consume. She waves for me to come in. I pull on the door and stop when a droplet of water splashes on my face. I look up at the dark clouds quickly forming in the sky. Petrichor fills my nose as I rush inside to evade what's to come.

Rush

"How does this look?" I ask Trixie while twirling in the mirror.

"I think you paired the shirt nicely. You gave more effort than me," she says, laughing.

The rush T-shirts are tasteless faded black with the letters P-N-M in white. I twist the sides of the shirt into knots to give it more oomph. My platinum bracelet, a gift from my parents, embellishes my left wrist. I opt for a half ponytail to ensure my face isn't hidden by my hair. Dark denim shorts and black tennis shoes complete my look.

"This is as good as it is going to get. There's nothing more I can do about this shirt."

"Looks nice. Can you help me get my shirt like yours?" Trixie asks.

"Of course."

She rushes to the mirror and stands in front of me. I admire her beauty before starting on her knots. We've only been on campus for a few weeks, and she has changed a lot. She has traded her big-rimmed glasses for contacts. The new highlights in her hair add volume. And her style, save for her cosplay, mimics mine to a T. But I don't mind. What's that quote about being flattered by imitation?

She takes one of my hair ties when I finish her knots. "Can I borrow this?"

"Sure."

She parts her hair with her fingers into top and bottom sections. She takes the top area and pulls it through the hair tie. After setting the ponytail, she wraps her loose hair around the band to veil it. She turns to me and says, "Twins."

I check my makeup and outfit in the mirror again and contemplate exchanging my tennis shoes for flats, but ultimately decide what I have on is great. Plus, we'll be doing a ton of walking during this round of recruitment. I hear that open house can be chaotic. "Ready to meet up with our group?"

"I sure am." Trixie grabs her notebook, and I follow her to the door.

We meet recruitment counselor Alice at the start of Fraternity Road, a street filled with sorority and fraternity houses. Trixie and I chat with the other PNMs. My nerves calm as I realize that the other women are just as nervous as I am, far from the confident feeling they expressed at the convocation a couple of nights ago.

Alice refuses to tell us which sorority she is a part of. "It's unethical to say, I'm just here to guide you," she states whenever someone poses the question. She takes attendance and reviews the schedule for today and tomorrow.

"You'll have twenty-five minutes at each house. Remember to be yourself. You don't want to end up in a house where you must constantly wear a mask. Trust me, it'll get old quickly, and you'll be miserable." She checks the schedule and walks us to the first house.

Luckily, I will visit all three of my top sororities tomorrow night. The practice today will, hopefully, prepare me to meet my favorites tomorrow.

We gather on the steps of the first house. Our guide stands in front of the door, announces the sorority's name, then steps aside. As the doors open, we can see a group of women screaming at the top of their lungs in a triangle formation. They do a stiff dance routine, including fist pumps, before welcoming us in. A sister grabs me by the arm, and we chat for a few minutes before another sister pulls me away to chat with her. This chaotic process continues for the rest of my time in the house. Is every house like this? Yes, they are all like this.

A group of screaming women greets us at the second house. At this house, the women form a square, waving their hands as they scream. Upbeat melodies blare from the sound system as they perform a short swing dance choreography. When it is time to chat, they still grab me by the arm and pull me in different directions, asking the same questions but with slightly different language.

I am more than prepared for the second night of open house. I slip on my denim shorts. I knot my PNM shirt and do the same for Trixie. My makeup is a tad different, influenced by some of the other PNMs' styles from yesterday's open house. I opt for black flats instead of tennis shoes. Trixie does the same.

The first house we visit is the Goddesses' house. They welcome us with shrieks and a ballet number. Their poise during the dance matches the character of the women that I met at the Activities Fair. Still on their tiptoes, they walk over and gently hook our arms one by one to be carried away for a chat. I mentally note the questions they ask and how they make me feel.

My game plan is to answer the question, then hit them with a "What about you?" to get insights into their values before another woman grabs me to ask a different question. It is working pretty well so far.

When we leave the house, Trixie catches up with me and asks, "How was that?"

"I really like them, and I love their questions. What about you?"

"I like them too. I have no idea what Marc was talking about," she responds.

I narrow my eyes and rub my chin. "Marc?"

She throws her head forward, shaking it, and a laugh escapes her throat. She gathers herself and places her hand on my shoulder, "Oh girl, that's just what I call Marcel. I know everyone's nickname for him is Cel, but that's, like, the last part of his name. I prefer nicknames to be the beginning of someone's name, if you know what I mean."

"I get it, but I think he prefers Cel. Does he know you call him Marc?"

"Yes, I asked him, and he said it was okay." She hugs me. "Come on, girl, you know me. I would never just rename a black person without their permission. That's super problematic."

It's more than problematic. I change the subject back to her thoughts about the Goddesses. We both agree that they don't seem that bad. In fact, they seem like a wonderful sorority to join.

We visit house after house, just like yesterday. My eardrums are buzzing from the screams and the loud music accompanying the dances. I take a deep, calming breath as we approach the steps of another house in my top three: Grox.

Shrieks welcome us in. The women partner up and begin to tango across the floor. The beautiful, sensual dresses flow in the air as the women shake their hips to the beat. However, I cannot take my eyes off their shoes. What beautiful heels. Custom, I think.

Once their dance ends, we clap before being pulled in different directions. Again, I answer the questions flawlessly and listen to their response.

I see someone rushing toward me from the corner of my eye. A familiar face. Deidra. She gently grabs my arm and pulls me away. "Hey, Destiny! Nice to see you again," she says in her sweet voice.

"Nice to see you again, too. Your sisters are so nice."

"Thanks, they're awesome," she says. "So, how was your summer?"

"It was great. I went backpacking in Europe with my best friend, Erika."

"Oh, sounds fun! So you're already used to being away from home, with you being away all summer, huh?"

"Actually, I left for Europe last year. I did a gap year. And I came home in July. I was gone for about eleven months."

"Oh, amazing. I would have loved to have done something like that," she says.

"You still can. It'll give you a break and a chance to broaden your horizons."

"I'll have to think about that."

"Time is up, ladies," Alice announces. "Time to go to the next and final house of the evening."

"Hope to see you again," I tell Deidra.

"Same," she replies.

She walks away, and I see her tap Lucinda, who I haven't seen at all during the open house. She must have just come out of wherever she was hiding. Deidra whispers something in her ear. They both look at me. I wave a quick goodbye to them and join my group as my guide leaves for the next house.

"Another awesome group," Trixie says as she buddies up with me on the sidewalk. "How are we supposed to choose from all of these houses."

"I know, right? So you're feeling all of these groups as well?"

"I am, but Qousa still has my heart." She does an animated spin with her hands on her chest.

I laugh. "You are so funny."

She lets out a snort, and we both burst out laughing.

"Alright, ladies,"—Alice turns to face us, walking backward—"this is our last stop of the open house phase of rush."

The beautiful gradients of gold, emerald green, and blush pink on the house are the first things that catch my attention. Kousa has the same gold and emerald green colors but swaps the blush pink for a nice azure.

"Ooh," we say in unison, admiring the building.

Our guide stumbles up the steps. A few women rush to help her, but she's already up when they reach her. "I present to you the Qousa Women." She bows and presents the front door as she steps aside.

The French doors open, and, once again, screaming women greet us. The women do a Hip-Hop dance number, which makes me believe some are on the school's dance team. Popping and locking, the Humpty Dance, and even the Harlem Shake make an appearance during the choreography. The original Harlem Shake. Their movements are smooth like butter and flow like a river. The way they isolate, control, and twerk the booty is revolutionary. They grab us by the arm after the dance ends to chat.

The last person I talk to at the house is Tammy, the chapter's president. "So, how was Europe," she asks. "Is it as racist as America?"

"That's a tough one." I pause and think for a moment. I didn't practice this question, and none of the other houses asked a question of this nature. "I would say that racism presents itself differently. I had an American passport, so I was treated better than the non-American black people, but some things were still noticeable."

"Interesting," she says, nodding her head. "Did the laws and policies there aid in structural racism?"

"I'm not sure. I didn't really do any research while I was there. But as they say, anti-blackness and racism are global." I say that last sentence confidently, trying to make up for the lack of knowledge of a region I spent such a long time in.

"Right on," Tammy replies. "I see that your group is leaving. I'll let you catch up with them. Hopefully, I'll talk to you soon."

I admire her wavy, Peruvian bundles as she struts away and joins the Qousa women waving us goodbye. I return the wave bye and join my group.

"Okay, that is definitely the group for me," Trixie nearly shouts. "It blows all of the other houses out of the park."

"So, you're definitely sticking with Qousa?" I ask.

"For sure. Aren't you?"

"I'm keeping my options open. I just want to know for sure if they're my match, you know?"

"I feel you, girl."

When we make it back to the beginning of Fraternity Road, we enter a large, empty building. Remnants of exercise equipment surround us. About eight basketball hoops, sans nets, are hanging from the ceiling. Chairs and tables are set up in the middle of the room. Chatter about the pros and cons of joining different sororities buzzes throughout the room.

"Alright, ladies," Alice starts. "We've visited several houses these past two days. Now it is time to rank them."

"What if we liked all of them?" a PNM, whose name I've forgotten, asks.

"Then think about which ones you like the best." Alice paces across the room and holds up her cell phone. "You can now open your app, which should let you rank the sororities."

The room grows silent as we find the app on our phones and see the list of sororities at the university.

"Now, there are two sections." Alice raises two fingers in the air. "In the top section, you need to list the sororities you want to see for the philanthropy round. It doesn't matter which order you place them in; you can choose up to eight."

"What if I only want to choose seven sororities?" another PNM asks.

"Then choose seven," Alice answers.

"Sounds good." The PNM turns back to her phone, satisfied with Alice's answer.

"The bottom section is for sororities you want to drop." Alice continues. "The order of this section absolutely matters. If, for some reason, one of your picks from the top section drops you, we'll pull from the bottom section, starting with number one if they pick you."

I scroll through the list, finding my top three sororities to put in the first section: Goddesses, Grox, and Qousa. I check my notes to see which other sororities I'm optimistic about joining. I enjoyed all of them, but I vibe more with some than others. I add two more to the top section for a total of five sororities I want to see on philanthropy day. I condemn the others to the bottom section.

Trixie nudges me, "Who are you putting in your top section?"

I show her my picks on my phone. "I have five in the top section. And"—I scroll up—"these are my top picks in the bottom section. Just in case."

She squirms in the chair next to me. "You know I was only going to put down Qousa, but since looking at yours, I think I should put down a few more."

"Definitely. Anything can happen. It's better to leave your options open."

"You right," she says in a slight accent.

A notification pops up on my phone. **SCHEDULE READY**, it reads. I hop on my bed and take a deep breath before opening the sorority app. I scream into my pillow, which barely muffles the sound.

"What's going on," Trixie asks, startled.

"Did you get your schedule?"

Trixie rushes to her phone and opens the app. She jumps up and down, her sundress flowing with her movements. "Yes! Ya girl will be visiting Qousa today!" She looks at me. "Why are you screaming? Did they not pick you?"

"No, they picked me," I say. "It's just that one of the sororities I picked didn't pick me back."

"Oh no," she says while walking up to me, her eyebrows drawing together. "Which one?"

"It doesn't matter, and I shouldn't even care. It wasn't one of my big three, anyway. The rejection just stings a little."

"Well, look at the bright side. You'll get to know Qousa, Goddesses, and Grox a little better and won't be distracted by other sororities," she says, trying to lift my mood.

"You're right." I rise up from my bed and straighten my sundress. I place my feet in my wedges and buckle the loop around my ankle. Bracelets, a sunhat, and sunglasses complete the look.

"Wow, what a fancy hat," Trixie says, staring at my hat, mouth slightly parted. "I wish I had one."

I place my hands on my hat and model it for her. She intentionally pouts, and I give her a hug. "It's okay that we're not complete twins today."

"I know. I just feel like we are getting too far from each other. I mean, we don't even have the same schedule today."

"Trixie, we live with each other, and we might be joining the same sorority at the end of rush," I assure her.

She nods and smiles. I smile back, relieved that everything is okay. Or so I thought.

We leave the dorm, but Trixie isn't her usual energetic, talkative self.

"What's on your mind?" I ask her.

"I don't know how to explain it," she replies.

"You know we will be spending a lot of time together. Right now, it is just hectic."

"I know, but it is like, you're spending so much time with Marc, your job, school, Tanner—"

"SSN," I quickly correct her. "SSN is related to what I want to study. Tanner could possibly hook me up with some jobs after I graduate. It's all about networking, girl."

"Yeah, but do you have to do so much right now? I mean, it's only our freshman year." She crosses her arms.

"You're in the Japanese club and"—I smirk—"that freaky deak club."

We both burst out laughing.

Trixie shakes her head, still grinning. "It's sex-positive. I guess I am busy with my own stuff, too."

"And that's on self-reflection." We hug. "That club is so stimulating, though. Pun intended."

"Haha," she fakes laughs. "It really is, though. I learn so much new stuff."

"I bet you do. Anything that I could test out with Cel?" I wink at her.

"I don't know," she says with a hint of shyness. "We went over oral sex tips and tricks. We watched a movie about pegging last week, under my recommendation, might I add. Your girl is contributing already, and I just got here..." she trails off. When she realizes she's been talking non-stop about her contributions to the club for at least two minutes, she clears her throat and looks at me. "Hey, we are having a toy party sometime soon. No exact date yet, but you should come!"

"Sounds fun. Maybe I can finally replace Apollo."

"Apollo?" Trixie looks at me, confused.

"Girl, my vibrating dildo that I carelessly left at home."

She snorts. "We can help you find one."

We walk silently for a bit before she asks, "So does that mean Marc isn't putting it down on you?"

I shoot my eyes at her. It's flabbergasting that she'll ask such a personal question. I chalk it up to her being in a sex-positive club and quickly fix my face. Maybe I'm just a little sex-negative.

"I enjoy it, but I haven't orgasmed with him yet," I answer honestly. "Cel isn't a very good listener when it comes to sex. He thinks the tactics he has experimented with on other women will work on me. But it doesn't. He gets me close but never finishes."

"Shit, that's tough." Trixie looks down at her feet. "Maybe I can get him to join the club. Sounds like he needs it."

"He could use a bit more sex education. But it's getting better. We are communicating, and I am sticking to it."

"Okay, let me know if you need anything." Trixie spreads her arms, indicating that she is back in character. "We have loads of resources."

We meet up with our recruitment group. Excitement emits from the other PNMs as they discuss their schedules for the next two days. Trixie will be visiting six sororities: three today and three tomorrow. On the other hand, I have a full schedule and will visit eight houses, including the ones I initially dropped. I hope there are no hard feelings. Maybe I'll even change my mind on some of them.

"Does anyone have any questions about the schedule for the next two days?" Alice asks the group. We all shake our heads. "Good. So, you have your schedule for today and tomorrow. We won't meet again until the end of the day tomorrow to do your rankings. If you have any questions or issues before then, you can contact me through the app. Okay?"

We all respond nervously.

"Okay."

"Sounds good."

"Okie, dokey."

"Cool."

I open my notebook to review the notes I took during the first round of rush, paying close attention to the ones I dropped. I've been so focused on my top three that I've neglected the others.

"Good luck, ladies, and I'll see you again tomorrow," Alice says. She turns around too fast and almost trips over herself. Why that woman continues to wear heels that she cannot walk in eludes me.

I join a group of women in going to our first house of the day. This round is much longer. We have fifty minutes at each house. I know we are supposed to talk about philanthropy, but I have no clue what we'll do outside of that. I had mandated community service in high school, so I plan to discuss my experience.

Fortunately, the first house isn't my top priority. It's just the thing I need to shake away my nervousness. After the first house, though, I'll be visiting my top three, so I will be on my game for most of the day.

We enter the house, and it is set up like a reception. Finger foods are abundant. Sparkling juice fills the wine glasses waiting for us at the standing tables.

The sorors present a slide show of the foundation they support in the welcome speech. They tell us the importance of literacy among children. Pictures of various members reading to children are on every presentation slide.

After the presentation is done, they join us in the crowd. I talk to a few of the sisters, who ask me about my philanthropic endeavors in high school. I tell them what I did, what I learned, and what I would like to do in the future. I tell them nearly everything, omitting that volunteering was a requirement at my school.

I feel more confident after leaving the house to go to my next house: The Goddesses. Same reception-like setup. They have sparkling juice, but it's in these beautiful amethyst wine glasses that almost resemble a goblet. Surprisingly, the squarish structure of the cup fits perfectly in my hand. The intricately engraved crystal gives the impression that it is handcrafted and not mass-produced. A fleur-de-lis with a diamond in the center, their logo, sits on the front of the wine glass, and right beside it is the engraved signature of the maker.

The finger foods include mini quiche, salmon stuffed red potatoes, marinated shrimp, Korean BBQ bites, fruit, and cheese. They even have peach cobbler in tiny cupcake liners. The toothpicks to pick up the food have lilac balls at the end of them.

Soft classical music plays in the background. The Goddesses are wearing black dresses and lavender statement pieces. I feel wildly underdressed but find comfort in seeing the other PNMs wearing more casual clothing.

"We need a better public image," Kiana, the chapter's president, states in her welcome speech. "The media tries its best to trash our reputation. Putting negative stereotypes front and center. I am personally tired of it. Aren't you?"

Loud cheers come from the PNMs. I clap my hands with the other women.

"The media is always looking for something to keep us at the bottom," Kiana continues. "How about we don't give them anything to find? Stop providing the ammo, and they'll run out."

Whistles float through the air, and roll calls come from the sisters behind Kiana. I cheer loudly with the other PNMs.

"With etiquette training, we are preparing the next generation of black girls to be more socially successful. Which will, in turn, lead to more opportunities. I'm talking about more options in career paths, mates, where to live, and where your future children can go to school. I truly believe that we can run this world. And it starts with passing down our values and uplifting the next generation of young black women. Thank you." Kiana bows to a roar of applause. I would say that we gave her a standing ovation, but we were already standing, so I'm not sure if that counts.

The Goddesses integrate into the crowd. I mingle with a few of them and answer their questions as best I can.

How do you balance your feminine and masculine energies?
What does it look like to be a liberated black woman?
How do you prioritize yourself?
Do you have a mentor?

What are your thoughts about the current portrayal of black women in the media?

How can black women be better protected in the black community?

How can black women be better protected around the world?

Warmth spreads throughout my chest as I leave the house and join the other PNMs. I eagerly discuss the event with them; they feel as pleased with their answers as I do. I might have a little competition if their talks went as well as they say. I shake away any doubts, lift my chin, and focus on keeping this positive vibe going for the rest of the day.

The Qousa house is a short distance from the Goddesses. I wonder if they ever do events with each other.

Sundresses are the chosen attire of the Qousa women. Their colorful sundresses flow freely while waiting for the PNMs to filter into the house. Relief wipes across my face as I realize that I was not underdressed at the Goddesses' house; they, in fact, were way overdressed.

The setup at the Qousa house is a little different. They have regular-sized paper plates, unlike the miniature plates at the Goddesses' place. I grab a few items: mini pizza, spinach dip with pita chips, buffalo chicken bites, black-eyed peas with collard greens, and deviled eggs. The folding chairs near the front are filling in quickly, so I hurry to claim one, forgoing the desserts. Ensuring the Qousa women can see my face and my positive reactions to their presentation is more important than my sweet tooth. That banana pudding is calling me, but I must focus on my mission.

Tammy is in the front in a folding chair facing us. She's still rocking the wavy black Peruvian bundle but with blue highlights. Her orange sundress compliments her skin tone perfectly. Her sisters sit behind her, chatting, pointing out certain PNMs, and writing in their notebooks. None of the women I met last time is here, save for Tammy. I keep my face relaxed with a soft smile.

Tammy finally looks up from her phone, her foot tapping vigorously. She gets up and paces to the microphone. "If everyone can have a seat, please. We are ready to get started," she says.

She smiles and waits a bit. The room is polluted with chatter, and women are still in the back, grabbing food. Some who were already seated are now getting up to get seconds. She twists her lips and speaks into the microphone again, "If you can just quiet down. You can still get food, but we need to get started. Thank you."

The room grows silent, and the Qousa women begin their presentation. We get a mini-lesson about Black Wall Street and similar communities that existed.

"We have more rights and more power than we did back then. So why don't we have a modern Black Wall Street?" she asks the crowd. "This brings us to our foundation."

Tammy points to the screen. I stare at the black and white photo depicting a burned-down Tulsa that has been up for a minute. With her free hand, Tammy massages her head before waving at her sister, who is working the slides. Unsuccessful at getting the gorgeous bald woman's attention, she does a familiar dance and sings, "Somebody's getting fired."

I bust out laughing with the other PNMs, remembering that iconic moment. The woman on my right side leans into me and says, "Don't you love it when we share these special moments together?"

I give her a nod and say, "Yep. It feels like we've known each other all our lives, but we only just met. It makes me feel at ease."

The woman closes her eyes and takes a deep breath. On the exhale, she sings a soft om. "I feel so connected here. This is where I belong." She opens her eyes and looks at me. "I'm Treena, by the way."

"Beautiful name. I'm Destiny."

"Nice to meet you, Destiny," she says in her raspy voice. "I think I saw you at the other two houses I visited today."

I definitely remember her from the other houses. How can I forget? Her smile radiates happiness and shows off those pearly whites embedded in her light pink gums. She is one of the few women who haven't worn any make-up during rush, showing off her clear, obsidian skin and naturally lined eyes. Her plump black lips are only dressed in lipgloss. The TWA that sits on top of her head pairs well with her modelesque bone structure.

"I saw you too. You really stand out," I say. "What are the chances that we have the same schedule? Are you visiting Grox next?"

She shrieks and does a small clap in front of her lips. "Looks like I found a walking buddy to my next house. Yay!"

Tammy taps on the microphone. "Back to our foundation. As you can see on the screen, we've been very successful throughout the years."

Pictures of black women and men in various stages of success fill the subsequent slides. Holding up college degrees in some. Standing in a room with well-known businessmen and celebrities in others. Behind the scenes of some of my favorite TV shows. New business openings. But most prominent are the ones that display checks written in large amounts, investment portfolios, accounts with hundreds of thousands of dollars, and racks in hands.

"We teach financial independence and wealth building to the black youth in the communities we serve," Tammy continues. "Generational wealth brings power. Brings opportunities. We teach youth how to raise their credit scores." She raises her hand. "Has anyone here ever heard of a secured credit card?"

Only a few women raise their hands.

"This is the type of knowledge our community needs to thrive. We can't rent particular apartments because our credit scores are low. We can't get loans; if we manage to get one, the interest rate will be through the roof. Ask my"—she points in the general direction of the Qousa women—"good sis, why she can't get a building here for her growing business. But we got her. She's building that credit and should have a good enough score to secure a loan by next school year."

The PNMs quickly applaud the testimony. Shouts of affirmations come from different parts of the room.

"And that's only half of the battle. Rich people have been coming here, snatching up the buildings, preventing us from owning property in our neighborhoods."

A lot of the women in the crowd are shaking their heads.

"But we're coming back for it. Succeeding in our short-term goals will allow us a chance to complete our long-term goals. And that's on bigger, better, Black Wall Street. Thanks."

Treena and I get up to join the standing ovation. The Qousa women bow and join the crowd, firing off questions in one-on-ones.

What is on your bucket list to visit?

What is an issue prevalent among black females that you are passionate about?

What are your thoughts on reparations?

Who are your role models?

How do you help in your community?

Have you ever participated in a boycott or a protest?

How can we end this so-called gender war we have with black men?

I feel increasingly connected with my blackness after each woman I talk to. I meet up with Treena, and she expresses the same sentiments.

"They really know how to speak to our souls," she starts. "I feel so elevated and uplifted. I cannot wait to bring my talents to this group."

"Same."

Treena and I walk to our last house of the day.

"Ready for this?" she asks.

"Yes, I am."

We enter the building with the rest of our group. The casually dressed Grox women greet us at the door and escort us to the reception area. Like in previous houses, I grab anything that speaks to my belly. Spinach and artichoke dip, cauliflower bites, and a spoonful of one of their grain bowls are on my plate as I sit and wait for their presentation. Treena sits beside me—sans plate because she overate at the Qousa house.

Lucinda takes the stage, her golden black skin shining like it always does. "Tell me the first word that comes to mind over the next few slides," she says.

The first slide shows a salad: butter lettuce, black beans, red onion, corn, avocado, and tomato.

I shout out, "Delicious!"

Someone else shouts out, "Healthy."

"Filling."

Lucinda changes to the next slide without acknowledging our adjectives. The next slide is a burger: Buns, patty, lettuce, tomato, onion, and cheese.

"Tasty!"

"Unhealthy!"

"Fast food!"

The next slide is a picture of chicken alfredo.

"Greasy!"

"Yummy!"

"Heavy!"

The following few slides have the same format: a picture of a dish and first impressions of that dish, except for the last slide. The final slide has one word with flowers, animals, and hearts surrounding it: vegan.

"Elitist!"

"Expensive!"

"Nutrition deficient!"

Lucinda returns to the slideshow's beginning and calmly states, "The food you've seen on the screen has all been vegan. Actual pictures of food prepared by my fellow sisters and me."

You can hear the breathing of everyone in the room. Nonetheless, Lucinda continues.

"We are aware of the constant mispronunciation of our name and decided to name our foundation, that's right, GROSS. That stands for Get Rid Of Systemic Starvation."

I hear a few claps from the audience.

"Are you sure it isn't gross because of the food?" someone shouts and then chuckles.

"The food is absolutely delicious and would make my grandmother proud," Lucinda says without missing a beat. "We wanted to create a foundation that helps our community while staying true to our values and beliefs. And that is how we came up with GROSS. Many of the complaints we receive about veganism are about the food, which is a small part of veganism but a large part of our everyday lives. You have to eat to live, don't you?"

Most of the PNMs nod their heads along with me.

"So some of the things you named earlier like... elitist, nutrition deficient, and expensive are some of the things you tell us that"—she makes air quotes—"prevents"—end air quotes—"you from becoming vegan. And we want to get rid of those obstacles."

"I don't think you can fully eliminate those obstacles," a PNM says.

"True," Lucinda says with a shoulder shrug. "We can't entirely eliminate many things in this system we're living in, but it doesn't stop anyone from helping others or trying to do better. So, a little about our foundation."

She starts a soundless video that displays the Grox women shopping for food. The next scene is of them cooking in a beautiful kitchen. Then, displays of their finished dishes before they are stored in small containers.

"Every week, a few of us cook for the underserved in our communities. The people in our community are overworked, exhausted, and mentally drained. Some have strenuous jobs, while others work two or three jobs just to make ends meet. They give us money or benefits they would have spent on food, and we do all the shopping and cooking for them that week. We prepare delicious, healthy, and filling food for them and their children. Three meals a day, seven days a week, all meal-prepped and just need to be reheated."

"That sounds awesome," one of the PNMs says while squirming in her chair, "but it still makes me uneasy."

"What is making you uneasy?" Lucinda asks.

"The whole animals being better than humans thing," the PNM replies while patting the top of her lemonade braids.

"Where did you get that idea? Because it certainly wasn't in this presentation."

"Never mind!" The PNM stands and grabs her things, her braids swaying.

"Don't go," Lucinda pleads. "Stay and talk about it. One of my favorite things to do is dispel myths about the vegan community."

"I don't want to hear it! I am tired of you all forcing your beliefs on me. And now you're targeting the disadvantaged? Nah!" She storms out. A few other PNMs follow.

Lucinda observes the bolting women. "Go ahead and run," she says, "filter yourselves out. Less work we'll have to do." Deidra elbows her, and Lucinda gives her a confused—*what did I say?*—look.

"And that is my cue to go," Treena says, turning to me. "A bad attitude and arrogance are major red flags."

"Agreed."

We get up to join the other vacating PNMs. Looks like I only have to choose between two sororities now. Thanks, Grox, for making my life much easier during this hectic time.

Today is preference day, the day that I've been waiting for. After visiting house after house, watching philanthropy presentations, and participating in skits, I have two sororities left on my list. Some eliminated me, but for the most part, I was scratching sororities off my list left and right because, frankly, they just didn't fit me. And what good is it to be in a group where you don't belong? I can feel the perceived loneliness as I shudder at the thought.

"Which sororities did you match with?" Trixie asks me as we get ready in our dorm.

"So, I matched with Qousa women, of course."

"Obviously."

"I think they really like us! But I'm not going to get my hopes up. There's so much competition."

"What's your next match?"

"I really want to give this group a try. When I met them at the Activities Fair, they didn't seem as bad as their reputation. So I gave them a chance. I really felt a connection with them throughout the rounds. So I chose them, and they chose me."

"Chose who?"

"Oh, uh." I shift before I say their name. "The Goddesses."

"What?"

"Yeah, I felt like I clicked with them a bit. They are just as friendly as the Qousa women and just as beautiful."

"I thought we've already been through this! They are a bunch of racists."

"Black people can't be racist."

"Okay, but they can be bigoted." Trixie places her hands on her head and turns in a circle. "And you know how they treated me during the skit."

"I know, but—" I stop to search for the right words. "They just want a safe space for black women only."

"They have you fooled," Trixie says, emphasizing the last word. "Believe me, I thought they were awesome on the first day of Rush as well, but that all changed during the skit."

"But—"

"How could they," Trixie cuts me off, "even suggests that I am a colonizer just by being in a historically black space? Why don't they see me as a symbol of unity?"

"Those are some good points, but I want to hear them out."

"Fine. But don't say Marc and I didn't tell you so." Trixie wags her finger. "Remember, he said the same thing about them at the fair."

"Well, I still want to give them a chance. I think they are just misunderstood."

"See, that's how they get you. They seem all nice and friendly in the beginning. Then you start to hang with them more and more. Your friends that you once had start to distance themselves from you. You start to wonder why everyone is acting so weird. And then you realize they're not acting weird. You're the one who has changed. You've turned into a big bitter sourpuss."

"Sounds like you need to get into storytelling."

"Plus, why would they let me go through all those rounds? It's not like I just turned white. Unnecessarily cruel." She slides to me on her knees. "Please don't join them!"

"Mmmh, okay," I tell her so she can stop hounding me about it. "Who else is on your list?"

Trixie lays back on the floor and says, "If it ain't Qousa, it ain't right."

"You're not worried about the competition and potentially not being picked?"

"Noped. I didn't click well with the other sororities or co-ed fraternities, so I crossed them off. Besides, why wouldn't Qousa pick me?"

"I strive for your confidence."

"You know we already have a leg in due to our connection with Marc and all, right?"

"I know, but dating a Kousa man doesn't mean you're automatically in the club."

"Girl, they adore Marc. And they love the story of how y'all met. They're definitely not letting you or your awesome roomie sidekick get away. We're a definite in!"

I chuckle along with her. "I guess we do have an advantage over the others, huh?

Trixie nods her head. "So you have two preference interviews today?"

"Yep."

"Good luck with both. I am going to the Qousa interview right now, and I know you will do well when you sit with them later. I hope your interview with the Goddesses," she pauses briefly and gets up from the floor, "will be enlightening."

"Thanks," I say. "Good luck to you as well. You got this."

Trixie opens the door, looks back at me, flashes a smile, and waves goodbye before closing the door to head to her interview. I wave back and continue to do my make-up. I take one last look in the mirror before leaving for my interviews.

A Quick Call Home

What are the clouds telling me? I alternate between looking up to the sky and looking straight ahead while on my way to my first preference interview. The clouds are moving rather quickly against the clear blue sky. Am I moving too fast? But what does that have to do with my upcoming decision? Maybe the clouds are rushing, and they want to tell me about rush.

I stop to study the shape of the fluffy cloud directly above me. It looks like a ship. A ship with two horns. A few moments later, the horns dissolve and resemble a leaping dog. I just need one sign about what sorority to pick or at least what to look for in these interviews.

"Doesn't look like it's going to rain," a familiar nasally voice says from behind me. I turn around to meet Tanner's green eyes. He looks back up to the sky. "Yep, looks like another beautiful day."

I smile. "I was actually looking for a sign of how my interviews will go today. Or who to pick." I regret saying the words as soon as they leave my mouth.

Tanner gives me a blank stare, then looks at the sky again. "I give you two months before you lose it."

I narrow my eyes at him, wondering what he could mean by that statement. I know I didn't sound that crazy. "Lose what?"

"That magical thinking of yours." Tanner turns to walk away. He throws up his hands and turns back toward me. "Or universal blessings, whatever you guys call it nowadays. Being in SSN will do that to you. You'll think more logically." He taps his noggin and continues walking away from me, and I can't do anything but stand there, stunned.

My gaze is broken by my vibrating wrist. I look at my smartwatch. **INCOMING CALL, MAMA**, it reads. I slide right on the watch face to answer the call.

"Hey, Mama," I say as I rummage around my purse, trying to find my earbuds before she says anything embarrassing through the watch's speaker.

"I can't see you!" she whines.

"Hold on, I have to get my phone." I locate my earbuds in the bottom of my purse and switch them on. One of these days, I will get a new case to replace the original one I broke months ago. I grab my phone and slide the screen to give video permission. "See me now?"

"Oh, I miss you so much!" she says.

"I miss you too."

"I am so happy to see your face," Mama says. She slightly goes off-screen, but I can still hear her voice, though faintly. "Paul, come say hi to your daughter." Mama squeezes back into the frame, now joined by my dad.

"Hello, princess, how are you?" Dad asks, sounding much older than when I left. You would have thought that I had been away for years.

"I am good. I am actually on my way to one of my interviews."

"For the sorority, right?" Mama asks.

"Yes, for the sorority. I am a little nervous."

"Don't be," Mama encourages. "Just be yourself, and don't let those catty girls bring out the worst in you."

"Ooh wee," Dad dramatizes. He then enunciates every single word of his next sentence. "There's about to be some drama in there. Just remember to stay true to yourself."

"Thanks," I say, the only word I can muster. "Where's PJ and Laila?"

"Oh, they are outside," Mama responds while getting up. "I'll let you talk to them; give me one sec." She starts walking.

"What have you all been up to?" I ask.

"Family functions, school, work, movie theater, the usual," Mama responds. "How are you liking college so far?"

"It's great. The best decision of my life."

"Sure beats pursuing modeling after your gap year, doesn't it?"

"Yes, it does."

"That is good to hear. That's what I want for my daughters," Mama says. "I want educated girls who don't have to depend on no man or their looks in life. Whatever they want, they'll have the brains to get it. Do you know what you want to study yet?"

"Not yet." I stop walking and find a bench to sit down on. I still have time before my interview; the first house is just around the corner. There's no need to show up early because they'll be interviewing another PNM anyway.

"Well, I will need you to do a job shadow, intern, take a career test... something. Your father and I did not fund that gap year you took for nothing. We need our investment back." Mama's tone is flat, and her face is expressionless. This isn't criticism but a disguised suggestion of what she wants me to do next. Mama: the queen of living vicariously through her children and tugging the strings through unsolicited advice.

"Once I settle down in a sorority, I'll figure out what I want to do."

"Hopefully. Are you getting the money we send you on Fridays?"

"Yes, I am." Both of us are quiet for a moment. I admire the new highlights in her hair. The side-swept bang brushing across her eyelashes is the push I needed to decide to get a similar hairstyle when my allowance hits my account next week. It takes a few more seconds to realize why Mama hasn't said anything in a minute. "Thanks for that," I utter.

"You are more than welcome," she responds. She looks away from the camera and shouts, "Kids, guess who's on the phone for you!"

"What's up, big head," PJ says playfully, poking his head into the frame.

"Hey PJ, how is school going?"

"It's alright. I can't wait to get out of here and start my rap career."

"Boy, you need to pass English class first," Mama says. PJ darts his eyes at Mama. She looks at him with her lips turned. "What? I'm just telling you the truth. You can't have good bars without good grammar."

"See, this is exactly why I don't mess with y'all now. AuthenticCap was right, like always," PJ says, slowly backing out of the frame, Homer Simpson style. "Going to Puerto Rico as soon as I turn 18. Going to get my passport, a foreign whip, a foreign girlfriend, a record label…"

"Whatever," Mama says. She sits down on the patio furniture. A little girl with two pigtails climbs onto her lap and then turns to face the camera.

"Laila!" I shout louder than I should have.

"Destiny!" she shouts back, matching my tone.

"I miss you so much! How is school going? Are you learning a lot? Did you get the books I sent you?"

"I miss you too," she says sweetly. Her big eyes lock with mine. "I bring my books to school with me to read. My teacher always asks where I get my books from, and I say, 'Boy, I get them from my sister.'"

I laugh. "I know that's right."

Dad pokes his head into the frame and says, "I've been giving her some books, too."

"Cool," I say, looking at him. I turn my attention back to Laila.

Laila looks at my dad, then looks back at the camera and says, "He tried to give me some books, but I said, 'Boy, my sister already gave me books.'"

I burst out laughing. I love the little personality she has developed. Laila laughs with me. A cute little squeaky laugh. Mama is smiling. Dad is frowning.

"What did I tell you about calling me a boy?" Dad asks Laila.

Laila wiggles her nose and turns to him. "But… but you are a boy."

"No. No, I am not. I am grown!" Dad says firmly, his nostrils slightly flared.

Laila shrugs and says, "Girl?"

"Don't get smart with me," he says.

I close my eyes and hope that Dad calms down. I start to say something, but for once, I don't have to.

"Oh, she's just using the new vocabulary she learned in school," Mama says.

"Yeah," I add, trying to defuse my dad. "She didn't use girl or boy a few months ago. And she used to call everyone he." I look at my baby sister, who is now a little teary-eyed. "You are growing and learning so much. I am so proud of you." Laila smiles back at me.

"But I've told her to stop saying it," Dad starts.

"Oh, Paul, give it a rest," Mama cuts him off. "How are you this upset over some words?"

Dad looks at Mama, mouth ajar and eyebrows raised. "I am trying to teach her some respect."

"Respect, where?" Mama says. "She is talking to her sister, and you keep interrupting her."

"I'm not interrupting her. I am trying to teach her. But you're over here with this new parenting technique crap we never agreed to do."

"I'm still trying to find out why this upset you so much. You're acting like a little girl."

My dad's eyes widen as if he has had an epiphany. "A little girl? Never."

"Lately, you have been. There can't be two females in a relationship. One of us is going to have to man up."

"Woman!" Dad stands up and grabs the phone. "Watch out! Let me talk to my daughter."

"At least let us say bye first," Mama says.

"I'll bring the phone back in a minute," Dad responds. Once at a safe distance, he says, "Your mama always has something to say. How's college going?"

"It's going good."

"How do you like your roommate?"

"She's great! Better than I thought she would be. I guess I shouldn't judge a book by its cover."

"She's white. I know how those white girls get down. She's wild, isn't she?"

What kind of answer could he possibly want to this question? I glance at my watch and see it is almost time for my interview. "I guess. Hey, I have to go. My interview is in a few minutes."

"So, you don't have time to talk right now? Interesting."

"Well, yeah. You guys called me on preference day. I have a tight schedule."

"You are avoiding me."

I don't say anything back. Truth is, he isn't my favorite person to talk to, so I don't make an effort to call him. We don't have that much in common or that much to talk about. Anything I say has to be carefully pieced together to avoid everything falling apart in a rage. It is honestly exhausting.

"You haven't called me since you've been away," he continues.

Why would I, I want to say. Actually, I should say it. He can't do anything over the phone. But then again, he can. I bite my tongue. Truth is, I cannot afford to lose my weekly allowance, especially with my minimum wage job. "I call and text y'all all the time."

"Y'all," he mocks. He awkiles. "I am talking about *me*. You don't take the time to call me. You only talk to me in the family group chat."

"I just figured you're busy with work and that you would see whatever messages I put in the group chat."

"Okay." He looks away from the camera. "You know who you got that from. Your mama."

"What?" I ask, genuinely confused.

"It's a damn shame, but mothers always turn their children against their fathers. I know we didn't have the best relationship when you were growing up, but your mama sure didn't make it any better. Look," he pauses. "I want us to have a good relationship moving forward. I am sorry if you feel like I didn't do the best I could have done in the past. But now that you are older, maybe you can better understand that your mama only bad-mouths me because she is upset, not because I am bad. Let's have a fresh start. A new beginning."

Mama never bad-mouthed you. All that woman did was worship you. I want to say my thoughts, but fear captures my tongue. "Sounds like I need to call you more," I say quickly. "I'm heading to my interview. Tell Mama, PJ, and Laila that I love them."

Dad chuckles.

I wave goodbye and hang up before he can say anything else.

And the Winner Is

My first interview is with the Goddesses. I walk up to their beautiful stone lair. Out of all the houses I've been to, this one is my favorite architectural-wise. The outside is a lovely grey stone carved with the faces of African Goddesses. The door is plated with gold paint. The inside is enormous, with tall columns and skylights. They even have a fountain. A very small one, but nevertheless a fountain. I walk up the steps, counting each one as some sort of self-calming meditation. One, two, three, four, five, six, seven, eight, nine...

Okay, I can do this. Just relax... be myself... I got this! I lift my finger to ring the doorbell. I hear someone on the other side. I step back and put on a friendly smile. The door slowly opens, and Kiana, the chapter's president, walks into view with a warm glow.

"Good evening, Destiny. Glad that you can make it. Come on in." She holds the door open for me, closing and locking it once we're inside. I admire the beautiful architecture of the house once again. She leads me to one of the side rooms and has me sit on a chair fit for a princess. They really get into their theme. She heads towards the door, but before exiting, she turns and asks, "Can I get you anything? Coffee? Tea?"

"Tea, please."

"Flavor?"

"Do you have mint?"

"Yes, I do. Do you take it with sugar or milk or anything?"

"Sugar will be fine."

"Cool. Be right back."

I look around the stunning room. The Goddesses' initiation fee is the same as the other sororities, but their money goes further somehow. The expensive furniture, the paintings on the wall, and even the house pet, a tricolored Coton de Tulear, scream luxury.

"Okay, here is the mint tea and a few cookies." She brings out a beautifully crafted gold tea tray with intricate details of a flower garden. She places one tea cup and saucer near me and another where she'll sit. The aroma of the tea instantly calms me.

"Thank you so much. Your tea set is gorgeous!"

"Thanks. It was my grandmother's. She gifted it to the house when she learned I had become a Goddess."

"Well, it's very nice."

"Yes, indeed. Shall we begin?"

"Yes, I'm ready!"

"Just to let you know, this session will be recorded so my sorority sisters and I can review it to make final decisions."

"Understood."

She sets up a recorder and says, "First Question: Why would you make a good sorority sister?"

I am prepared for this question. Actually, I think that I am ready for any of the questions that Kiana is going to ask me. Trixie had found a list of questions on a sorority website, and we went through them together. We rehearsed until we found the perfect answer for each of the questions. I gave her my prepared answer without a flinch.

Kiana checks the recorder a few times during the interview to ensure it is still recording. I use those moments to sip my tea to calm myself for the next question.

"Okay," she says. "Final question: How do you plan to cultivate your black-ness in our sorority?"

"I kind of grew up isolated from blackness, going to a predominantly white high school and all. I rarely hung out with my extended family because they were too far away. I was in the burbs, and they were in the city. My best friend, Erika, and I created our own safe space and passed knowledge between each other. We didn't learn much about our culture in school outside of the slave trade and the Harlem Renaissance, so we took it upon ourselves to learn about the things that our school intentionally omitted. I have connected more with my blackness in the short time I have been in college than I ever have in my entire life. I am an activist at heart, and I believe the Goddesses have the resources to help me cultivate my destined path. And I believe that I can help grow this organization through my activism."

"Wow, what an answer! You didn't seem nervous at all." Kiana says.

"Well, the tea kind of calmed me down."

"Yeah, tea always helps. But you have a really wonderful, genuine personality as well."

"Thanks!"

"Have you met a lot of people on campus?"

"Not really, just my roommate, a few people from a couple of clubs I joined, and my boyfriend."

"Is your boyfriend Marcel?"

"Yes." I let out a slight laugh. "I feel like everyone on campus knows now."

"I saw you walking with him at the Activities Fair." She twists her lips. "He and that white girl mean-mugged us every time they walked by."

"You know, I think you all got off to a bad start. I think that we all need to just start all over. And I can help with that. If I become a Goddess, I can help build a bridge between the Kousa men and the Goddesses."

"You think he will still be with you if you become a Goddess?"

"Well, of course. We're soulmates. Since we've been together, Cel has supported everything I do."

"He won't be supporting this. Trust and believe."

My stomach begins to roil. "I already told you that you two got off on the wrong foot. I'll tell him how amazing the women in your house are, and he'll be cool with it."

"That won't work. I don't understand why you're with a guy like Marcel. Like I said, you have an amazing personality and can do much better. Get yourself a Tanner."

I cringe when she says Tanner's name. "Okay, this is very inappropriate. You shouldn't be this invested in my relationship. I'm not even a Goddess yet, and you're already trying to control who I date."

"Sorry, didn't mean to be controlling," Kiana says, raising her hands peacefully. "I just want to warn you about how much of a sexist pig your boyfriend is. If you even heard half of the things he has said—"

"My boyfriend isn't a sexist pig!" I shout at her. "Some nerve you got!"

"I'm just trying to warn you. I would hate for you to go down the same path I went down when I first started college. Your man hates black women and—"

"Hates black women? How? He's dating a black woman."

"Listen, you are conventionally attractive, you're joyful, you are his idea of respectable, and I can go on and on. You are the exception. He doesn't like black women and—"

"I am not the exception. Cel has a whole group of black women, the Qousa women, whom he interacts with daily. Explain that."

"The Qousa women don't like black women either."

"I am—" The laugh I let out has a slight edge. "I am so done with this. You seem to be more emotional than logical. Just listen to yourself. None of what you're saying is making sense."

"You will see soon enough. There have certainly been red flags that you have ignored to keep this ideal relationship going. But how long can you ignore them? How long—"

"Enough! I'm leaving! Don't even bother putting my name down because I'm not putting yours down." I get up from my chair, grab my things, and head to the door.

"Please, just listen to him and the Qousa women if you join their clan. Listen to how they talk about other women. Listen and observe who gets the most support and who doesn't. Listen and observe who gets the most vitriol and who gets all the compliments. Listen to how—"

"Yeah, my boyfriend was definitely right about you all. And he should have added materialistic as hell as well. Y'all all about y'all designers, aren't y'all."

"What?"

"All this expensive shit up in here. I guess you're royalty, and everyone else is peasants, huh?" I say as I open the front door to exit.

"Before you go, just know that the other Goddesses and I really like you. If things get rough, you can always talk to us if you need anything. We can be your..."

I slam the door. I can still faintly hear Kiana babbling on. Storming down the steps, I almost trip. I turn around to see her poking her head through the window. I throw my middle finger up and model-walk out of the yard. I can't believe this heifer has me in such a bad mood! I thought for sure that this was the house for me. But then again, looks can be deceiving. Marcel was right. Trixie was right. I should really listen to them more. And even worse, I'm down to only one sorority. Maybe I should have picked a third and fourth. I can't change it now. I can only return to my room and try to calm down before my interview with the Qousa women.

"See, I told you," Trixie says. I try to put her on video, but it isn't going through. Whatever. I put her on speaker phone while I, yet again, do my make-up. Wiping away the mascara tears and painting my quivering lips.

"I was just in disbelief. Everything was going so well, but Kiana had to poke her nose in my business."

"I told you not to trust them. Even Marc told you not to trust them. You need to listen to us more often."

"I know, I know."

"I knew they were trouble when they said they didn't feel safe around me during the skit."

"For the last time, there's nothing wrong with black women wanting to have a space to themselves." I wince from my sudden tone change. I am so tired of her bringing this up so much. I've been avoiding it, but I must talk to her now. Get it over with.

"But they acted like I didn't belong at this school at all!"

"Girl, let's settle this. As a white person, you will never understand some things about blackness."

"I am so ingrained in the culture, though. I adopted the language and style, and I even get black dick and black pussy every once in a while."

"Woah, slow down. It is starting to sound like fetishization."

"That's another thing. I think that no matter what I say, it will sound like a fetish," Trixie says. Although I can't see her, I know she is pouting.

I sigh. When race discussions come up with her, it's like talking to a brick wall. "I don't think you'll ever see our side of things. And it isn't like you can't join any other sorority on campus. It's just that the Goddesses is only for black women."

"Certain black women. You said they think the Qousa women are racist against black women."

"True, but—"

"How would you like it if white people made a club you couldn't join simply because you're black?" Trixie asks.

"Totally not the same thing!"

"Explain to me how it isn't!"

Just then, I hear a familiar voice in the background. The phone statics as Trixie tussles with them.

"Cel?" I say. The other end of the phone is dead silent. I pause for either one to answer, only hearing the thumping of my heart. When no one answers, I shout, "Marcel!"

"Yes, sweetie, I'm here," he replies back.

"You're hanging out?"

"I saw your friend Trixie when she left the Qousa house. We were just talking about how her interview went."

Trixie chimes in, "Yeah, he was coming, and I was going, and we just bumped into each other."

"Oh. Well, where are you now?" I ask.

"We're still in front of the Qousa house. I wanted to see you before your interview." Marcel says.

"But my interview isn't for another hour."

"Oh really? They must have gotten the times wrong." Marcel explains. "I'll be here waiting when you arrive. I wanted to wish you luck before your big interview. I know how much this means to you."

"Okay, I guess I'll see you in a little bit," I say, quickly hanging up the phone afterward. I don't know what to think. First, Trixie is fed up about being unable to join a club for black women only, and now she's hanging out with my boyfriend. Maybe I'm looking into this too much. Regardless, talking to her didn't make me feel any better. In fact, I feel even worse than before. How am I supposed to go to the Qousa interview like this? I reach for my phone to call Erika.

"Best Friend!" Erika's soft voice says on the other end.

"Hey, girl..." I say to her.

"You don't sound too good. Is everything okay?"

"Not really. Everything was okay, but today has been so horrible."

"Tell me what happened."

I spend the next few minutes telling Erika everything that went wrong today, from my meeting with the Goddesses to what happened with Trixie and Marcel.

"It'll get better. Do you think that the Goddesses were right about Marcel?"

"I don't think so. Even though he didn't stand up for me at all when I was arguing with Trixie, what Kiana told me about him just doesn't add up. He is just so caring towards me."

"Do you think anything is going on between him and Trixie?"

"No, I believe what he said. It isn't so unusual they bumped into each other and started talking. I mean, they know each other. I think I'm just overthinking it because of the argument that Trixie and I had."

"Yeah, I can see that. But be on the lookout just in case."

"I know, I know. I am so glad that I called you. Talking to you has always made me feel better. When are you coming to visit?"

"I don't know. We are so far away from each other. I'll let you know after I check my calendar." She lets out a sigh. "College has been crazy busy so far."

"I know, right? I can barely find time to eat with rush and everything going on."

"Same here. I forget to swipe most days. Can't be wasting all that money I spent on room and board."

"Haha, I keep forgetting that you can only swipe at certain times at your university. Why do they only allow you one swipe during each meal? What if you want to skip breakfast and go for seconds at dinner?"

"I don't know. I wish we had 21 swipes a week at any time, like your school has. Or hell, even 3 swipes a day at any time. It's just so frustrating trying to get those swipes during the allotted time."

"Yeah, I told you about going to that white ass school. It's such a rip-off. They bet on you missing those periods to save them some money."

She laughs. "It sure does feel that way."

"Yeah. Let me get off this phone so I can head to this interview. Hopefully, it goes better than the Goddesses interview."

"Yes, you don't want to be late. And please, I know we're far from each other, but if you're ever going through anything again, do not hesitate to call me. You know I'm always here for you. You're always welcome to stay at my place if you need a break or anything."

"The pleasures of having a single room. I wish I had that. Then I probably wouldn't be dealing with this Trixie drama right now. I can't believe I called her anyway. What was I thinking? I usually call you, don't I."

"Haha, yes, for everything. Everything!" Erika roars, hinting at our inside joke.

"Haha, no need to bring that up again!" I start bugging up over the phone. I hear Erika laughing uncontrollably on the other end.

She stops laughing. "Good luck with your interview tonight. I'm sending you nothing but positive thoughts and energy."

"Thank you so much! Love you!"

"Love ya like cooked food!"

"Cooked food!"

I end the call and stare at myself in the mirror, ensuring my makeup is perfect. Talking to Erika always brings up my spirit. Even so, I am still nervous. I take a deep breath and leave my room to walk to the Qousa house.

I traipse the steps to the beautiful mini-mansion known as the Qousa house. The confidence that I had while talking to Erika has vanished. The incident at the Goddesses' place escapes from the back of my mind and is all I can think about. And my conversation with Trixie. And Marcel.

The doorbell has a peculiar sound. But everything sounds strange right now. I try to give myself one last pep talk, but I hear footsteps slamming against the pavement before I can finish. I turn around to see Marcel, carrying flowers, running toward me.

"Marcel Moore," I grunt his full name and make eye contact so he knows I mean business. "You were already supposed to be here."

"I know, sweetie. I came here and realized I had forgotten the flowers I was supposed to give you. I made a quick stop around the corner just to get them. Here," he says while handing them to me. I take the flowers from him, never breaking eye contact.

He tries to give me a kiss, but I step back to dodge his attempt. He smiles softly and grabs my free hand. He brings it to his lips, pressing sweet kisses on my moistened skin, and says, "Good luck, sweetie. I know they'll love you just like I do. You'll do great."

I can't stay mad at him. For all I know, he probably wasn't even near Trixie when I argued with her. I kiss him and smell the flowers. "I love you, too," I say.

The door to the Qousa house swings open, and a gorgeous light-skinned woman stands in the doorway. She has the same Peruvian bundles she wore at the philanthropy presentation, but this time with pink highlights.

"Getting some good luck kisses before the interview?" she asks.

"Yeah, you know," Marcel responds. "I gotta support my girl."

"And you brought her some Kousa flowers. She must be special."

"Why yes, she is." Marcel turns to me and gives me one last kiss on the cheek before waving bye to Tammy and disappearing down the steps.

Tammy welcomes me into the house and takes me into a room where the interview will be held. She asks if I want tea and does the usual things a good host does. "I'll be back," she says, "I just need to grab my notepad."

"Okay."

My hands are shaking so much that I can't grab the tea to drink without the risk of spilling it over myself. I grab a few sugar cookies and snack on them until she returns.

"Do you not like the tea?" she asks as she appears beside me, cradling her notepad.

"No, it's fine. I'm just waiting for it to cool down."

"Okay then. Are you ready to begin the interview?"

"Yes, I am."

She turns on a tape recorder. "This is just so the other Qousa women can hear this interview since they can't be here tonight."

"That's fine with me."

"So, Destiny, why do you want to become a Qousa woman?"

I give the same answer I gave Kiana at the Goddesses' house. Already having a script calms my nerves. In fact, I can comfortably sip my tea without spilling it halfway through the interview.

"How do you expect to cultivate your blackness as a Qousa woman?"

"I kind of grew up isolated from blackness, going to a predominantly white high school and all. I rarely hung out with my extended family because they were too far away. I was in the burbs, and they were in the city. My best friend, Erika, and I created our own safe space and passed knowledge between each other. We didn't learn much about our culture in school outside of the slave trade and the Harlem Renaissance, so we took it upon ourselves to learn about the things that our school intentionally omitted. I have connected more with my blackness in the short time I have been in college than I ever have in my entire life. I am an activist at heart, and I believe the Qousa women have the resources to help me cultivate my destined path. And I believe that I can help grow this organization through my activism."

"That's a great answer," Tammy says.

I smile, knowing that I nailed that delivery. "Thanks!"

She opens and then just as quickly closes her mouth. She exhales deeply. "Can I ask you something?"

My heart starts racing. Please let this not be a repeat of what went down with the Goddesses. "Sure," I say, my voice shaking.

"How did you meet Marcel?"

"I met him at the protest for Quintin James."

"Oh, so an activist couple. How cute!"

"Yeah, we are already discussing doing a few more protests."

"That's great! We need more people like this at our university. You know, the person who did your Rec letter, Rose, started just like you! Qousa woman with a Kousa boyfriend who did activism together."

"Oh, Rose!" I exclaim, remembering the sweet elderly woman I had tea with in the South of France. "Does she come to campus often?"

"Yep. Rose and her husband, Earl, come to alumni events we cocreate with Kousa. She is my biggest role model. How did you meet her?"

I straighten up in my chair and think about how to put my words together. I was desperate to network during my gap year, but I don't want it to seem that way. "Well, during my gap year, I wanted to reach out to alumnae of different sororities to get a feel of my future. I saw that she had a speaking engagement and decided to attend. What a wonderful speaker she is."

"I know, right," Tammy affirms. "I want to get to that level someday."

"Yes, me too," I agree. "One thing led to another, and she invited Erika and me to tea!"

"Did she talk about how she used to pass?" Tammy asks, wide-eyed.

"No, she really just talked about her activism. I had no idea she had that kind of history."

"Yep," she giggles. "She used to pass, but once she met Earl, she changed her entire path. Went to a black school, rushed a black sorority, fought for black causes, and the rest is history. It is amazing what love can make you do, isn't it?"

"Yes, it is."

We talk about Qousa women and their relationship with Kousa men as she walks me to the door. We connect very well, and I am sad that it is over. I am leaving more energized than when I came in. We say our goodbyes at the door, but before I go, she raises her fist and says, "Black power."

I repeat her action. Wow, she must have really gotten a Rose-like activist vibe from me. I think it's safe to call myself a Qousa woman now.

Hair

"I'm sorry I made you feel that way," I say to Trixie as we walk to the park. It has been nearly a day and a half since we had that argument over the phone. We haven't spoken much, both of us are extremely busy with Rush. Today, while we were sitting awkwardly in silence in our dorm room, we received a text simultaneously. I opened it to find that it was a group text and that Trixie was among the many recipients. The text instructed us to meet at a particular spot in the park this evening dressed to impress. This could only mean that we got into the same sorority. "We should let bygones be bygones."

Trixie looks at me for a second, then smiles. "I'm sorry too," she says.

We hug, and it's as if we've never even had that argument. We start to talk about how excited we are about being a Qousa woman.

"So, what do you think we're doing tonight?" I inquire of her.

"I think that it'll be some kind of getting-to-know-everyone activity. You know, like those icebreakers we do in school. What do you think?"

"I think that it's going to be a fancy dinner."

We show up at the park and join the ecstatic group of women already present. There are so many questions being thrown around:

"Did you receive the text?"

"Yes, I did, but did you see how many people it was sent to?"

"Do you think it's from the Qousa women?"

"It has to be from them, but is it good or bad?"

"They wouldn't have us get all dressed up if it's bad, would they?"

"Of course not, but what if this is the final test?"

"Yeah, what if we have to prove how fashionable we are?"

You can practically feel the excitement and the anxiety in the air. The park lights come on, and underneath one of them stands three women dressed in all black with hoods covering their faces. I point out the three figures to the other women.

"Are we supposed to go up to them?" one of the women asks.

"I don't know," another woman responds.

We all collectively decide to walk toward the three mysterious women. Statues—or so I thought. I see one of them scratch an itch. And then I rest my eyes on their shirts. They each have one word on their shirts: **GOT OUR TEXT?**

Some women give a verbal yes. Some try to show them the text on their phone. Watch alarms start to go off. The three women instantaneously raise their wrists, turn off their alarms, and turn around. The back of their shirts read three new words: **GOOD, FOLLOW US.**

We follow the three women through the park on the paved pathways heading towards the main streets outside of campus. I regret wearing heels. The women finally stop at the steps of a recreational center and point to the door.

"Are we supposed to go in?" a woman asks.

"I'm quite sure we are," I respond to her. I lead the way to the doors and swing them open. It's dark and quiet inside. I unsuccessfully try to feel the wall for a light switch. I turn to see the mysterious woman directing us to enter the building. "I think they want all of us to come in."

All of the women gather in the pitch-black building. We huddle up as we don't know what is in the building. Once all the women enter, I see the mysterious women slowly clapping their hands together. The doors close, and the mysterious women are still clapping. Neon lights come on. Hand in hand, the women and I follow the path made by the lights, anxious and curious about what will happen next.

"Ouch!" a woman right in front of me exclaims. "It's a wall!"

We all try to push it, thinking it might open somehow, but with no such luck. "What do we do now?" another woman asks.

"I don't know," I answer. "There is only one possible path to follow the lights, and now we're left with no clues."

The sound of footsteps comes from behind us. I feel everyone turn. The lights click on, and the building is crowded with people. "Congratulations and welcome to Qousa!" they all scream.

The other women and I all scream in excitement. The Qousa women hug us one by one. The Kousa men, who are there with their new recruits, also come to us and welcome us to the family. Trixie comes over and hugs me. "It looks like it's going to be a party," she says.

I look at the details around the room, and she's right. There are bowls full of punch. Finger food. Glow stick stands are in nearly every part of the room. And there is a DJ booth with a gigantic dance floor. A man heading to the DJ booth, sporting red light-up headphones, grabs the mic, "Let's get this party started!" Everyone shouts and hurries to the dance floor.

I spot Marcel. He takes my hand and leads me to the dance floor. "I'm so proud of you," he says.

After dancing my butt off, drinking many cups of the spiked punch, and eating all the food I can get my hands on, Tammy pulls me off the dance floor. She has been pulling off the new recruits one by one all night.

"Are you enjoying yourself?" she asks me.

"Yes, this is so much fun!" I yell over the loud music. "I want to stay here forever! Wooooooo!"

She laughs, "You're having a really good time. I want to introduce you to your big sister!"

I squint my eyes at her. "I don't have a big sister. I have a little sister named Laila."

Tammy chuckles. "You are so drunk. No, this is your big sorority sister. She will be the one to personally show you the ropes. And will prepare you for the initiation ceremony."

I throw my head back, almost spitting the punch out. "Oh, yeah, that big sister," I say after gathering myself. "I get to meet her tonight! Who is it?"

"Her name is Jennifer. She's right over here."

Tammy leads me to a light-skinned woman with dark red, naturally curly hair. She's wearing a beautiful cut-out red dress that hugs her curvy figure. Her acrylic nails have the Qousa designs on them. "What is up, lil sis?" she says in a smooth, deep voice.

"Hey, hey! I'm Destiny. Nice to meet you!"

"I see you like to party, yeah?"

"Yep, this party is lit!"

She laughs, "Well, if you ever need anything or want to know about anything, just hit me up, and I will try my best to make it happen. Here, let's exchange numbers." She hands me her Qousa-adorned phone.

"Where did you get your phone case?"

"I ordered it off of our official website. It was $30."

"Oh, cool. We have an official website?"

"Yep, and only Qousa women have access to it. One of the many perks of being a Qousa woman."

"Damn, that's exclusive. What are some of the other perks?"

"The men. I see you already have yourself a Kousa man."

I smile. "Yes, I do, and we're going to get married one day."

"So y'all serious?"

"Yes. Yes, we are."

"Black love is good love. We are in the best position possible to marry a good black man. We go to the same parties, attend the same events, and we even do the same volunteer work. May your love continue to grow, sis." She gives me prayer hands, and I return them—an accompanying silent thank you.

"Do you have your eye on someone?" I ask her.

"Yes, I do. I've had my eye on him for a few months now." Jennifer looks up to the ceiling. "We met this past summer, and he is a king. Let me tell you, girl."

"Are you guys talking?"

"No, I'm a pussy when it comes to this stuff. It's like, I'm one of the guys, ya know, so I'm comfortable talking to them, but I get nervous when shit gets all romantic."

"Girl, if you want it, you gotta go get it. That's how I got my man, and I haven't regretted it since. Is he here now?"

"Yes..."

"Well, point him out. What does he look like?"

"Okay, but you can't tell him 'cause I'm not ready yet."

"I won't."

"Okay, he's the one sporting the full green Kousa outfit."

I turn my head until I spot the only person in the room with all green Kousa attire. "Oh yeah, he was among the first people I noticed at the party. He stands out a lot!"

"I know, right? His name is Mike. He's one of the dopest people I have ever met. Everything he wears is custom-made, and he even has a Kousa grill. He is adamant about how much he loves his queens. "

"He seems hella dope. And he's handsome!"

"I know! And he's ripped as fuck."

"So when are you going to make your move?"

"I don't know. I don't even go up to guys for real. I wouldn't even know what to do to see if he's even interested in me."

"Girl, your little sister is a professional! I can have him taking you to fancy dinners in no time."

"You look like a professional! I still can't believe how fast you were able to swoop up Cel. You have to show me your ways!"

"As much time as we will spend together, you are bound to pick up some of my tactics. I'll teach you, no charge!"

"Thank you so much, sis. I'm so happy that they chose me for you. I can see us being very close. I hear that you're into activism."

I can't believe the excellent reputation that I already have. "Uh huh, one of the first things I did when I arrived on campus was march for Quintin James."

"I hear you, sis. One of the best things we can do to protect our black men is march and fight for them."

"I am so tired of seeing unarmed black men being shot by these police officers."

"Those racist pigs. We need a change. The entire system is racist against black people and especially racist against black men. I can't wait for the day we'll have our Black Wall Street again."

"I wish I knew more about my history. Would you believe I just learned about Black Wall Street? I am so embarrassed."

"No worries, sis. I can help you out with that. After all, I am your big, and you are my little."

"Thanks so much, Jenn! Sorry, Jennifer!"

"You can call me Jenn or Jennifer. I answer to both," Jennifer says. "Have any idea what you would like to learn about first?"

"Well, the dorm where I live has carvings of prominent women figures on the building. I only know a few of them, but I wish to know all of them."

"The Ashford dorms are full of history! We can meet up there, and I can tell you everything about that building and the people carved there. And you can give me some tips on how to pick up Mike." Jennifer winks.

"Deal! When can we start?"

"We can start next week if you want to. I'll hit your line to compare our schedules and shit."

"Awesome!" I shout.

Jennifer motions me to stay where I'm at. She stands up and waves a young woman, another Qousa woman, over. Jennifer sits back down as the light-skinned woman walks over. She looks just like Jennifer, except she has straight blonde hair.

"This is my twin," Jennifer says to me. "Her name is Jessica. And Jessica, this is my little, Destiny."

"Nice to meet you," Jessica says, holding out her hand.

"Nice to meet you too," I say, meeting her hand. "Your sister is so nice! I'm fortunate to have her as a big."

"She aight. I would let you meet my little, but I had to take her home. She got too drunk."

"Wait, I think I saw her. Was she the one who was trying to eat the fish in the aquarium?"

"Yep, that's her."

We laugh.

"She was wildin'," Jennifer says, still laughing.

I look at them both, "So both of you decided to join the same sorority? Do you do everything together like those twins on TV?"

"Yep, pretty much," Jessica answers. "We're so much alike that people can't tell us apart."

"Except for the hair," Jennifer chimes in.

"Yep, except for the hair," Jessica continues. "We have different hair types. She got the good curly hair, so she can go natural, but I got left with the nappy shit."

"It's because she was the second born!" Jennifer laughs.

Jessica laughs, "Yep, her greedy ass took all of the good hair. But it's okay. This relaxer and weave stay on point."

"You never thought about wearing an afro?" I asked.

"Girl, nah." Jessica flips her hand. "Men do not like that type of hair. This is just my opinion, but if you don't have a good hair texture, you probably shouldn't go natural."

"Afros are so cute, though," I say, trying to change her mind.

"Girl, I'm saying this as a hairdresser. When these naturals come to my salon, I recommend them to go elsewhere. I can't work with that stuff. You should not go natural if you don't have my sister's texture or something finer. They get mad when I use a small amount of perm to do their hair. Like they expected me to do that shit without it."

"You put perm in their heads?" I search her face for amusement.

"Only when it's super nappy."

Nah, she's deadass. "Isn't that wrong?"

"They should be thanking me for helping them out with that shit. Maybe they'll acknowledge that they can't go natural and return to the creamy crack they make fun of."

I laugh at how bold Jessica is.

"It's funny now," Jessica starts. "But it don't be funny when they break my comb. And niggas be clowning them in the street. They don't seem to understand that men only like afros and nappy hair on redbones. All others need not apply. Treena really thought that she was going to join the crew with that mess."

Treena? Treena! That's who I haven't seen all night. I am shook, but I can't be. Not if I want to be off to a good start with my new tribe. I quickly fix my face and say, "Yeah, I've noticed that many people only like natural hair with certain aesthetics."

"Are those tracks?" She asks, pointing to my hair.

"No, it's just my regular, relaxed hair."

"You got some pretty, long, good hair."

"Thanks! I'm actually glad I met you. I don't have a hairdresser here yet, and I won't be going home for fall break because I live too far away. I was actually looking for someone to do a touch-up."

"Ohh yes, girl. I would slay that hair. You see, me and my sis, we're a team. She does nails, and I do hair."

"That is great. I will set up an appointment with you soon."

"Just hit my line."

The party is starting to thin out.

Marcel walks up to me, "Are you ready to go?"

I look at my watch and learn it is the next day. I can't believe the center let us stay this long. I tell Marcel to give me a minute as I walk toward Jessica to schedule a hair appointment. All of this dancing really sweated out my edges. I know my hair will not look too good if I wait any longer to get my relaxer. I grab my purse and my light jacket. I search for the heels I had thrown off my aching feet when I was drunk. I ask Marcel if he saw where I threw my heels, but he is already holding them.

"Looking for these," he says, smiling. "I retrieved them after you threw them in the crowd."

"Thank you so much, sweetie!" I kiss him on the cheek. I really do have the best boyfriend ever. "Okay, I think I'm ready now. Oh, wait. Where's Trixie?"

"She's with Mike. They're waiting for us outside. I don't want to leave them alone together for a long time, so we have to rush."

"Cool, let's go."

We make our way to the door. I hug all of my new sisters as we exit. Then, I get a sinking feeling in my stomach. Did he say, *Mike?* I hope he's not talking about Jennifer's Mike. And if it is Jennifer's Mike, I hope he and Trixie aren't trying to get together. Wow, talk about a rock and a hard place.

We open the door to find Trixie and Mike hugged up and making out on the porch.

"Man, I thought I told you not to touch her!" Marcel yells at Mike. His face is hard, something I've never seen before. This is rage. I pull him to the side, away from Mike and Trixie, who are still hugged up but now looking at us in terror.

"Baby, it's okay. She's a big girl. She wanted a Kousa man, and now she has one. Is there something wrong with him?" I ask him.

"He just isn't loyal. And I'm still finding that out."

"I'll talk to Trixie about it later."

Cel shifts nervously then smiles. "Thanks."

"Let's go back to your place," I say flirtatiously.

Cel smacks my booty. "Sounds really good! Let's go!"

Fall break is when most students who live close by go home to recover from the lifestyle changes of college. Reconnecting and getting the motivation needed to finish the rest of the semester on top. The rest of us stay on campus because we are not about to splurge on plane tickets just to spend a few days with the family we saw a few weeks ago. Jessica is among the students who chose to stay on campus, and today, I have my hair appointment with her. I open a text from her.

It's a black car with a busted side door.

Vague. I've seen so many cars on campus that fit that description.

Coming down now!

I walk out the front door of my dormitory to find only one car in sight. Black and busted.

Jessica jumps out of the car, hugs me, and helps open the side door. Once in her barely functioning vehicle, we talk about typical Qousa stuff as we take a short drive down the road. She stops on the side of a nondescript building.

"So, this is you?" I say, checking out the size of the building from the passenger window. "Business gal!"

"Not exactly," Jessica mumbles. "It's more of a salonshare."

"What's a salonshare?"

"It's like a timeshare, but for salons," she says, sneering.

"Oh, I've never heard of a salonshare," I say, my voice a little more high-pitched than usual.

"It's all about that sharing economy." She sighs.

"Makes sense," I say. I look around to see what she can be waiting for. We've been sitting in the same spot for five minutes. I look at her, and she is staring at the building. "Are we waiting on someone?"

"We need to wait for the other people to leave, and then we can go in." Jessica shrugs. "The only con to salonshares."

"The people you share the salon with?"

"Yeah, they should be leaving in a little bit, and then we can get started on your head."

I stare at her momentarily and then turn my head just in time to see two older white women departing the building, locking the door behind them, and driving away in their cars. Jessica finally starts driving again and parks right in front of the building. Two other cars pull up next to us. Four women get out of the vehicles. The one with the braids opens the building door. Jessica, who is carrying a big box of hair products, and I follow suit, and she introduces me to two of the women who are also hairdressers.

We enter the salon, which is breathtaking. Everything from the chairs to the rinse bowls creates a good homey vibe. One of the hairdressers turns on a diffuser, letting out a warm cinnamon smell. Jessica punches in the security code as soon as we enter and asks me to sit in one of the chairs. I am so not used to this. Back home, I usually wait and read magazines for at least 30 minutes because of overbooking.

I choose the comfiest-looking chair and wait while Jessica gathers her products. She puts the cape around me and starts to part my hair in four equal sections. She lines my forehead and my ears with some petroleum jelly. And then she puts on gloves.

"Now," Jessica says to me. "You haven't been scratching, have ya?"

"Just a little bit, but it usually doesn't bother me much."

"Okay. Hopefully, it doesn't burn too much." She starts to mix the activator in the perm base. The unpleasant smell brings back memories. Great-grandmother Mary used to perm all of the girls' hair when we would spend the night.

Jessica starts applying the chemical to my head. The women engage in typical salon talk about celebrities, dating, and hypotheticals. I barely participate, except when Jessica tells me about a weird video Trixie tried to show Jenn. But other than that, I am too busy checking out the other hairstylists' work. The way they are adding hair to their client's hair. My parents never let me wear weave. They always said that it was too grown for me. The only time I ever had hair added to my own was for cornrows going to the back. Other than that, I wasn't allowed to have a weave, Senegalese twist, or even micro braids, something my little cousins wore regularly. Perhaps it's time for a change. I'll be aiming to get some braids next time I come.

The client across from me is getting her hair cornrowed for a new install. The beautician starts with a perimeter braid and then twists the leave-out. She then gets started on a typical braid pattern. The hairdresser takes the hair that the client brought out of the packages: 22in, 24in, and 26in Brazilian straight hair. She grabs an already threaded needle and sews the hair as flat as she can on the braids. I can already picture how beautiful and flawless this look will be.

Sitting next to me, another client's hair is in a bun while the stylist inserts inches to her kitchen. The hairstylist sections off her hair with a rat tail comb, moisturizes the area, and then pins it off. She grabs the jumbo synthetic hair and loops it around a small portion of her client's hair. She twists the synthetic hair so that it has a hold on the client's real hair. She adds the client's hair with the synthetic hair and braids it all the way down. Eventually, she'll neaten the braids by dipping the tips in boiling hot water. Box braids.

Jessica is smoothing the perm in my hair when I see a shadow come across the window. Someone knocks on the door.

"Were either of you expecting any clients at this time?" Jessica asks.

The other stylists shake their heads. She puts down the activator brush and walks to the window. She takes a quick peek before ducking. "Shit! It's the cops."

"Open up!" a baritone voice yells from behind the door.

"What's happening?" I ask, panicking.

"Shit, shit, shit, shit, shit!" Jessica repeats as she gathers her stuff.

The door begins to unlock, and a few police officers enter. The two women that I saw earlier accompany them.

"So you decided to come back," one of the white women says to Jessica. The woman smoothes the blue streak in her blonde hair. The rest of her pixie cut has pink tips.

"I'm sorry," Jessica says in her telephone voice. "I just need to rinse her hair, and we'll be out of here in a few minutes."

"No, we've given you several warnings," the other white woman, a redhead, says while stepping forward. "I'm afraid you must deal with the police now."

"Okay. I'm so sorry. I will never come to your property again," Jessica pleads.

"It's too late for that," the redhead says. She looks at the other clients and me. " For the rest of you, if I catch you on my property again, you will have the same fate as your friend here."

I scrunch up my nose. "The same fate? What do you—"

One of the police officers grabs Jessica's arm and begins reading her Miranda Rights. Another officer helps place cuffs on Jessica's wrists. I can't move, frozen as I fear for Jessica. But Jessica just rolls her eyes.

"I need to wash my client's hair," Jessica says firmly. "You don't understand. It's crucial."

I come out of my shock. My hair. *My hair.* I stand up and yell, "She needs to wash out my hair. This chemical can damage it permanently."

"Well, you should have thought about that before you came to this property," Blonde Pixie responds.

"But I didn't know. Please, just allow her a few minutes to wash it out. Or at least let me wash it out." Tears start to well in my eyes. "Or you. I'll pay you to wash it out. And then you'll never see me again."

The redhead smirks and crosses her right leg in front of the other. "No."

"But it could ruin my hair."

"Take it as a lesson learned." The redhead looks at the officers. "Can you escort them off my property?"

The officers look at us. "You can leave on your accord, or we can do this the hard way."

The room is still. My head is spinning as I look over to the sink, thinking, how much of the perm can I wash out before the officers eventually grab me? Or, I saw sinks in the other room. Maybe I can lock myself in and wash the chemical out.

"This is bullshit," one of the clients, Box Braids, shouts. She points to her head. "I know you don't expect me to go out looking like this?"

The officers start moving forward. I glance behind me to see how far away the door with the other sinks is. An officer stands guard in front of it. Shit. I don't have time for this. I go to the front door, resisting the urge to flip off everyone in that salon.

"Does anyone else want to follow her lead and leave..." I hear one of the officers trailing as I exit.

I bolt back to my dorm. I'm grateful that hardly anyone is here to see me, a caped sweatpants-wearing woman with a perm in her head, darting through campus. I grab my shampoo, go to the bathroom, turn on the radio, and head for a shower stall to rinse out the relaxer.

Shower Radio

[Whispers] I Know it's hard for a
black man in this world. So here's a
little appreciation from your favorite
girl.

[Slow R&B music starts to play]

Just worked 9 to 5, and I'm glad to
be home

Saw that my man left some flowers in
the dome

What did I do to deserve a man like
you?

Been together for years, and I'm glad
our love grew

You weren't always faithful, but I
stayed cause I knew

A love like ours will always break
through

Sistas don't give up on a love that's
so true

Listen to me when I'm trying to tell
you, (ooh)

Smooth, Swagga, Natural protectors

Providers who guide us

Real heart collectors

Braids, afro, low cut caesars

Dreadlocks make us drop

Real box pleasers

Dark-skinned, light-skinned, all
shades of ebony

Baby, don't you know that you come
from royalty?

Who can make me such a fan?

Ooo, nothing but a black man

Now I'm cooking your favorite meal

Wearing lingerie and 6-inch heels

I don't mind catering to you

With what you give me, it's the least
I can do

All of the knowledge you give me,
boo

Now I can innerstand you, too!

I feel like we connect on a level so
new

Glad I have a man to look up to,
(ooh)

Smooth, Swagga, Natural protectors

Providers who guide us

Real heart collectors

Braids, afro, low cut caesars

Dreadlocks make us drop

Real box pleasers

Dark-skinned, light-skinned, all
shades of ebony

Baby, don't you know that you come
from royalty?

Who can make me such a fan?

Ooo, nothing but a black man

[DISTORTED VOICES]

DJ MAC N' CHEEZY: Hey, y'all, welcome back to The Chow. This is your favorite DJ, DJ Mac N' Cheezy. You've just heard "Nothing But" by the beautiful Queen Petoh. I'm here with our usual panelist this week in what is sure to be a very heated debate. We got a letter from a woman named Rochelle. She states that her man pays for her beauty treatments, such as manicures and pedicures, and he even pays for her waxes. But he flat out refuses, I say, REFUSES to pay for her to get her hair done. Is he right or wrong about this? Appetizers. Let's start with Wings.

WINGS: I say she needs to pay for her own hair. You know how expensive weave is? In fact, why is he paying for all of the other beauty treatments? Women have to take responsibility for taking care of themselves. I say he is right and wrong. Wrong for paying for the other vanity expenses, and right for refusing to pay to get her hair done. Where are our natural, independent queens?

DJ MAC N' CHEEZY: So your take is that she should be self-sufficient? That makes sense. Raisin Potato Salad—I mean Potato Salad, what is your take?

POTATO SALAD: Thank you for correcting yourself this time cause last week was a mess.

DJ MAC N' CHEEZY: It's called growth. I'm still learning.

POTATO SALAD: Funny how you can keep this show gender pronoun neutral, disguised voices and all, but you're still learning to respect the nickname YOU gave me. Anyway, I am sick and tired of the black community having these conversations. They are pointless and don't really do anything for our community. How about we focus on lowering crime rates in black-populated areas? How about we focus on something we can control, like black-on-black crime?

DJ MAC N' CHEEZY: It always goes back to crime with you, doesn't it? Pudding, what's your take?

PUDDING: I think females should pay their own way. It is nice that he is paying for all her other beauty treatments, but it shouldn't be expected. It is more of a courtesy. Thank the man for paying for all of the other stuff. And make paying for your hair your responsibility. Females need to be more aware of their entitlement because it is ruining relationships. I mean, come on? The man pays for everything except hair, and you had to run and tell the radio? Does common sense even exist anymore?

DJ MAC N' CHEEZY: That take is sure to stir the pot. Cobbler?

COBBLER: Honestly, he should be paying for everything as a man. Why wouldn't he want his woman to look good? Her entire body is fly except for her hair. Huh? That makes no sense to me. Did he run out of money? A wash and blow dry ain't nothing but $40 and a tip. Honestly, if he can't afford to fully take care of a woman, then he shouldn't be dating. Why are you dating while broke?

DJ MAC N' CHEEZY: Another one. Damn, are y'all trying to get us canceled? Greens, what is your take?

GREENS: In our society, men make more money than women. So, he is expected to pay for most of her expenses. But we must remember that black men are also poor and may struggle financially. It looks like he is helping where he can, but there's a red flag here. Why is he specifically refusing to pay for her hair?

DJ MAC N' CHEEZY: That is a good question. Moving on to our final panelist, Black-eyed Peas.

BLACK-EYED PEAS: Listen, men should spoil our queens when they can. But it sounds like he can't afford to spoil when it comes to hair. I know how expensive hair can be. Appreciate that he can spend the money that he does spend on you. Stay patient, and a time will come when he can buy you more than just beauty treatments and hair. When will my community focus on building together instead of growing apart?

DJ MAC N' CHEEZY: We are definitely stronger together. We are going to cut to the music real quick. But we'll be back. This is "Dope Kingz" by Dem Powda Boyz.

[Trap Beat]

Call us the Dope Kingz, nigga

Thc Dope Kingz, nigga

Don't fuck with us

We got the finga on the trigga, nigga

Nigga, nigga, nigga, nigga

Don't fuck with us

We got the finga on the trigga, nigga

[Ya verse]

Yeah, this Ya, one-half of Dem Powda Boyz

While y'all were playin' with toys

I bought somethin' to cancel out
noise

While I'm shootin' at cha

Don't forget who you fucking wit

Got labeled a dope king

Before I was even doing this shit

This rapping shit

When you say my name, put some
honor on it

Or else you will end up at the bottom
of my pit

Jack off my hose to a picture of yo
bitch

And make sure that you catch all of
the spit

Called yo ho over

Now she ridin' in my rover

Got her selling ludes, but the streets
are getting poorer

But that's alright though

Just change the plans, ho

Now she in the kitchen whippin' up
eggs and yayo

You finna watch yo ho sin

She bout to suck my dick, all ten

You betta listen nigga

Or you'll get the hose again

Go tell your friends to

Call us the Dope Kingz, nigga

The Dope Kingz, nigga

Don't fuck with us

We got the finga on the trigga, nigga

Nigga, nigga, nigga, nigga

Don't fuck with us

We got the finga on the trigga, nigga

[Yo verse]

Yo, this Yo, and I'm the chemist of
this group

You can't be this creative; I mix my
yayo with my fruit (cook!)

Kiwi flava, color camouflage, like the
troops

You try to steal my green; yes, I'm
gonna have to shoot (goodbye!)

Mix it with grapefruit and get that
pink color

This the type of shit that I sell to
your mother (OD!)

That purple grape mix'll have you
feelin' all good

This yo cousin's favorite; they like it
in the hood (Lean!)

Lemon is the best cause we sell it to
white girls

In the sorority house, and they all

wear pearls (swirling)

The watermelon flava ends up dark

red

Don't cop my shit, or you will end

up dead (R.I.P.)

Blueberry blue puts antioxidants in

yo head

They should call you Heisenberg;

that's what my daughter said (leg-

end)

But they

Call us the Dope Kingz, nigga

The Dope Kingz, nigga

Don't fuck with us

We got the finga on the trigga, nigga

Nigga, nigga, nigga, nigga

Don't fuck with us

We got the finga on the trigga, nigga

Yea, we out here, nigga! Gettin work!
Actually, we got all the work! If you
ain't getting your work from us, you
ain't getting that real shit, my nigga!
Aye, free my nigga Coupon. They
out here lockin' us up and shit. The
feds stay hatin' on a nigga!

DJ Mac N' Cheezy: Ladies and gentlemen, you are listening to The Chow. Before the musical break, we had our appetizer. If you missed it, stream it on our app. Now, it is time for the main course. Or shall I say main discourse? Panelist, you have the floor.

GREENS: Why do y'all assume she was getting a weave? And why such negative connotations around weave? Our people have been weaving for centuries. Why be ashamed of such a tradition?

WINGS: This is just my opinion and personal preference. But weaves, wigs, tracks, whatever you choose to call them, are downright disgusting. They get raggedly, strands fall out, and hair is all over the apartment.

DJ MAC N' CHEEZY: Do real hair not shed?

WINGS: Of course it does, but the texture is totally different.

PUDDING: I agree. Why wear all of that fake stuff when you can just be natural? Natural hair, no makeup, no filters. Just the real you.

COBBLER: I agree to an extent. Black women have this beautifully unique, Goddess-like texture that no one else on the planet has. But you're covering it up with this dull, lifeless hair.

PUDDING: So, we agree then?

COBBLER: No. A lady should always be made up and ready for new opportunities. Don't leave the house without mascara and lipstick, at the very least.

BLACK-EYED PEAS: I prefer entirely natural. Besides, what's on the inside matters much more than what's on the outside.

POTATO SALAD: I couldn't disagree more. We need to look like we belong in society instead of on the streets. Dress up. Stop wearing pajamas in the grocery store and sagging your pants at the parks. Learn how to speak properly. Learn how to stop being a victim.

GREENS: It is true that what we look like affects how society interacts with us, but it shouldn't. Now, if I speak on the other nonsense...

DJ MAC N' CHEEZY: Say whatever is on your mind.

GREENS: I'm just going to get back on topic. The man not choosing specifically to pay for her hair just seems like a punishment for having the hair that she has or wants.

WINGS: Damn right, it's a punishment. If the man is paying for the hair, he should be able to choose what she gets.

PUDDING: Exactly. He's doing you a favor by paying for you to get your hair done. Return the favor by getting something that he likes.

Black-eyed Peas: A relationship is a partnership. You give what you receive. He gives her a little somethin' somethin' for her hair, and she surprises him with his favorite hairstyle. Everyone is happy and can do community work again.

Greens: Her body, her choice!

Wings: His money, his choice!

Cobbler: A stingy man is a broke man.

DJ Mac N' Cheezy: Damn! Just throw that in there. Greens, you said something earlier about the wage gap; how does that fit into this situation?

Greens: Simple. The more money you make, the more you can spend. Men make more money than women, so it is a given that he pays for most of her stuff.

Black-eyed Peas: But do black men make more money than black women?

Greens: If controlled for profession and location, black men most certainly make more money than black women.

Black-eyed Peas: Yeah, I don't know about that one. I'll have to do my own research. That sounds very "stats that came from white people to break up the black community" to me.

Greens: Why would that break up the black community?

Wings: Because for the longest black women believed that they were the breadwinning patriarchs of the black community.

Cobbler: That doesn't even make sense.

Pudding: I can see Wings' logic.

Potato Salad: Yes, there is some logic there. No men are in the home, so the community might as well be labeled a matriarch. Society has convinced black women that they make more money. Convinced them to kick out the man. When in reality, it is just handouts from the government.

Greens: You had me, then you lost me.

Black-eyed Peas: No, what Potato Salad said is absolutely true. The government did conspire to get men out of their homes, and look where we are now.

Cobbler: Why didn't black men take a leadership role and just say, "No, I am not leaving my women and children behind," instead of letting it dissolve into what it is now?

Greens: Because black men didn't have the power to do so.

Wings: So you agree? The government convinced black women to facilitate broken homes.

Greens: Wow, what an oversimplification of this situation. There are several reasons black women had no choice but to take the money, including power imbalances and domineering men.

Pudding: I don't think it is black men's fault that our community is how it is today. We must look at the government's role in this and the role of black women.

Cobbler: Typical. Blame everyone and anyone but the culprit. Did you want to fault black children, too? I agree with Greens; black women needed a way to escape domestic violence. It's sad that the government, instead of the community, had to provide an out.

DJ Mac N' Cheezy: Do y'all want to get back on topic?

Pudding: I'm just going to say this final thing. Females look better natural.

Wings: Yep, naturally long, straight hair for the win. No need to spend money. Especially your man's money.

Black-eyed Peas: Natural short hair looks good on our queens as well. I love a good wash-and-go. What if they don't have long hair?

Wings: Then grow it.

Potato Salad: Long hair is beautiful. But what's more beautiful is family values.

Cobbler: Both long hair and short hair can look beautiful and feminine. It just depends on your face shape and how you style your hair. Hair consultations are a must and should be paid for by your man, especially since he wants you to look good.

Greens: Be a loving and caring partner. If you can help out, then do. If you can't, then don't.

DJ Mac N' Cheezy: And with that comes our last song before our commercial break. You've probably heard of the beef between Lil Cady and Shaundra. I am proud to bring you an exclusive, leaked diss by Lil Cady. You heard it here first. This is Lil Cady with "Keep My Name Out Cha Mouth."

[Talking] I'm ruining hip-hop, huh? Sounds like your ass is ruining hip-hop with all of those lame ass songs you've been putting out lately that get no airplay. You've never seen a platinum album in your entire life. I've been in this game for a lil bit. Imma need yo rookie ass to go back to the projects. And yeah, I called you a rookie with your old, one-hit-wonder ass. I'm too busy making millions over here. Ya, dig? [Beat drops] Let's go!

[Rapping]

Yo, I'm a classy chick

Working on my albums and shit

Never been to the projects, yeah

But bet yo ass I can spit

Just cause I ain't from the hood

Doesn't mean that I can't rap

All the records I make good

While you still making that crap

Why the hell you all up in my biz

You should be focused on yo kids

All of them baby daddies

How bout you not focus on Cady?

You mad cause I'm living the dream

White-bone on stage with huge
screens

Sold-out tours, making crowds
scream

Making this paper, getting cream

Don't know how you still rapping

Yo albums ain't doing shit but
scrapping

So instead of coming for me

Wonder why your albums are free

[Singing]

No need to be dismissive

No need to be aggressive

You ratchets are hating

Cause this white-bone is winning
(yeah!)

Keep my name out cha mouth

Don't forget I'm from the south

I keep an extension on me

I will fuck that ass up, baby!

[Rapping]

When I say I keep an extension

Just know I'm talking bout my gat

My hair long, and real like a pension

No extensions on my scalp

You hos think that I'm playing

Check out these baby hairs I'm laying

You think you got some edges?

Ooo, baby girl, just keep praying

You over there looking like roaches

I'm over here buying out coaches

You over there looking like Queen
Petoh

I'm over here stunting on you hos

Don't open your mouth no more

Don't wanna hear nothin' from you
whores

My world will keep on revolving

Don't get mad cause we evolving

[Singing]

No need to be dismissive

No need to be aggressive

You ratchets are hating

Cause this white-bone is winning
(yeah!)

Keep my name out cha mouth

Don't forget I'm from the south

I keep an extension on me

I will fuck that ass up, baby!

[Talking]

Yeah! Keep my name out cha motherfuckin' mouth before I take your man! And you know I will. A bad bitch just over here making magic happen, and I attract all of these ratchets who want to stop me at every turn. But I ain't worried about y'all. I got too much shit to do. And too much work. Something you don't know nothin' about over there collecting welfare all day. Anyways, shout out to Dollarstar for working with me on the beat and lyrics. I can't wait for y'all to hear half of the rap game on the remix. If you ain't on our team, the winning team, then you're not getting paper. We out!

DJ Mac N' Cheezy: Don't you love a good beef? Can't wait to hear Shaundra's response! Now let's—

Wings: Ay, let me say something real quick. I love Cady's demeanor. She makes money and buys her own.

Greens: Mmm... You give them an inch, and they—

DJ Mac N' Cheezy: Before this gets any further, we must have our favorite course: Dessert! As always, YOU, the best audience in radio history, will have a chance to tell us what meal you're fixing this week. Or do you have another meal in mind? We'll open our line after the commercial break because, let's face it, we all have bills to pay.

The Aftermath

I leave the stall and rush to the mirror, examining the damage to my head. Okay, it's not that bad. It could've been worse. Maybe a little trim. My hair still tingles as I part different sections to look at my roots.

Click, Click, Click.

I hear the door swing open behind me. I turn around to meet Kiana's wide eyes.

"Are you okay?" she asks, her bushy brows raised. "I saw you running across campus looking distressed."

I think about ignoring her. I haven't gotten over what she said at the Goddesses' house. I give her a reluctant head shake.

"What happened?" she asks.

"Jessica got busted using those white women's shops without permission."

"Oh no! That's terrible! I know she can't afford to open her own shop, but I thought she was renting from them this entire time."

"I did, too. And I wouldn't have gone had I known. She told me they were salonshares."

"Haha," she laughs. I dart my eyes at her, and she covers her heart-shaped lips. "Salonshares?"

"Yeah, some shit she made up. I knew it sounded suspicious."

"Next time, trust your gut."

"You and this unsolicited advice. Had she told me sooner, I wouldn't have made an appointment. She only told me about this salonshare when it was too late."

"My bad, just trying to help."

"Well, I don't need your help or advice, and I would appreciate it if you would stop trying to offer it," I demand.

"Sorry, I do that sometimes. Can we start over?"

"Start over when? Are you talking about when you started advising me about my boyfriend and friends?"

"I'm sorry for that, too."

"I bet."

"Let's just start all the way over. Because I really like you, and we would make good friends." Kiana extends her long arm, expecting a handshake. But I just ignore it. "Really?"

"I'm really not interested."

"We took some of your advice," she says quickly.

"What advice?" I say, now intrigued.

"When you called us materialistic. We're taking the sorority on an entirely different path."

"Well, that's good."

"Yeah, we realized we only had the materialistic things all over our house because we wanted to attract more women to the sorority."

"Yeah, getting rid of all that trickery."

"I want to thank you for that. For now on, we'll be more upfront about ourselves."

"No problem."

"So, what happened at the salon?"

"When the cops came, I still had the relaxer in my hair. They wouldn't let Jessica wash it out at the salon, so I had to rush back to the dorms and do it."

"Good thing you live close. Were you able to wash it all out?"

"Yeah. The only thing is, my hair is still tingling, and I can't figure out why."

"Did you use neutralizing shampoo?"

I turn away from Kiana, wiping my eyes.

"Shit!" My chin trembles as I try to let out more expletives. Shit, shit, shit, shit, shit! I want to shout, but tears choke my words and dampen my face. Instead, I let my hands express my anger, banging them on the basin.

"Don't worry," Kiana says, comforting me with her arm wrapped around me. "I know a few hairdressers. I'm sure they'll know what to do."

Kiana introduces me to Ebony, a hairstylist who specializes in natural hair. Ebony is as sweet and patient as a first-grade teacher. She's in school for her MBA and is a Goddess.

"That should take care of the relaxer," she says after rinsing my hair.

"Thank you so much," I say. "Can you tell me what kind of damage I can expect?"

"Umm," Ebony pauses. "You will have to cut most of it off."

My eyes start to well up again. I've never in my life had short hair before. I was always known as the black girl with good, long hair. I can't imagine how I will be seen in the world now. What will my identity be? What will I be known for now? How will Marcel react to my new hair? "Is there any other option?"

"I'm afraid not. This must be cut off so your hair can be healthy again."

"But I don't want my hair cut short just yet."

"We can do some long protective styles if you want. Getting a protective style will be better than leaving the relaxer in."

"I've never had a weave or braids or anything."

"Will you consider wearing a wig?" That way, your hair can rest."

"I don't like how fake they look."

"I have some really good ones on hand. Considering what all you've been through, I'll give you one at a discount." She goes into another room and comes back holding a natural hair wig. "I think this one fits the shape of your face."

I twist my lips. The wig is long, though shorter than what I am used to. It's beautiful and looks natural, but it doesn't match the texture of my relaxed hair. I run my fingers through the strands. "It will have to do."

Another Protest

I thought about going home midway through fall break, especially after the hair debacle. But staying and using that time to catch up on studying and get used to my new wig was more effective. Plus, I got to know Kiana a little better.

Since I joined Qousa, it feels like I've been out partying, or at socials, or at some event every night. The study sessions we set aside on Sundays ultimately become gossiping for hours as we are all too hungover to do anything that day. When I ask the other women how they do it, late nights and early mornings are always the answer. But I value my beauty sleep way too much.

I hear a car door slam outside; nothing unusual as most students return today. I go to the window of my room to investigate just in time to see Trixie wave goodbye to her parents as they drive off. She walks to the dorm, pulling her overnight suitcase behind her, when someone stops her. Marcel. He is wearing a tight-lipped smile and clenching his fists. The balled fists stay, but the smile disappears when he starts shouting at her. I open my window to hear, but they are too far away to make out anything. Trixie starts to shout back at him. My intuition tells me to run downstairs and approach them. And I follow it, just like great-grandmother Mary always told me to do.

When I open the door to the building, I see them walking towards the entrance, all smiles like nothing happened.

"Hey beautiful," Marcel says, hurrying towards me. "I miss you! I ran into your roomie Trixie, and she said that I could come up and surprise you. But I guess it isn't a surprise now, is it?"

"Yeah, I guess," I say, still suspicious.

"I love the new haircut. It looks good on you. The bangs really fit your face," he says, commenting unknowingly on a wig. He comes closer. "Listen, I just wanted to give you these." He hands me flowers, the same type he always gives me. "I must go because I'm already late, but we'll catch up soon."

He kisses me on the cheek and runs off. I hold my flowers, not content at all. I narrow my eyes at Trixie. "So, what were you guys talking about?"

"Oh, he was just asking me how my vacation went."

"What about before?"

She furrows her brow, "Before vacation?"

I cross my arms. "No, when you were yelling at each other. I saw it from the dorm window."

She shifts her eyes. "Oh, he was mad about Mike."

"Why would he be mad about Mike?"

"Because he doesn't think that Mike is good for me."

"Why the hell is he all up in your business, though?"

"What do you mean?"

"Why does he get over the top over someone you're dating?"

"Oh, I don't know," she says, looking away. "I think that Marc is just a really caring person. You're lucky to have him as a boyfriend. A Kousa man like him."

I head back to the room without saying another word. I have to talk to Marcel later because something is not adding up. Trixie senses my anger and confusion. She keeps talking to me about what she did during the break. A socially aware person would try to have an honest conversation or at least stop talking, but what does Trixie do? She cracks jokes and continues asking questions while lying in bed, still dressed in outside clothes.

"I really like your hair," she says.

I run my fingers through the natural wig. "Thanks." I go back to my desk to finish studying for my upcoming exam.

"Did you cut it?"

"Yes."

"Was that weave you were wearing before?"

"No, it was all mine," I say, rolling my eyes.

"Like, you bought it, so it was yours?"

I turn to face her so she can see the stern look on my face. A warning. "No, like it grew out of my scalp, so it was mine."

"Oh, it was just so long."

"Yeah." I quickly grab my backpack and fill it with my books and notes. "I'm going to the library to study and heading to the protest. I'll be back later."

Trixie rises from her bed, holding one of her stuffed anime characters. "Oh, there's a protest going on? For what?"

"We're protesting that new song by Lil Cady. She's coming to do a concert on our campus, and we don't want her making money off of us."

"Oh my god! I love Lil Cady and can't wait to see the concert!" She throws her stuffed cuddle buddy in the air, grinning from ear to ear. She is about to catch it on the way down but misses it as a baffled look comes across her face. "Why are you protesting her song?"

"Did you hear the new diss record?" I ask.

"Yeah, I thought that she did well. I think she really put Shaundra in her lane."

I massage my temples. "Well, it was very anti-black."

"I didn't get that message at all."

"Well, more specifically, it's anti-blackness towards black women. It's hard to miss. Maybe take a look at the lyrics?" I try to quickly open the door and leave because I don't want to get into it with this girl again. "See you la—"

"I think you're confused," she says with one eyebrow raised. "How can it possibly be anti-Black when she worked with black people to produce the song? And how can it be anti-women when she is a woman?"

I turn around to look at her. I let out a deep sigh. "It is more complicated than that."

"How?" Both of her eyebrows are now raised.

"Trixie," I start, "I am exhausted and do not want to deal with this right now. There's so much going on. I need to get to the library and prepare for the protest." I rush out and close the door behind me.

Kiana claps her hands and lets out a loud gasp. She covers her mouth and looks around the library before turning back to make eye contact.

"It's not funny," I whisper to her.

"I know, I know," she says. "It's just... How do they work up the nerve to tell us about our own experiences?"

"I know, right? And they say this shit with the utmost confidence. I'm thinking about moving out."

"You should definitely move out. I know Trixie is a part of your sorority, but all she will do is cause you to stress all year."

"I've already emailed my R.A. Hopefully, there is an extra spot in the Ashford dorm. I love it there and wouldn't want to move somewhere else."

"Why don't you consider rushing our sorority again? We have a rush coming up soon for the spring semester. Then you can just move in with us. And I promise our house isn't as materialistic as before."

"That would be nice, but I'm still with the Qousa women. I already signed a pledge with them."

Kiana shrugs her shoulders. "Just break it. Say it's not for you and rush our sorority."

"Yeah, but I still like them." I tap my pencil on the table, searching for anything to justify my wanting to stay with them. "They haven't been anything but great to me."

Kiana twists her lips. "Now Destiny, you said they keep you busy with parties and events. And also, the things you've been telling me, it sounds like they have some colorism going on in their lil clique." That last sentence came out with a neck roll, which is very out of character for Kiana.

I shift in my seat. Kiana's usually sultry almond eyes are now intense and staring into my soul. She wants to know why I would stay in such a sorority, but the reason isn't apparent. The truth is, I don't know why. I feel connected there, and this is the type of sorority that Aunt Vanessa, who I strive to be like, would join. I pull at any reason I can to defend my chosen sorority. "But there are only a few women who are colorists. Maybe I can help change their ways?"

"Okay." Kiana exhales. "Just think about it. We would love to have you as a new sister."

"I will." I give her calculus test back. "Thank you for letting me study off this."

"You're welcome. I saved all of my tests from the previous years, so if you need to review and study for anything, just let me know!"

"That will be a godsend. College is so different. I wouldn't say it's as hard as high school. But there's just so much content, and I never know what to study for."

"Just hit me up. I got beaucoup notes!"

"Haha, you remind me of my friend Erika back home."

"You always say that to me!"

"I do? Really?"

"This is like your fourth time saying it to me. But it's good, though. Ready to head to the protest?"

"Yes, I'm ready. I texted Cel to see if he's coming, but he hasn't replied yet."

"You think he'll come?"

"Well, yes. Cel is pretty into protesting and is a perfect activist. That's how we met." I smile while thinking about the first time I saw him. That curly black hair. That chiseled face. My daydream breaks, and my smile drops when I see the annoyed look on Kiana's face. "What," I whine.

"I guess he is a... protester," Kiana says, air-quoting the last word. She opens this large, plain white binder. She finds the section for freshman year tests and places the calculus paper in its chronological order. "So you're not mad at him anymore?"

"No, I don't know why I was mad at him before. I guess I thought something was happening between him and Trixie, but I just overreacted."

"Mama always says to trust your first reaction."

"My grandmother used to say the same thing. But I legit think that I just overreacted."

We grab our bags, leaving the library to walk to the protest.

The sprawling campus fills with students, car doors slamming, and students waving their goodbyes to their parents. First day on campus déjà vu.

"I just want more positive representation in the media," Kiana says. She looks over her shoulder at me without breaking her gait. Her perfect, evenly-spaced strides avoid the structured cracks in the sidewalk. It takes me two steps just to keep up with her.

"I am so tired of seeing the sidekick, token, or sassy black friend," I respond. "Or the nurse or social services friend. Erika and I talk about this all the time. That's why we want to go into the sciences. Help little black girls see that they can be in STEM too!"

"That is a good strategy. Battling the negative images with the positive." She opens her purse and pulls out a tube of tangerine-tinted lipgloss. Two quick swipes and the color on her lips are as vibrant as when she first applied it at the library. Orange really does look better on dark-skinned women. She focuses back on me and continues, "Sometimes I feel that us giving attention to the negative images works against us."

I stumble but smoothly restart my gait, but Kiana doesn't notice. "Do you think protesting Lil Cady is a bad idea?"

"I don't think it is a bad idea," she says. "But I also don't want to give her attention for disrespecting black women."

"I understand that," I say.

"It is a struggle. What can we do? If we don't say anything, her disrespect gets swept under the rug and possibly grows. If we say something, we platform her, and her disrespect possibly grows."

"It is a catch-22," I say, looking at her. The tiredness of these situations clearly shows in her eyes. I wonder if my eyes have the same fatigue in them. "I feel like," I start to say, but someone catches my eye in the distance. Deidra, waving. I can recognize her tall, slender frame from any distance.

We wave back and hurry to join the rest of the women. Deidra opens her arms for a hug, and I embrace her. Even though I ultimately didn't join her sorority, we still have a connection through sisterhood that can never be tarnished.

"I'm glad to see you!" I say to Deidra. I look behind her, and Lucinda is also in attendance. I haven't really spoken to her since the whole vegan slideshow thing. "Hey, Lucinda! Glad you made it."

"Hey!" Lucinda stands beside Deidra. "I wouldn't miss an opportunity to protest for the world." We all laugh. I've seen her flyers around school, asking students to join Grox in various protests. I never attended any. Now I feel guilty.

There are a handful of women waiting with signs behind the Grox women. It isn't nearly as big as the protest we held earlier for Quintin James, but it will be. Flashbacks of me placing flyers at the Qousa and Kousa houses make me giddy. I even attached a personal note so they know it's from me. I put flyers in my residence hall and told a few coworkers about the protest. The Goddesses who stayed during break placed flyers nearly everywhere and even made an online invitation. Leaflets are handed to students as they arrive back on campus. This protest will be massive. And campuses across the map are protesting at the exact same time as us. This is the first protest I had a significant hand in organizing, and I couldn't be more excited.

Our crowd grows larger as more women appear, but not as large as I expect it to be. The women from Grox and the Goddesses' house are pretty prominent, making me wonder about my own sorority. Where are they? I text Jennifer and Tammy to see how far away they are. I scan the crowd to see who has accepted my invitation. A few women from the Qousa house, some women from the

Ashford dorm, students from the Black and Queer Organization, and black women from the surrounding community.

I text Marcel once again.

Where are you?

He replies by calling. I answer the phone on the first ring. "Hey, babe! Where are you? The protest will start soon," I say, not exactly containing my excitement.

"I'm not coming." His voice is cold. Hard. Distant.

"What? Why not?"

"It's not my fight."

"What do you mean?"

"I just think we have more important things to protest than a silly song."

I close my eyes and take a deep breath, trying not to let the tears fall. I step away from the other women so they won't hear me painstakingly explaining to my black boyfriend why this protest matters.

"It's more than just a silly song," I respond. "If this goes unchecked, people would feel they can take swipes at black women without consequences. And this has the potential to get worse."

Marcel sighs. "Yeah, but it's not like your lives are in danger because of it. And it's not like Lil Cady was talking about all black women. This was a song about one person."

"What?" I pause in disbelief.

"Look, baby, we need to pick and choose our battles. And I'm not choosing this one. I am choosing to protest police brutality."

My lips are quivering. My eyes burn. I try my best to calm my anger so he doesn't hear it in my tone. "You can protest more than one thing at a time, you know? I'm doing it right now."

There is a long pause. Marcel sighs and says, "Look, I just don't believe in this protest. It isn't for me. I can't fake it." The words stumble from his mouth so hard I almost want to ask if he is okay.

"You can't fake it?" I say, shouting into the phone. "Fake what? Fake caring about black women?"

"I didn't say that. I care deeply about black women. The women in my family are black. I just think that y'all are overreacting."

"We are not overreacting!"

"I think you're hanging around those Goddess women too much. They're making you upset about things you shouldn't be upset about. You even caught some of their attitudes!"

If pressing the end button swiftly was an Olympic sporting event, I might have earned a gold medal just now. World reigning champ. I power down my phone and jam it into my backpack. My body is shaking again. Deep breaths, deep breaths. I pace back and forth, observing the flora on the campus. Whenever Marcel pops into my head, I look at the flowers and think about how easy life could be if I were one. Then again, their life isn't easy either, considering how complex some of their mating systems are. I don't know how, but it makes me feel better.

I join the other women. The crowd size doesn't live up to my expectations, but this is my very first protest, so I lower the bar. I introduce myself as the organizer, something I'm proud to do. We talk briefly about some of the issues black women uniquely face. My favorite speakers are the older women from the community. Hearing about how they grew up mirrors my life. Though I am happy that I am not alone in what I went through and can finally bond with others who get it, my blood boils at the thought that we haven't progressed much since they were little girls.

As we discuss protests we've been a part of, a large, boisterous truck pulls up in the parking lot and captures our attention. I check out the truck: spikes on the rims, defensive plates, and tinted windows. It's like a military vehicle, but the paint job gives it away. Guns and zombies are splashed on the sides. The driver hops out, wearing blue jean leggings, white tennis shoes, and a simple white top, which she covers with her camouflage jacket. I've never seen Jeanette outside of work before. Although I invited her, I wasn't expecting her to show up. I didn't know that she took part in things like this.

"Hey, boss! Glad you can make it," I shout, still checking out her whip.

"Glad to be here. I think it's about time we fight for our voices to be heard. I made a few signs just in case anyone needs them." She goes to the back of her truck, grabs several signs from the trunk, and sits them on the ground.

"Wow, thanks. This will help a lot."

"No problem."

I help her carry the signs to the protesters.

One of the protesters grabs a sign and reads it aloud, "You model your entire image after us and then diss us. Nah." She looks at Jeanette. "Oh, I love your signs!"

"This isn't Pokemon. You're not evolving. Quit saying that!" Another woman says, reading another sign.

"Black women are the definitions of class and regalness," Kiana reads, holding the sign in the air. "I'll take this one. I think it really fits my sorority."

"I'm tired of black women being disrespected," I read. "I'll take this one."

"I don't think this is a good idea," a soft voice raises the hairs on the back of my neck. I turn around to see Deidra looking solemnly at one of the signs. "I just think that there are better tactics."

"Destiny and I were discussing that earlier," Kiana adds. "I feel like this is a very masculine way of getting our point across. If anything, it brings more attention to the song and doesn't make us look good."

Lucinda steps next to Deidra and says, "These artists see all press as good press. Lil Cady may very well see her streams go up if we do this."

"So, what do you suggest?" I ask.

"I suggest we hold off and brainstorm together," Lucinda replies.

Brainstorm. That isn't such a bad idea. That is what Marcel says makes a good protest. Researching the subject and hitting them where it hurts. I turn my phone back on to see if Marcel texted me. Nothing from him, but quite a few texts are waiting in my inbox. "Yes! Jennifer and Tammy texted me back. They probably want to know where we are now."

I open the text message from Jennifer. I read it to the other women.

Hi, sorry for the late reply.

Unfortunately, I won't be able to make it to the march.

But keep up the good work.

Like I said, girl, love your activism.

No worries!

There will be other protests to join.

"Wow, that's pretty surprising," Kiana responds. She's twirling her favorite protest sign like a color guard member. "I thought that she would've been against the march."

"See, they're not all that bad." I open the text from Tammy and begin reading it.

Hello, Destiny.

I will not be joining you in your march.

You should have consulted with the Qousa women beforehand.

This protest you have going on is giving us a bad rep.

It's giving sensitive.

I saw that you put fliers with your name in both the Qousa and Kousa houses.

That is unacceptable.

We shall have a swift meeting about it today.

What time works best for you?

Busy with the protest.

I will be free tomorrow! Anytime!

"Now that's the response I was expecting," Kiana says. She throws the sign in the air, watching it spin, then catches it behind her back.

"I don't understand. I thought that she would be interested in stuff like this. She said that she liked the activist in me."

"Yeah, but it's all about what you protest," Kiana says. "Black women can be mammies to nonwhite people as well."

I look down, then look at Deidra. It seems like she is still unsure about the protest and has every right to be.

"Shall we go back to the library to brainstorm ideas?" I suggest.

Kiana rubs her stomach. "We should grab something to eat first!"

"I know a place," Deidra shouts, the loudest I've ever heard her voice.

"Your excitement about this place is all the convincing I need," Kiana quirks.

"Great, let's go," Lucinda says, leading the way.

The bus eases to a stop. The horrified faces of the people at the bus stop waiting to get on the bus make me giggle. Kiana elbows me, "Girl, leave those people alone." My giggle turns into loud snorts.

"It's just that I can see all the thoughts on their face," I say, still laughing. "Why is this bus so full? Is there an event today that I didn't know about? Am I in the Twilight Zone?"

My last sentence snags a laugh from Jeanette, who is sitting right behind us.

"This is our stop," Deidra says.

Relief sweeps across the faces of the awaiting passengers as we get off the bus one by one. A bus that was once standing room only is now completely empty. Maybe I should be proud of the size of my protest crowd.

"Well, I'll be," Jeanette says quietly but still loud enough for us to turn in her direction. "I've always wanted to visit this place but never got around to it."

The large brick building has red paint splattering down it. A large sign sits atop the building and reads, **Apocalypse Eats**.

"I knew you would be a fan of it," Lucinda says, winking at Jeanette.

We enter the building and smile at the servers, who are kind enough to accommodate a large group on such short notice. We are seated at five large tables, which we eventually push together. There are three different menus in front of us: One for drinks, another for humans, and the last for zombies.

"Our entire menu is served all day," the waitress says while placing silverware on the table. "If you have any questions about the menu, feel free to ask!"

The drink menu is mostly alcohol but can be made alcohol-free, which is helpful since a few of us are underage. I choose the housemade kefir. Grapefruit, blueberries, and rose petals sound like a fantastic combination for a drink. Kay, one of the new Goddesses I vaguely remember rushing with, tries her luck ordering a margarita. When the waitress asks for her ID, she swiftly changes her order to a ginger kombucha. Pretty much everyone orders the kefir or kombucha.

"Is this chair taken?" The raspy voice sounds familiar, but I can't place it. It isn't until I look up from the menu that I see her obsidian skin in front of me.

"Treena!" I shout.

"Hey, sis." We hug before she takes the seat in front of me. "Sorry, I'm late. Had a photoshoot. How was the protest?"

"We decided to brainstorm new ways to get our message across," I tell her. I keep staring at her beauty. It still radiates like the first time I met her, but more powerful and confident. I don't think I'll ever get used to it. Her TWA is gone, a lilac-dyed fade in its place. "When did you cut your hair?"

"When I needed a new start," she says without hesitation. She sweeps her hand across her shoulder. "I needed extra cleansing from the ridiculousness I went through during rush. I'm glad to be a Goddess now."

I finger the waves of my human hair wig, wishing I possessed the same confidence as Treena about my new short hairdo. Her boldness is a trait that I admire. Maybe I should rock a fade once I move into my new room. A cleansing for a new beginning. I like that.

"So what will we have today," the waitress says. She has her pen and pad out, ready to take notes for the large order ahead of her. Her lax posture says that she has done this many times before.

I order the tofu scramble with crispy potatoes. There are stars on the human menu beside both dishes, indicating them as customer favorites. Kiana orders from the zombie menu. A heart. One made up of beets, of course. The waitress takes the other orders in our group and hurries away to the serving hatch.

"Must everything here be vegan?" Kay complains.

Deidra shifts in her seat and turns to Kay. "Well, we are in a zombie apocalypse," she starts. "Would you rather we use the land to grow crops to feed animals that also take up land or grow crops and eat them directly?"

"Something to think about," Jeanette adds. "My fellow zombie enthusiast has a point. In this situation, we must decide how to better use our resources. Hypothetically, the lands and climate will be devastated. We'll be left to seek alternatives such as greenhouse gardening or vertical farming. If we find healthy land that can grow food, why waste it by giving that food to animals to eat them?"

Kays rolls her eyes. "Wow, information overload," she says quickly before reaching for our Brussels sprouts appetizer. "Zombie nerds." She sniffs the Brussels sprouts on her fork. The leafy green ball might be small, but its scent is pungent. She dips it in the sweet, nutty sauce that came with it and sniffs it again as if that is supposed to cover the smell. She twists her face. "Has anyone tried these?"

Treena grabs a Brussels sprout from the plate, dips it in the sauce, and pops it in her mouth. "Taste great to me," she says.

"You just ate it like it was nothing," Kay says. She finally places the veggie in her mouth, chewing for a long time before finally swallowing. "It's alright." She discreetly spits what she didn't swallow into her napkin and grabs some fried okra. She pops one in her mouth and then two. "Now, these are delicious!"

"While waiting for our entrees, let's get down to business." Lucinda's elegant voice pauses all side conversation, and all eyes are on her. "How do we go about the Lil Cady situation?"

"I think we should protest outside her concert," Kay suggests.

"How?" Kiana asks.

"I don't know yet," Kay responds, "I can't come up with everything." She shrugs her shoulders and goes back to gobbling down the fried okra. The hair of her slick bob accidentally goes into her mouth with one of the cylinder-shaped veggies, and only then does she realize she needs to slow down. She peers up and notices a couple of eyes on her, except mine; I turn away to save her the embarrassment. She dabs her mouth to show that she is still ladylike to the other women. I have to poke Deidra with my elbow to stop her from laughing. "How do you ladies suggest we protest?"

"I think we should only focus on representation," Kiana says. "Just focus on the image of the black woman so we wouldn't even have to deal with the disrespect that comes our way so often."

I build up the nerve, swallow my pride about my failed protest, and utter, "I agree. A protest will just give Lil Cady the attention she is craving. Let's promote a positive image of the black woman instead."

Kiana gives me a warm smile and a nod. "We must show the world how intelligent, beautiful, successful, and feminine we can be. A protest doesn't do that. No one is standing up for us because we have portrayed this image of strength and independence for so long that no one knows we need help. That we hurt, too. That we can't continue to fight for ourselves on our own."

My eyes start to water. Treena reaches across the table to grab my hand, comfort for both of us, as I see the tears beginning to build in her eyes as well. Kay, as stubborn as she is, has moved from dabbing her mouth to dabbing her eyes with her folded napkin. Kiana has always known how to grab a crowd by the heart.

I look at the Grox women. Their heads tilt and nod at Kiana's words. A clenched half-smile is drawn on most of their faces. I reach out to touch Lucinda's hand. She pats the back of my hand, but it feels wrong. The touch doesn't have the same connection as Treena. It's cold. It's distant. Her lips are pressed together to make a straight line; sadness fills her eyes, and she nods at me. But something is still off.

"Do you not feel moved and enwrapped in sisterhood?" I ask, making eye contact with each of the Grox women.

Deidra is the first to break the long silence of the Grox women. "We just don't see it the same way. Not all black women fit in that little box. What about them?"

"WhAt AbOuT tHeM?" Kay mocks. "Like Kiana said, they are represented and can protect themselves with their masculine energy. We are not. We need to let the world know that there are black women out here who are harmed by what happens in the world. That soft and vulnerable comes in black too, not just white."

Lucinda clears her throat. "But why only offer protection to a small group of black women? Why not all black women, or all beings for that matter?"

"Because other beings already have protection," Kiana snips. "There comes a time when we have to care for ourselves. We don't have unlimited energy to expend on all issues of all groups." Kiana presses her hands together in prayer and closes her eyes. She takes three deep breaths. "As for the other black women who would not be included in our activism, they've already decided they do not want protection."

Lucinda crosses her arms. "How? How did they decide that?"

Treena takes her hand from mine and raises her index finger. "When they took on the strong, independent black woman trope. Those who want to protect themselves should be able to do it. But the ones who didn't decide this, i.e., us, should be able to shape an image that offers protection."

Lucinda sits there, frown upon her face and arms crossed. The rest of the Grox women join her in shaking their heads. "This isn't something I can join you in doing," Lucinda says, her tone assertive and confident.

"Well, what are you going to do instead?" I ask.

"Our activism will focus on being a good human," she responds. "I don't like how we have to fit certain constructs to be protected. Protection should come with just being a sentient being. I say this as a black vegan woman."

Kay smiles and says, "Well, you have your good human campaign, and we will have our campaign that focuses on representation. No reason why we can't do both."

"Fine," Deidra responds.

None of us know what to say next. It is silent until the waitress comes with our entrees, and we return to discussing the delicious food. In high school, this spirited discussion would have ended our dinner, and we would have gone our separate ways, forming two rival cliques. But in the maturity of college, we agree to disagree and share bites of our entrees with one another.

A buzzing in my purse stops my admiration of the women before me. I take out my phone and read a text from Tammy.

Emergency meeting in thirty minutes!

I go into my purse to grab some money to pay for my portion of the bill. "I wish I could stay longer," I shout to no one in particular, "but I have a meeting with my sorority in a bit."

"Wow! They couldn't wait until tomorrow to have the meeting?" Kiana says, blinking her eyes.

"Nope, apparently, it's urgent."

"They are making you come this late to the house over a protest? Unbelievable." Kiana rolls her eyes and takes a sip of her kombucha.

"They didn't like my advertising of the protest, and I'm pretty sure they will also talk about other components." I shake my head. "Wish me luck."

I hug them all goodbye. I want to stay and connect, but I don't want to get in even more trouble with my sorority for missing a meeting. I exchange contact information with my new connections and suggest making a group chat. I would love to explore more of their interests and do something I've never done before.

Kiana and I talk briefly. Her usually tense, dark-brown eyes are filled with sympathy. "Do you need me to come with, you know, for emotional support?" she asks.

"I got it, I think," I respond.

Kiana opens her arms to the women at the tables, then turns her head to me. "Notice who showed up for you," she says.

I look at the women who barely knew me but showed up to my event because they believed in my protest. My lips start to quiver. "I am grateful," I say.

Kiana nods her head. "I want you to know that you have a community outside of that sorority you joined. The black women who attended your protest this evening will always have your back." She hugs me, and I hold back tears.

"Thank you," I choke out. "Thank you."

I say goodbye to everyone, and we do one more round of hugs before my departure. A tradition that has grown on me and that I now find warmth in.

Three Conversations

I know what I am in trouble for. My protest. Specifically, organizing a protest and kind of associating it with the Qousa women. But my activism is part of why they wanted me to be a part of their sorority in the first place. I thought they would be proud. What do they expect me to do? I look at the text again, one sentence, straight-forward, no context. I have no idea of the tone. *What will I say once I make it to the Qousa house?*

I can see the house in the distance. Tammy stands in front of the large French doors I once admired. The doors that I thought would jumpstart my career with study sessions, networking, and exclusive programs. Now, all I see are late-night parties, holding my sisters' hair as they purge their insides out over the toilet, undone homework, and wasted time.

I pick up my pace. Tammy greets me when I finally reach the house, leading me to the official meeting room. The Qousa women are seated on an elevated platform, making them look like judges, and I, the defendant, forget how to walk for a second. I shuffle across the floor, head down, my heart rate increasing whenever I accidentally make eye contact with one of them. Spotting Jennifer in one of my quick glances makes me think the meeting can't be that bad; I'll have at least one person on my side.

"So," Tammy starts. As president, she is seated in the center of the platform. She opens a folder and grabs a piece of paper. "We are here today because flyers were distributed in our house and the Kousa house without our permission. That is simply unacceptable."

Tammy looks at me and holds up one of my flyers. She gives a flyer to each of the women sitting next to her. They pass them down the line to the other women, who receive the flyers with a head shake and lip twist. A feeling of déjà vu sweeps over me as each woman repeats the same motion after reading my pamphlets.

I speak up while they are still observing the evidence. "I am so sorry for leaving those flyers in the house. I should have gotten permission, and next time, I will do so."

"There won't be a next time." Tammy snaps back.

"What do you mean?" My voice shakes.

"I don't like what you were protesting." Most of the women nod their heads in agreement. She continues. "Your protest made black women look horrible, and the fact that you collaborated with different campuses means this bad representation was spread nationwide."

I blink my eyes, waiting for anyone to speak up. "How did I make black women look horrible? All I did was try to give black women a voice. A protest for us to start standing up for ourselves. Plus, it ended up being a brainstorming session."

"Negative. And it doesn't matter if the protest happened or not." Tammy walks towards me as close as she can without falling off the platform. "From now on, before you organize any protest, you will come and get our permission first. You are connected to us. Our name could be dragged because of this. I have the Kousa men calling me, angry about the protest that you started."

"Why would they be angry? It has nothing to do with them."

"They believe that if you start protesting foolish, non-important things, then our important protest, like the one we have now for police brutality of black men, will not be taken as seriously. And I agree with them." She points to the flyer on the wall for the upcoming police brutality march that the Kousa men are organizing.

"How could you say that this isn't important? This rapper said some nasty stuff about black women on her diss record, things that affect us in our personal lives, and you're alright with her coming here to perform?"

"I didn't say that I was alright with it. I said that we need to prioritize, and right now, we're doing police brutality against black men. Our issues, which aren't causing any deaths, can wait."

"What about police brutality against black women? A woman sitting in her car was dragged out by police officers last week and died while being beaten, yet we don't know her name, nor have we marched for her."

Tammy shakes her head. "This is the first I've heard of that incident, and I will review it, and it might get added to the upcoming protests. However, police brutality affects black men more than it affects black women. We need to wait and look at—"

"Wait!" I shout, my cracking voice turning my cry into a two-syllable word. "What is up with you and all of this waiting? You really should have joined us today. You would have learned a lot from the older black women there. They were great activists for black people back in the day. When they wanted to speak up about the violence against women in our communities, you know what they were told? To wait! They are still waiting because none of it has been addressed."

"That is an entirely different issue, and I'm going to need you to—"

I throw my hands up. "No, no, it isn't. If we choose to wait, we'll be waiting forever. They chose to wait, and each time the black community got a little piece of the equality we were fighting for, these women would bring up issues affecting black women. And they were once again told to wait."

"We need to look at issues that affect us as a community and not just part of the community."

"So we'll be marching for the woman who was beaten by those police officers, correct?"

"As I said, I will look into it. If it fits our agenda, I will add it to the upcoming protest."

"Great, so an afterthought?" I place my hand on top of my head and exhale. The icey faces around the room are silent as I await a response. I look back at

Tammy. "Look, I've seen the downside of my protest. That's part of the reason why it never happened. I've discussed it with the other women who showed up and can't wait to spread their knowledge to you. I think we would be stronger if—"

"Strong women wouldn't be protesting some rapper," Tammy says sharply. "This is what I'm talking about with the sensitivity and making us look bad. And as far as spreading knowledge, are you serious? We have a model that works and has been working for decades. We'll stick to our tried and true method."

I roll my eyes and shake my head. "You know what? I am done with this meeting. I thought you wanted innovative ideas. Growth in the movement. No. You're okay with receiving the small crumbs you've been getting for years." I grab my purse and head to the door.

"So you can dish it but can't take it? WoW, yOu'Re BeInG sO sTrOnG." Tammy is sporting a big, closed-mouth smile.

I ignore Tammy and the snide remarks I hear as I walk out. It's cold outside, but my entire body is hot, and my heart is racing. Before I hit the sidewalk, I pull out my phone to call Mama. We usually would have talked tomorrow, but I need to talk to her about what happened.

"Hey, Mama," I say over the phone.

"Hey, baby," Mama whispers. I can hear her heels click on the floor, and the music in the background fades with each click until silent. I hear a door close. "You sound upset. What's going on?"

"I just got into an argument with my sorority."

"Uh oh, baby, what for?"

"I tried to do a protest today, and they disagreed with it. I feel like I can't explain anything to them. They only see it from one perspective, and that's it."

"Well, that's girls for you. That's why my group of friends has always been men. Men are much more fun and not full of that drama."

"There's more to it than that," I say, trying not to raise my voice. I massage my temples with my hand.

"Too bad you couldn't join a fraternity," Mama chuckles. "Everything would have been more easygoing."

I sigh, "Yeah."

"Are you okay?"

Tears start to well up in my eyes. "Yes, I'm okay."

"Good. Listen, baby, I'm at a party right now. I will call you tomorrow at our regular time. I love you!"

"Love you too." I end the call. I immediately call Erika. No answer. I dial again and again. She finally answers.

"Hey, girl, what's going on?" Erika says when she finally picks up. The concern in her voice causes me to burst into tears.

"I can't anymore," I manage to get out.

"Can't what?" Erika shouts more than she asks. "Talk to me. What is happening?"

"I just... I think I want to leave the Qousa house," I sob. I find a nice patch of grass to sit on in front of a random fraternity house. My hand brushes against the soft blades of grass, so soft that I almost forget that it is artificial. I lay back and sniffle. "Yeah, I think it is time."

"As they say, great minds think alike," Erika says.

"What?"

"Yeah, the chapter on my campus has been saying a lot of offputting stuff lately," she continues. "I've been thinking about leaving as well."

"It's like, no matter how far apart we are, we're always on the same page. Are you thinking what I'm thinking?"

"Girl, you know I am."

My eyes dry as I wipe away the remaining tears trailing down my cheek. "Goddesses' house this spring?"

"Of course."

Winter Break

My one-word description of the first semester of college: hectic. I reach for my vibrating phone on my desk. One new message from Mama.

Around the corner. Be there in 10!

Okay! See you when you get here.

I grab my suitcase and head out the door, closing it behind me. The RA in my new building finally placed a decorative cookie placard on the door for the new roommate I'll be getting when I return from winter break. The chocolate cookie bears my name. And the sugar cookie next to it reads Cat. Let's hope the few weeks I'll spend with her are pleasant until I enter Goddesses' house.

Dad's car pulls up, and Mama hops out the passenger's side and gives me the biggest hug she has ever given me. Dad grabs my suitcase and puts it in the trunk while Mama dotes on me.

"I missed you so much," Mama says, kissing my cheeks.

"I missed you too, Mama."

I peer into the car and see PJ on his phone, watching videos. I knock on the window and wave. He jerks a little, almost dropping his phone. He smiles and waves at me, phone in hand, swaying back and forth as if trying to hypnotize me. The words of the website on his phone slowly glide toward me, trying to get inside, but I blink, turning my gaze back to PJ, effectively knocking them off course. He rolls down the window and says, "The favorite is back."

I roll my eyes and say, "Whatever." Obviously, neither one of us is the favorite. That title belongs to Laila. I look past PJ to where Laila usually sits in her booster seat. But instead of seeing my little sister's sweet face, I see an old man's hardened, wrinkled face. Herbert, my dad's father. I look back at PJ and ask, "Where's Laila?"

"She went to see some kind of ballet with her class. A weekend field trip," PJ says without taking his eyes off his phone. He's back to consuming that website, Blue Rugs In The House, affectionately known to its followers as BRITH. PJ's favorite, my least. In fact, the Goddesses hope to get it shut down one day. Their About page should get them shut down alone.

Our name comes from the blue rugs commonly found in black homes that let visitors know that there are black male children present that need emasculation. We exist to eliminate these rugs and prevent them in the future by providing educational guides, insightful articles, and knowledgeable mentors.

And if you get past their About page and skim through their most popular articles, that should be enough for you to start protesting in the streets.

He Has Risen: Jesus Spotted Baking Pastries in NYC... and He's BLACK!

Language Courses for Black Men: Learn Thai, Portuguese, Spanish, and Dutch today for Free!

Free Game Classes: How to Play Your Cards Right

I'm Hebrew: Introducing Intersectionality to Our Egyptian Roots

Become the Next AuthenticCap! Catch the Early Bird Deal and Pay Only $2500/month NOW!

Why is She Lying: A Thinkpiece

But knowing that they are the reason why we have the infamous Authentic-Cap is reason enough to become a vigilante and hunt the owners down.

I walk around to the other side to say hello to my grandfather. "I bet you don't remember who I am," Herbert says, the same thing he said a decade ago when I met him for the first time.

"Hi, Grandpa," I say, fighting the urge to call him Herbert. He gives me a fist bump. I spend the next few minutes with them, discussing who should get the middle seat, a common disdain of backseat passengers. I give up and volunteer to take the despised seat. I have the longest legs, but their argument—*two men shouldn't sit beside each other*—beats me.

I stretch my legs out on each side, invading their space, until finally, Dad pulls over because PJ wants to trade seats. I try not to show the excitement for the secret battle I've just won, but I can't help the little smile that pops on my face as I hop out of the car and take the window seat I deserve. My smile disappears as PJ, now in the middle, starts showing Herbert an article on BRITH. Their whispered conversation works my nerves.

"We didn't have all this knowledge when I was little," Herbert whispers. "You kids today are lucky that you get to avoid many of the pitfalls my generation was never warned of."

"Did you pay child support, Grandpa?" PJ asks.

"Yep, that was one of the things that kept me down," Herbert replies. "Baby mamas constantly said I did not care for the kids."

"These females stay using the system to keep us down. I don't know if you heard about the football player about to lose his scholarship because a female lied about him, but I hope she goes to jail for being a liar!" PJ emphasizes the last word and clenches his fist so hard that he might have to buy a new phone if he uses any more strength.

Herbert rubs PJ's head and says, "My boy!" He grabs PJ's phone and starts scrolling through the article. "You are taking the initiative, learning what this world is really about. I'm so proud of you, grandson!"

I grab my earbuds from my purse because it will be a long ride without them. Just when I am about to hit play on my audiobook, a notification pops up. I elbow PJ, show him the display on my phone, and read it out loud because he isn't reacting fast enough.

"Local football player found guilty of all charges!" I say. I go into the article and start reading. "Despite the widespread public opinion of his innocence based on unsound news sources, including a debunked video, the local legend will be sentenced to jail based on the evidence prosecutors presented to the court."

"That doesn't mean he was actually guilty," PJ says.

"Right," Herbert asserts. "The system locks up innocent black men all the time. I can't begin to tell you how many times I got locked up because of unpaid child support when taking care of your daddy and his siblings."

"Plus, the system protects liars," PJ adds. PJ and Herbert high-five. "I'll wait until I see AuthenticCap's take on it. I'm sure it is going to be good."

I place my earbuds back in my ears and start my audiobook. I do not have time for this nonsense.

Once home, I go straight up to my room and start unpacking. My room has, for the most part, been left untouched except for some light cleaning. I pull off my wig and toss it on the rack beside my door. I hop in the shower, cleaning off the ickiness of being in a packed car for hours. The notes of lemongrass and rose from my old body wash hit my nose, relaxing my body. I massage my scalp with my favorite shampoo, smiling as I feel how much new growth I have.

After my shower, I towel wrap my hair and hop on my bed. I grab my phone to text Erika.

Ready when you are!

Okay, let's meet at the café down the street.

Sounds good.

Be there in 20 minutes.

Okay! Can't wait!

My closet is full of the winter items I had not packed for college because I thought I would be home well before winter break. Now, I have a new wardrobe in my closet on campus and at home. How lucky! I sort through the pieces, landing on a cute textured sweater and tight black pants. Thigh-high boots complete my look. I do my makeup at my vanity and am ready to go.

Mama is the first person I see on my way out the door. Her wide eyes and open mouth are tell-tale signs that my hair is the first thing she sees.

"You like?" I ask.

"What—what did you do?" she emphasizes each word. "What happened?"

"Perm accident. I had to cut it all off. I am pretty used to it now."

"So, that was a wig earlier? I thought that was your hair."

"Yep, a perfect wig. Had you fooled, huh?"

"Are you going to put it back on?" Mama circles around me, looking at my hair from each angle.

"I think I am just going to wear it like this now. It's easier to deal with. I just wash it and go."

"Okay," Mama smiles. "Wow, I've never seen you with short hair before. It really fits your face. You have the bone structure for it."

I grin widely. "Thanks!"

"You know you got that structure from your mama." She pinches my cheek, smiling even harder now. "Who are you going out with?"

"Erika. I'll be back later tonight."

"Alright. Just be back at a decent time. As long as you are under this roof, you still have a curfew."

"Will do." I frown when she leaves. How is it possible that an adult still has a curfew?

I put on my coat and gloves. The front door creaks as I pull the knob. The snow-covered grass and icicles hanging off the fountain are visible through the screen door. With one push of the screen handle, I will be connected to the outside world again.

"Where do you think you're going?" My body freezes at the deep, stern voice. I turn around to see my dad. He is also frozen, staring at my hair. "Did you cut your hair?"

I clear my throat, mentally thanking my hair for the distraction. "Yeah, I got a perm at a salon, and it burnt most of it off, so I had to cut it."

Dad smirks. "Didn't I tell you and your mama about those perms? I knew one day this would happen. Hopefully, y'all stop getting them. Are you going to do something to it before you go out?"

I scrunch up my face. "It's already done. It's called a wash-and-go."

"I didn't ask you what it was called. I asked if you'll style it before leaving this house."

What the fuck does he want me to say? I keep my body still. "No, I'm just going to go out like this."

He chuckles and says, "Okay. You and your mama are going to listen to me the first time I say something one day."

I bite my tongue and nod my head. "See you later. I'm going to the café with Erika," I say shakily, hopeful that this will end the conversation.

"Don't try to change the subject," Dad says. "And how are you going out when those dishes in the kitchen are piled up in the sink?"

Ignoring that I haven't been in the kitchen since I got home less than an hour ago, I go to the kitchen to start rinsing the dishes and place them in the dishwasher. I text Erika.

Going to be about 10 minutes late.

Obligatory chores before going out?

Girl, yes! I hate it when they do that. SMH!

I was almost out, but big-mouth AJ had to dry snitch.

Now I am stuck vacuuming floors I haven't seen in months!

I hate that we have to pay to have fun.

Trading money for tea and labor to even step outside.

What is free in life?

Nothing!

As I turn on the dishwasher, I hear footsteps approaching me. Dad is standing behind me, quietly chuckling.

"All done," I say. "I'll be back later."

"Back when I was growing up, there was no dishwasher," he says. "My grandma cooked huge dinners from scratch and then cleaned all the dishes herself by hand."

"Wow, no one helped her?" I asked. "She always told me she hated washing dishes because it took hours out of her day. It all makes sense now."

Dad stays silent, wearing an awkile on his face. I walk past him, smiling. Yep, you're dealing with an entirely new woman now.

Our favorite café is catty-cornered to the park we frequented growing up. When we were children, we used to grab the free oatmeal cookies they offered in between playing hopscotch and double-dutch. As teenagers, the café doubled as a study and gossip catch-up spot. Erika isn't here yet, but I'll wait for her inside.

"Destiny! It has been months!" Carmen, the owner of the café, runs up and hugs me. Her deep voice always swathes me in warmth and makes me feel safe at home. When I last saw her, pops of gray appeared in her hair, and she wanted advice on coloring it. Now, she is rocking a head full of silver confidently and beautifully. She helps me remove my coat and hangs it on the coat rack. "How's college going?"

"It has its ups and downs." I take a menu and skim through it. "I hope that the second semester is better."

"Oh, honey," Carmen says sweetly. "I hope that whatever you went through during the first semester washes away." She pats me on the back and hugs me, and I thank her. She straightens some napkins on the counter before walking behind the cash register. "Now, will you be ordering your usual? It is on the house!"

"Yes, please!"

"And will Erika be joining you today?"

"She is on her way."

"Alright! Hibiscus tea and a hot matcha tea latte are coming up." The machine in front of her prints out the order. Carmen rips the label from the device, peeling the backs before meticulously placing them on the ceramic cups. "You can sit in your usual nook," she says, pointing to the chaise longue in the corner next to a bookcase, "or you can check out our new heated deck. I'll bring your orders out shortly."

"Ooooh, a heated deck? Fancy," I say.

"I try to fancy it up every once in a while."

I go out to the deck, and it is unreal. I'm outside, surrounded by snow; naked trees are now wearing icicles, yet I don't feel the least bit cold. I take a selfie on the side facing the park, documenting my first time being on the deck in winter. I upload the cute seasonal photo on all my socials. When I look up from my phone, a tall, dark-skinned woman stands before me, smiling from ear to ear. I scream, and she screams back.

"Destiny, girl, it has been forever since I've seen you!"

"Erika, I have missed you so much!" I am the first to go for a hug. We hold each other for a minute, tears soaking our cheeks. I take a napkin from one of the holders on the table and dab under my eyes. I do the same for Erika, being careful not to mess up her makeup even though the tears have damaged it a little.

"Girl," Erika starts. "Do I have to start calling you DD now?" She laughs.

"Hush," I can barely get the word out through my giggle. Our tear-soaked cheeks were just touching as we embraced, closing the distance we've had between us for months now, and now she wants me to use a different napkin to wipe her cheeks.

"Alright, I'll stick with DL. Oh, and by the way, I have to tell you about my own DL moment." She rolls her eyes, and we both crack up laughing.

"Just like old times," Carmen says, coming out to the deck to meet us. Our usuals sit on the tray she is balancing. She places two napkins on the table and sets our cups on them. We sit down in front of our respective favorites. "I miss hearing your sweet laughter. I was hoping to talk to you, just for a little bit. To catch up mostly," she says. "And also to discuss some serious business."

"Oh," I say. I look at Erika; she is already looking at me, head cocked. I look back at Carmen. "Is everything okay?"

"Honey, everything is fine," Carmen says. "Sorry, I didn't mean to startle you. Have a sip of your tea, and let's talk about your college life first. I'll be back. I'm going to grab my coffee."

"Um," Erika utters.

"Yes, dearie?" Carmen asks, stopping in her tracks. She puts her hand on Erika's shoulder, encouraging her to spit out whatever is on her mind. She looks down at the matcha tea, observing the microfoam, which is still in the perfect shape of a heart. "Do you not drink matcha anymore?"

"I do," Erika utters. "Just not with cow's milk. I'm vegan now and—"

"Ah, no worries," Carmen says. She picks up the cup and places it on the tray. "We have a lot of different options now. Do you prefer oat, soy, or almond milk?"

"Soy," Erika responds.

"Alright, I'll be back with a soy matcha tea latte. We have more to catch up on than I thought," Carmen says while walking away.

"Shit, we do, too," I say, looking at Erika.

"Sorry, I would have told you over the phone, but I want to explain in person."

"Vegan?" I tap my fingers on the table. There goes my plan to tell her about this new BBQ spot I passed on my way here. She sits across from me, fiddling with a cyan bracelet on her wrist. My eyes widen. "Wait... are you... are you rushing Grox in the spring?"

My friend looks down. Her full lips are twisting. "Yes," she finally answers. "But I am also rushing Goddesses," she quickly adds. "I'm still undecided but leaning more toward Grox."

"Why?"

"The Goddesses have been turning me off lately, and the more time I spend with Grox, the more things make sense."

"To tell you the truth, they've also been turning me off lately. They keep sticking their nose in my relationship." I laugh. "They definitely hate Cel."

"I... I agree with them on that part," she responds. "I think you can do better."

I let out a sigh. "Ugh, let's not talk about Cel right now." I take a sip of my hibiscus tea.

Erika shoots me a look—*Girl, you brought him up*—and reapplies her lip-gloss.

Carmen comes back with Erika's soy matcha latte, sits down at the table, and takes a sip of her coffee. "So, what sorority did you end up joining?"

"Well...so...um," Erika starts.

"So we were both Qousa women," I take over, nodding to Erika. "But they were not right for us."

"At all!" Erika adds.

"So, we're not in a sorority now." I shrug my shoulders.

"But we have good prospects." Erika smiles and nods her head. "Actually, I'm glad we went through this process. It gave us more time to spend with the two sororities we are considering."

"Right? Rush felt so quick and superficial."

"It felt like we were settling."

Carmen puts her hands on our shoulders, lightly tapping and pulling back. "I'm glad you'll be with a better group now." She raises her mug to her lips, steam infiltrating her nose, and for a brief moment, I can smell the caramel notes of the nutty drink. "Leaning toward one in particular?"

"Uh." Erika rubs the back of her ear. "So, we like both sororities, but we're not leaning toward the same one."

"Ah, so you might be joining two different groups?" Carmen shifts her eyes from Erika to me. "There's nothing wrong with that. It might be good for you two to start making decisions for yourselves."

"I agree," I say.

"To new beginnings," Carmen says while raising her cup.

Erika and I mimic Carmen's action and repeat, "To new beginnings!"

We sip our beverages, completing the spontaneous toast. Carmen scoots her chair back to get up. "Now, down to business." She lifts her index finger. "I'll be right back." She hurries away, leaving her coffee in the center of the table. Once she's gone, I make eye contact with Erika.

"What do you think it could be?" Erika asks.

"No clue!" I shrug my shoulders. "Maybe something that has to do with sororities."

Erika finishes the rest of her matcha tea. She dabs her mouth and pulls out her phone. She looks at me and frowns, flipping her phone screen to me. A snap of a woman with butterfly locs and a red crop top is on the screen. "Isn't she beautiful?" Erika asks.

"Yes," I say, moving closer to the screen for a better look. "Is this who you're dating?"

"Yeah," she says, sighing.

"Why are you sad?"

"Remember when I told you I had my own DL moment?" She waits for me to nod my head before she finishes. "Well, it was with her!"

"Oh, wow!" My mouth is sarcastically wide open. "So what you're saying is that you get it now? You had to experience it first, huh?"

"Well, mine is different. You were overly dramatic with yours!"

Carmen comes back with a folder and places it on the table. "Why those faces? What's going on?"

"We'll ask Carmen her opinion," Erika says.

"I don't even know what happened to form an opinion yet," I say. "I'm just saying you gave me a hard time, calling me DL, and now you're a DL." I laugh.

"Fine! I'll tell both of you what happened." Erika clears her throat. Carmen and I are silent; our eyes are glued to her lips. "So, I went on a date. We went to this lovely restaurant, and our orders of fries came. This restaurant has thick, long fries that are extra crunchy. Seasoned perfectly. Some of the best fries I've ever had. My date takes a fry, dips it in the ketchup, takes a bite, and dips the bitten end of the fry back into the ketchup."

"No!" Carmen shouts. She covers her mouth, but I can still see the horror in her eyes.

I roll my eyes. "Well, duh, mine isn't as bad as yours. Double-dipping food is like the blueprint. I'm saying, maybe we should consider DL as well."

"What is DL?" Carmen asks, looking from Erika to me and back to Erika.

Erika giggles. "I'll let you tell her."

In Erika's fashion, I clear my throat. "So, this happened a long time ago, and only once, yet I'm still branded DL. After a great night, my date suggests that we shower together."

"And your parents allowed this?" Carmen asks.

"Kind of. They took Laila and PJ to the amusement park that weekend. I had the house to myself."

"Oh. Reminds me of when I was younger," Carmen sneers. "Go ahead, honey."

"I had this beautiful rose-shaped soap that smelled as good as it looked. My date loved the smell of the soap. We were washing each other with the washcloths when he picked the soap back up and started rubbing the washcloth with it. The same dirty washcloth we just used!"

"Oh my," Carmen says, repeating the same horror and shock she gave Erika.

"Was I wrong to not like that?" I twist my lips and look at Erika. "Now she calls me Double Lather, or DL."

"Well, both of those are quite gross," Carmen says. She shivers and scrunches her nose. "And I agree with Destiny. Now you understand where she is coming from."

"See! I told you I wasn't being dramatic when I decided not to see him again." I cross my arms and look at Erika.

"You decided not to see him because of that?" Carmen lightly taps her forehead. "That is a tad bit dramatic. You could have just told him to use a different towel."

"See!" Erika crosses her arms and looks at me. "Looks like we were both kind of right."

After a few more good laughs, Carmen finally opens the folder to show us what's inside. "So, I bought a new house," she starts. "It is on the beach." She shows us pictures.

"The view from the deck is gorgeous!" Erika says while sorting through the photos.

"Large windows? An outdoor shower? You're about to live your best life," I say.

"Oh, I am already living it." Carmen turns her hand. "Kind of. Right now, I am splitting my time between the beach house and the café." She sighs. "It is exhausting. Even with the extra staff, I am tired of running back and forth. I would like to enjoy my retirement. That is why I need to sell the café."

"No!" Erika and I shout in unison.

"Hold on." Carmen holds up her hands, signaling she isn't done. "I want to know if you would like to run the café. Become the new owners."

Our wide eyes and smiles are the only signs Carmen needs to continue discussing the business's plans and the eventual handover to us.

I quietly close the front door and glance at my watch. Five minutes before curfew, nice! Nevertheless, I still jump when I see Dad in the chair beside the coat rack. That image is all I need for chills to run up my spine. He used to sit in this chair, waiting for me to enter when I would get in trouble at school, when a phone conversation didn't go as he wanted, when I snuck out, or when I broke curfew.

"I guess some things do change," he says. He gets up from the chair and walks toward the staircase. "You're finally growing up and obeying rules." He heads up the stairs, and without looking at me, he says, "Good night, princess. I'll see you tomorrow."

I follow behind him, quietly mocking his words. His slow pace causes me to be a step behind him. When we finally reach the top, he turns right to head to his room, and I quickly make a left, going to mine. I can hear his footsteps stop and feel his eyes burning into the back of my head, but I don't turn around. I quickly enter my room and lock the door, never looking back. I shower quickly, grab my laptop, and hop on my bed, hoping to get a few items finished for the upcoming campaign I'm leading.

Knock, knock!

The knocks are heavy, almost banging. I know it's my dad. As much as I want to pretend I'm asleep, I unwisely left the lights on so he knows I'm awake. He knows that I heard his knocks. I open the door to my bedroom slowly.

"I need you to get off the internet," he says sternly.

"I'm not on the internet," I respond.

He peers into my room, eyes squinting as they land on the laptop still on my bed. "Don't lie to me."

"I'm not. I am offline, designing pamphlets for a group I am a part of at school." He pushes the door open, dashes to my bed, and grabs the laptop. As he looks up from the screen to me, I cross my arms. "See, just work for school."

Dad shakes his head. "I still need you to get off of the computer."

"What, why?"

"Because I said so."

"But I need to work on this."

"You should have thought about that before you went out earlier. Maybe you'll learn to manage your time better." He closes my laptop and places it on my desk. "Look, I know you think I am being mean, but I don't like the type of people on the internet at night. There are some dangerous people out there, and I think it is disrespectful of you to be on the computer during this time. I don't know if you are on the internet or not." He closes his eyes and shakes his head. "You can become distracted, stop what you're working on, and suddenly get on the internet."

Younger me would have been angry and felt belittled or manipulated, but grown me is trying to hold in my laughter. "I understand," I say, smiling.

"Good," he responds. "I'll see you tomorrow." He waits for me to get in my bed before turning off the light and closing the door.

I grab my phone and open the folder to my project, hoping it synced before Mr. Domineering decided to close my laptop. Thanks to the cloud, all of my work is there, and I can continue to work on my project from my phone. A text from Erika pops up.

Hey, business partner! Made it home!

But walked into some BS! Haha!

Thanks for letting me know.

And girl, same!

I'm not coming back home next break.

One day was enough for me! Lol.

They tried to provoke you, too?

Provoke ain't even a strong enough word!

It was just so silly that I had to let it go.

I feel you.

Mine was just straight goofy!

Did you snap?

Nope.

Not about to give them any ammo.

Right!

They love throwing around bad attitude accusations.

Especially toward black women.

You ain't lying!

Stay strong!

I will! And you do the same.

I spend the next few minutes working on the pamphlet. It looks great and has a lot of information, but I wonder if it achieves the goals the Goddesses set. I email the draft to Kiana, who quickly responds that she loves the design. I roll over and end my night thinking about my future campaign.

Christmas Eve is for family, food, and our tradition of opening up one present of our choosing. We usually go to my aunt's house, but my parents are hosting the festivities this year. Family members go in and out of the front door, dropping off their potluck dishes in the kitchen and their presents below the Christmas tree. My parents are annoyed with the constantly open door, but save their exclamations of "You're letting all the heat out!" for the children who run between making snow angels in the front yard and sipping hot cocoa in the dining room. They make it a point to remind everyone, adults included, to remove their shoes when entering the living room, which houses the artisan rug they had shipped from Persia. I don't think they'll be hosting next year.

Family tradition says we go to Laberto's Farm to pick the tree we want to decorate. According to Laberto, this is supposed to provide a connection with nature, ensuring you'll get the present you wished for. But this year, a musty, white, pre-decorated artificial tree stands next to the fireplace. Mama sprays it with her homemade mixture of camphor and thyme essential oils, which masks the smell a little, but I can still smell the fakeness up close.

"Should have left it outside a bit longer," Mama says, fanning the tree, hoping the smell will eventually disappear.

I touch one of the branches of the tree, the tips brushing against my palm, reminiscent of an old hairbrush. "The smell isn't overwhelming," I say, trying to make her feel better.

"I have a sensitive nose. It probably isn't as bad as I'm making it." I nod, and she smiles. She gives the tree two more spritzes and places the spray in a cabinet. She turns around and immediately starts straightening out the pillows on the furniture. "Can you check the kitchen for me? Make sure that each dish has a serving spoon." She turns to meet my gaze and holds up her finger. "Also, make sure there are no crumbs or spills on the floor. God forbid we end up with roaches."

I dutifully go to the kitchen. Instantly, the blood-red puddle under one of the tables catches my eye. Punch. There's no way someone spilled this without noticing. I soak up the liquid and then spray the spot with cleaner. The only thing worse than seeing a spill is the sticky floors after the spill. I sweep the floors, the dustpan being the fullest I've ever seen. Each dish has a serving utensil except for the 7-layer salad. I find the salad tongs and sit them next to the bowl, but not before helping myself to a generous serving.

Bowl in hand, I walk to the dinette where my cousin Ciera is devouring the last bit of mac and cheese on her plate. "That looks good," I say while taking the seat across from her. "Who made it?"

"I have no clue, but whoever made it put their foot in it," Ciera says between gulps. She wipes her mouth with the cloth napkin balled up on the table. "Too bad I'm going to pay for it later." She frowns and rubs her stomach.

"It is like every person I know is lactose intolerant," I reply.

"Same, but what choice do we have?" Ciera grabs her plate and heads to the kitchen. "It's not like we can stop eating it. Literally, everything has either milk or cheese in it."

"That's true," I say while she walks away. I eat a tomato from my salad. I wonder what the other layer would be if not cheddar cheese. The base of the salad dressing would no longer be mayonnaise. I shrug and take another bite. At least I'm not eating a lot of cheese. Stomach cramps won't be a problem for me later.

"Destiny!" The loud screech almost makes me choke on the little food I've taken in. Ciera runs out of the kitchen before I can say anything. Her eyes are wide, a bewildered expression on her face. "You will not believe who made the mac and cheese."

"Who?"

"Aunt Vanessa." Ciera hands me the placard that accompanies the dish.

Made with love by Vanessa. Mac and butternut squash cashew sauce.

This is the second time Aunt Vanessa has made my jaw drop in under a year. I look around, expecting her to be behind me like last time. I then slap my forehead. See, this is the shit that Tanner was talking about. I need to let go of that child-like magical thinking of mine. Aunt Vanessa isn't some ghostly figure lurking around the dinette. I gather myself and say, "But I haven't seen her. When did she have time to drop off an entire pan of mac and cheese, or whatever it is, in the dead of winter and then leave without no one noticing?"

Ciera shrugs. "Maybe she had someone bring it." She glances at the card. "Looks like my stomach won't be upset after all. There's no dairy in the mac and cheese." She licks her lips. "When you see Aunt Vanessa again, tell her to send me the recipe."

I nod, and we go to the kitchen. Ciera gets a new plate and fills it with the dish. I push my salad over to make room for a serving spoonful of Aunt Vanessa's mac and sauce. The flavor hits my tongue as soon as I bite down, and I am instantly transmitted to one of PJ's trances.

There might have been a few bites here and a few second plates there, but we still need to officially pray over the food. My family circles the food in the kitchen, linking our hands, heads bowed. One of my god-fearing cousins leads the prayer, imitating the authoritative cadence we are used to hearing on Sundays. After grace, everyone grabs plates and loads up on their favorite dishes. Well, almost everyone.

Herbert returns to the family room, rolling dice with a few of my uncles. "That's that shit!" he exclaims after throwing the dice and collecting his winnings.

Laila, who is playing with her tablet on the couch next to them, covers her ears. She has grown sensitive to cuss words and claims they hurt her heart. But that doesn't stop anyone from cussing around her. I grab her and bring her to my room for a sister chat.

"Did you like the ballet?"

Laila smiles and does a spin. "It's my favorite!" she exclaims. "I want to be a ballerina."

"You can definitely be one," I affirm.

"I know."

I smile and grab a hairbrush. "Here, let me lay your edges."

She squirms away from me. "I don't like that."

"Oh. Okay." I place the hairbrush back on the dresser and cuddle beside her in the bed. A role-playing game on the tablet captures her attention. Of course, the character she is assuming is a ballerina. The ballerina has cute afro puffs, just like Laila. I help pick an outfit, and we support the ballerina training for her performances in different countries. We learn dance movements such as plié, relevé, and sauté and practice them ourselves. Laila moves effortlessly after watching the character on the screen perform. "I'll talk to our parents about enrolling you in ballet class."

She grins, ear to ear. She practices foot positions as the character does them on the tablet. I make a note on my phone to send her books about ballet and to find more role-playing games. She is going to see herself in whatever she chooses to do. I try a sauté and end up falling in a split. We both bust out laughing. She mocks my fall over and over but gracefully. Even when she is trying to copy my mistake, it looks good. A natural. Her laugh gets harder with each iteration. She stops, and her smile disappears. So does mine because I hear it, too.

"What's that?" she asks.

"I don't know." I crack my door open and peer out. I can't see what is happening downstairs, but I can hear Herbert's grumpy, old man's voice. "I'll be back." Laila hops back on my bed, attention captured by the tablet again, and I go downstairs.

"I'm hungry, God damn it!" Herbert yells.

"Then make you a plate!" I hear one of my cousins answer back.

Herbert is sitting on one of the couches, arms crossed and lips stiff. Most people are heading to the dining room, trying to ignore the situation. Some are behind Herbert, trying to hold back laughter. Others revel in the drama, clapping when they agree, shaking their head, and shouting dissects when they don't.

"I need a woman to make my plate!"

"Come on, Pops," Dad says. "Everyone here made their own plate."

"Except you!" Herbert points at my dad. "Diana made your plate. I need someone to make my plate." He bangs his fists on the arms of the couch.

Dad looks at my mom, and she twists her lips so he knows not to ask. Dad looks around the room, and everyone gives him the same look. "What do you want?" he asks.

"You know what I like, boy!" Herbert shouts.

Dad enters the kitchen and comes out with a plate with a little of everything on it. He hands it to Herbert, who is shaking his head. Herbert takes his first bite.

"This is good, but is it worth the trouble of getting it? I tell ya, these new-age women are something else."

"They are more independent and expect you to be," I say promptly.

"Whaaaa," Herbert exhales, then turns his head until our eyes meet. "They are independent because they are doing men's work."

"What is men's work?"

"You're in college. You should know." Herbert's eyes are cold.

"You worked as a janitor, right? You didn't need to use your penis for that job, so what makes it a man's job?"

"It's a man's job because women would be shocked at the shit we see!" Herbert shouts. "Piss, shit, blood, vomit, anything, and everything."

"Do women not have bowel movements? We've seen all of that. In fact, I remember granny cleaning up after you drunk vomited in her sitting room."

Herbert violently puts his plate on the table and stands up. He points at me but looks at my dad. "P, you better get your daughter."

"Destiny, quit playing," Dad shouts. That's his usual phrase when he doesn't know what to say or isn't taking me seriously. "Kids play too much these days."

Herbert rubs his temples while sitting back down on the couch. He looks at PJ, then me, then my dad. He chuckles. "They think they know everything once they go to college, huh?"

"Yes, indeed," Dad agrees. "I can't believe I have a college kid."

"My boy, you are getting old!"

"You are, too!" They both chuckle. Dad rubs the top of his head. "I still remember the day the acceptance letter came in the mail. I'm holding this thick envelope with the name of my daughter's first pick, and I knew it was something good." He motions the thickness of the envelope.

"They ain't going to send anything that big for a rejection," Herbert, who is now back to eating his food, says between bites.

"My exact thought. I opened it, read it, and couldn't stop shaking. I was so happy. I called my princess to deliver the good news. She played it cool, but I knew she was happy." He looks at me, a smile—*proud dad*—is drawn on his face.

I clear my throat. "I wasn't playing it cool. I just wanted to be the one to open the envelope." The smile leaves. I stand there, wondering what he is going to say next.

"Well, I had to open it because what if it was a bill," he says quickly.

"I got a full scholarship, and that isn't even—"

"That you only knew about because it was detailed in the envelope," he cuts me off. "I open all the mail that comes to my house. You should have sent it to your house if you wanted to open it." He awkiles, but this one is different because of his eyes and stance. But especially his eyes. They are focused on me as if I am his prey. His head tilts up, and his chest is pushed forward. "I pay all of the bills. If there was a bill in the envelope, I would need to know about it."

"Okay," I muster out. Erika always said that my dad lived vicariously through me, and now I finally understand what she was talking about. He has always taken my big moments and turned them into his big moments. I shake my head and start back to my room. They loudly talk about me as I make my exit.

"There she is," Dad starts, "always walking away instead of facing the problem."

"That's how those teen girls are," Herbert says.

I flip the bird once I make it up the stairs and out of their sight. It fills me with some kind of justice. When I open my door, Laila is on my bed, ears plugged and face in the tablet. I scoot next to her and kiss her cheek. It dawns on me that she is the only girl in the house now that I am in college, and all of this negativity could be directed toward her in a couple of years. I bite my lip as I watch her dress her ballerina. She can't have my childhood. I won't allow it. I think of ways to keep her out of this house as much as possible.

Laila takes out her earbuds and asks, "What's that?"

I can faintly hear Herbert downstairs yelling about a second serving. I turn on the TV to drown out the noise. Laila plugs her ears and turns her attention back to her tablet. My eyes are glued to the television. It can't be. I rub my eyes, but the image is still on the screen. My eyes blink slowly as the rest of my body cannot move. The headline of the news broadcast reads **Missing College Woman**.

The woman in the photo has long black hair with bangs, but the heart-shaped lips, the bone structure, and especially the eyes are what give it away. I've seen this woman. The night of my cousin's party. Imagine her with lime green hair and mascara tears; it is an exact match. I text Kiana to let her know that I want to organize for missing black women. And I know the first person that I want to advocate for: Pina Morgan.

New Crew, Who This?

I watch Kiana grab a sandwich and salad from the walk-up bar, which we frequent often. The Goddesses always preach a healthy diet, and I try to stick to it as much as possible. I barely ate any fried foods when I was home. I sneak a hug from behind as she contemplates which soup to grab. She doesn't react. She's used to it by now.

"You've ruined me," I say.

She chuckles. "I remember my first break home after joining the Goddesses." She taps her finger on her face. "A real eye-opener."

"How's your relationship with your family now?"

"Distant." Kiana clears her throat. "I mean, I tried to enlighten them. Tried to get them to treat me better. But it wasn't worth the energy. They didn't see how they were hurting me, nor did they care to understand. Stuck in their ways, I guess." She moves her head back, and I catch a wince.

"Hopefully, I can get through to mine, but I doubt I will," I say while grabbing a salad from the bar. "It's like whatever I say or do is not good. They want me silent to keep up appearances."

"Oh, you have one of those," Kiana responds. "Bougie folks?"

I nod my head, and we find a seat in the cafeteria.

"Are you ready to move a second time?" Kiana laughs.

I steal a fry from her plate. She must have taken the last box because I didn't see any fries at the bar, and I certainly didn't see her take any. "Ugh, I can't believe there weren't any extra rooms in Ashford. I'm suffering at this new dorm. There is absolutely no support here, and it is so loud! I cannot wait to be a part of the Goddesses' house. Save me from this nightmare." I respond.

"You have the energy to rush again?"

"Yes, but I should have chosen y'all the first time. Then I wouldn't be in this mess."

I steal another fry from her plate. Kiana picks up the box and dumps half of it on my plate. I pull at my collar as I dip the donated fries one by one in the ketchup she passes to me. It is the day before classes start back up, and the cafeteria is still empty. Kiana and I are here early to print the newsletters we created for the Goddesses' house. It's better to hang them up before the students arrive rather than trying to when the halls are crowded. We also want our sheets to be the first thing the students see when they arrive on campus.

"Anyway, I'm afraid Marcel was right," I say.

Kiana nearly chokes on the chunk of sandwich she had bitten off. She coughs a couple of times before drinking a big gulp of water. She grabs a fry and pops it in her mouth. "I knew I deserved a cheat meal today. What was he right about?"

"About your influence."

Kiana puts down her sandwich and moves her glass of water to the side. She lifts her hand to her mouth, resting her chin on her thumb. Her lips are sandwiched between her index finger and middle finger. She has a New Year's resolution to keep certain thoughts to herself. I think she is doing well.

"I see things completely differently now. Even things that Erika explained to me years ago make total sense now. And it is all because of your influence."

"Was your sister there?"

"Yeah, she was." I dab my mouth with my napkin. I rub my eyebrow. "I kind of wish she wasn't around all of the chaoticness. She is really into ballet, and she is obsessed with gravity. I guess I'm not the only Lowry who fixates on things. I'm looking into ballet schools around here."

"That's good. Laila will be close to you and away from them."

I nod my head and take a bite of my salad. "How was your break?"

"It was okay. This is the first time I've seen them in months because I've been spending all of my breaks with the Goddesses. I saw my brothers and sisters. You know my daddy had a lot of kids, so I'm not even sure I saw most of them," she says, twisting her lip. "How are you and Marcel doing?"

"Girl, it's still off and on. We get into fights regularly now, and it's so stressful. I feel like the more I learn, the more red flags I see, and whenever I try to talk to him about these red flags, we always end up in an argument."

"He's pretty toxic."

"I know, but he is so fine, and I like leading the police brutality protest with him. He has opened up a lot more, though. He offered to help find missing black women. So, in a way, I think our talks are going somewhere."

"Oh, he's joining in on our march?"

"Yes, Pina Morgan went missing and lived right around the corner from me. I think he's worried that it could have been me. We have a meeting with her loved ones tomorrow."

"Well, that's good. Looks like Marcel has changed a little. Is he okay with you rushing our sorority?"

"I still haven't gotten him on board yet. He wants me to be a Qousa woman. He says that we are supposed to be a king and queen."

"Well, now you can be a Goddess and king, but I guess they aren't equally yoked."

"I guess," I say, ignoring the shady comment. "Have you ever thought about having a counterpart to your sorority?"

"We have, I mean, it has been discussed at our national meetings. But I don't think that such a thing will ever exist. We try to decenter black men as much as possible. I think we're too radical."

"I don't think you're all that radical, to be honest."

"Oh, trust me, we are. Our public image is just the tip of the iceberg. We have so much going on behind the scenes that any potential fraternity would be intimidated or, worst, try to control what we do."

"Really?"

"Our radical views are why we are very selective in our rushing process. We are cautious to only let in certain women, and we often question them on their problematic ways to see if they are ready."

"Oh. Is that why you asked me about Marcel during our interview?"

"For the most part, yes."

"Well, damn. I'm still with him."

"I know, but I feel like you can see how problematic he can be, and we can discuss it now."

"I see. So I already know the questions y'all are going to ask me. This should be a lot less nerve-racking."

"No, we still have other things to discuss. I know you have been doing a lot of reflecting this past semester, which is great! Remember those reflections because we might question you on a few of them."

"Thanks for the advice."

I get bread for our soups, something we always forget to grab. Our school bakes fresh bread every morning, and we can grab as much as we want for free. We always have a good selection. Today, my school offers French baguettes, sourdough, and three-cheese bread. I take a basket and place a couple of slices of the three cheese breads in it. I hear snickering behind me as I place the bread in the basket. I turn around to see Tammy and Jessica whispering to each other.

"Hi—" I start but remember that I have been excommunicated from them. Ever since that meeting, Qousa women have stopped talking to me. Even the new members overlook me. I still speak to Jennifer, but only in secret. She told me that the Qousa women had a vote to not communicate with ex-members as they have been dethroned. It's funny how I gained so many friends in one night and then lost them all the night of the protest.

I pass them as I walk back to the table, trying not to make eye contact. I can feel their eyes following me as I return to Kiana.

"Are you okay?" Kiana asks as soon as I set the bread basket on the table.

I raise my eyebrow, "Yeah, I'm okay. Why?"

"Just want to ensure the Qousa women didn't say anything to you."

"I noticed them laughing but didn't think they were laughing at me."

"Oh."

"What could they be laughing at? They need to get over the fact that I left their sorority."

"I saw them pointing to your hair."

I realize this is the first time they have seen my natural hair. I've been wearing my teeny tiny afro all break, and while it garnered a few comments from my family at first, the comments soon trailed off, and it became nothing special. Jessica has some nerve since she is part of why I had to get a haircut.

I look at Kiana, " It won't last long. It's something they've never seen on me before, and they'll get used to it."

"Always the optimistic one."

I spray perfume on my neck and check myself out one last time in the mirror. Cel texted me a few minutes ago to come down. We spoke a few times during break but didn't video chat like usual; he wants that spark when we see each other for the first time again on campus. I look at my new roommate, Cat, a soft-spoken black girl, and ask her if I look okay.

"You look beautiful," she says, her voice barely over a whisper. She smiles and gives me two thumbs up.

"Oh, you're so sweet." I grab my purse and coat. "Okay, I shall return."

I leave the room and squeeze between the noisy men in the hallway having a makeshift dunking contest. They haven't been back from break a full day yet, and they are already back to their ways. And to make it worse, they have subwoofers in their room, allowing them to blast music while they have their dunking contest. Yep, can't wait to move. And poor Cat spends most of the time in the room with her headphones on. I wish she would consider joining the Goddesses, but she says she doesn't do socials.

I walk out of the building and head to Cel's car. I can see him in the driver's seat, texting on his phone. I hop in the car and kiss him on the cheek. He smiles and starts to kiss me back, but jumpingly stops. He stares at me briefly before he lands a wet one on my cheek.

"New hair," he says.

"Yes. You like?"

He hesitates a little. "Baby, I'm going to be honest with you. I really don't like short hair on women."

"Baby, I thought we talked about this. Remember, women have bodily autonomy."

"I know, but this is different. When I met you, you had long, beautiful, straight hair. But now you have this. This is a big change for me."

"It was a big change for me as well. I've gotten used to it. And you will, too. Besides, it's growing relatively quickly, so it should be long in no time."

"Okay, so it would be long, but what about it being straight? When I met you, your hair was straight. I don't like this texture."

"We literally have the same texture." I run my hand through his hair and then through mine. "Yep, feel the same to me."

"Yes, but I had this texture when you met me. And even though I like this texture on myself, it doesn't necessarily mean I want the same on my woman."

"It's my natural hair. What do you expect me to do about it?"

"I don't know. I just like it straight."

"So you want me to relax it again? I remember you always telling me, back when my hair was relaxed, that relaxers were damaging and that black women need to go natural."

He shifts in his seat. "Yes, but not this type of natural. If it was longer, I would be okay with it, I guess."

"So you will be fine with my texture if it were longer? Is that what you're telling me? Because you were just saying something different a few seconds ago."

He twists his lip. "Yeah, I think I will be okay if you had a big afro. Like those women in the 70s. I think you'll look beautiful."

"Awe, I think I'll look beautiful too. Thank you for understanding."

He starts up the car and starts driving. "I think it will add to our activism. This will sound hypocritical, but I never thought I would be in this situation. Would you consider wearing a wig or weave?"

"Babe, I like my hair. Plus, you don't like wigs or weave."

"Yes, but if it's a curly natural texture, you have my word; I will be okay with that."

"My hair isn't curly. It's kinky. My natural texture wig will be an afro."

"And I will be perfectly fine with that. You just have to realize this is a big change for me. How would you like it if I changed something major?"

"Like what?"

"You wouldn't like it if I wore a speedo in public daily. You'll be embarrassed."

I laugh. "No, you did not just compare my natural hair to you wearing a speedo. I actually thought we were getting somewhere."

"We are getting somewhere. But you have to see my side of things as well. You're the one who changed up on me. I'm just reacting to the change."

"I'll consider it."

"Thank you. That's all I'm asking." He takes his hand and massages the back of my head. I love his touch.

We start driving, heading to meet the family of Pina Morgan. We are meeting at a library halfway between my college town and hometown. I'm glad they agreed to meet away from the city because it saves me an obligatory visit to my family. Cel and I talk about the protest in the car. He states how much progress he thinks this will be for the black community.

"Because we need our black women home," he says. "Who will raise the kids if black women are missing?"

When we get to the library, the Morgans are already there. They have a box of personal items belonging to Pina. They share stories about Pina and what she means to the family.

"I'm glad there are activists like you out here trying to find our girls," Mrs. Morgan says.

I give her an easy nod. "I knew I had to do something, especially since I didn't do anything when I first saw her the night of her disappearance."

Mrs. Morgan's eyes bulge, and her head draws back quickly. "You saw her?" she shouts.

"Yes...Yes. Didn't the police tell you?"

"No, the police didn't tell me anything. I call every day, but they have no updates to provide."

I step back away from her. "I don't understand. I told them I saw her in the car with an aggressive, strange man that night."

Mr. Morgan crosses his arm. "Goes to show that they are not taking my daughter's disappearance seriously." He shakes his head. "I'm glad that you young folks are on the case. I've heard about your protests. I've seen the videos on social media. Please do your best to bring my daughter home." He shudders and looks away.

"We will do everything we can," Cel says.

"Starting with getting an accurate picture of your daughter out there," I add.

"What do you mean?" Mr. and Mrs. Morgan ask in unison.

"Well, when I saw her that night, she had green hair and a lot of makeup. I think our best chances of finding her will be to get more current pictures of her to the media."

Mr. Morgan grimaces. "You want me to release unflattering pictures of my daughter."

"Well, no. I scoured Pina's social media pages, and her gorgeous selfies are on there. Green hair and all. Also, it looks like she wears makeup every day. I just think that it—"

"You can keep that thought to yourself," Mr. Morgan says sharply. "Do you really think the media will take her disappearance seriously if they find out she had green hair? That she caked on the makeup? That she wore those hoochie clothes?"

They already don't take it seriously. I shake my head and take the Morgans' hands in mine. "I'm sorry. You're right. The media wouldn't take it seriously. Maybe we can focus on finding the suspect."

"Good idea, sweetheart," Mrs. Morgan says while patting the back of my hand. "Do you remember what he looks like?"

"Oh, I remember what he looks like to a T," I say. "He's dark-skinned with thick, curly sideburns, cartoonish, I know, like the 70s and—"

"Hold on," Marcel cuts me off. "He's black?"

"Yes."

Marcel crosses his arms and gives me a stern look. "We can't release a description or even a sketch of this man. That would put every black man in the vicinity in danger."

"I agree," Mr. Morgan says. "Why don't we just focus on the pictures that we already have of Pina and add our personal stories? It will pull on heartstrings. And hopefully, someone will come forward with some information." He puts out his hands, and Marcel quickly gives him a handshake.

Mrs. Morgan gives Mr. Morgan a look—*we will discuss this at home*—and offers a handshake to Marcel as well.

"Besides," Mr. Morgan continues, ignoring his wife's side-eye. "She could be with a totally different person by now. She switched men like she switched hair colors."

What I want to do is sigh and roll my eyes. But I do neither. Instead, I swallow my words and shake Mr. Morgan's hand.

When I shake Mrs. Morgan's hand, she whispers, "I'll work on my husband and give you a call later."

I receive her message with a smile.

Spring rush is much shorter and less eventful than the fall rush. We still have the standard rounds, but they aren't as exhausting. Not every sorority participates in recruitment this time of year. But I am so grateful that the Goddesses do. I have gone through each of the rounds, as usual, this time with only one sorority in mind because there is no other place I'd rather be than the Goddesses' house.

I still met with Grox just to see what Erika saw in them. And what do you know, I made it to the final round with them.

Today, I will have my interview with both Grox and the Goddesses. The same day turned me off from the Goddesses last semester. And I didn't even make it his far with Grox. But I have grown so much since then that I am willing to listen to whatever criticisms they have to say. I did prepare my answers to the questions again but using an outline instead of a script. I wrote down a few points I would like to hit for each question. I want to be natural and genuine in my answers instead of being an actress following a script.

Cel, like the good boyfriend he is, walks me up to the Grox's house and kisses me on the lips. He looks me in the eyes. "Even though I don't like this sorority, I wish you nothing but good luck in the interview. You will do great, and they will love you!"

"Thanks, baby. Love you!"

"Love you too." And with that, he gives me a few more pecks on the lips. He blows more kisses to me as he walks away, and I blow them back before ringing the doorbell to the house.

Lucinda opens the door, arms wide, welcoming me to their house. I follow her down a long hallway, walls adorned with photographs of their events through the years. A black and white photo that had to be from the 70s shows a masked woman cutting a fence with chickens on the other side. A more recent photo shows sisters operating an ice cream truck with the phrase "cow milk" crossed out and the words "soy, oat, almond," and "cashew" all over the truck instead.

She brings me to an office with walls filled with more photos of rescues, events, and protests. A buffet awaits me.

"Help yourself," Lucinda says. "The ingredients are on the placards in front of each dish. There's ice cream in the cooler." She points to the freestanding freezer in the corner. "I'm going to gather some papers, and we will begin shortly." She hurries out of the room.

I look at the snacks and desserts on the table, but the brownies on the other side catch my attention. The brownies are individually wrapped, sitting on a stand in the opposite corner of the freezer. Round stickers, with a price of $15, stick to the plastic. *It's a little pricey for a brownie, isn't it?* It must be leftovers from a fundraiser they had. I grab one and take a half-pint of oat milk ice cream from the freezer. I open the small ice cream and break the brownie over the container.

The smell of the vanilla from the ice cream and the softness of the brownie between my fingers bring back memories of my great-grandmother Mary, who always topped off hers with pecans. She is the one who taught me the brownie ice cream trick. I always used to do a dramatic stink face when she sprinkled the nuts on top, and she always laughed. *Don't knock it until you've tried it*, she would say. Today, I'm feeling open-minded. Several bowls of crushed nuts are displayed on the table. I scan until I see pecans; one bowl is salted, and the other isn't. I opt for the unsalted ones, sprinkling a tablespoon on my creation. I wipe my fingers with wet wipes and spoon the DIY ice cream into my mouth. My great-grandmother was right; this is delicious!

Lucinda comes back to the room, and we sit in the chairs. Her smile is infectious.

"I'm glad you decided to go through this process with us again," she says.

"I am, too," I say, crossing my legs. "I had some discussions with my best friend over break and concluded that I was wrong to judge you so quickly."

"That's good progress!" She writes in her notebook and then taps the pen against her chin. "You've sat through our presentations and spoken to many of our members. So, I am going to ask you one question. Have you had any mindset changes, and if so, have you applied any changes to your lifestyle to fit that mindset?"

"I kind of see a new perspective now." I sit up in my seat as Lucinda scribbles in her notebook. "I talked about this with Erika during winter break. She no longer drinks milk, and we are supposed to be running a café together after Carmen retires. She wants to make the café fully vegan."

"A vegan café in that town can shake things up," Lucinda says.

"It can and will because my best friend and I can do anything together. Carmen and I are on board, especially after Erika explained her concerns." I take a deep breath and expel it slowly. "Hopefully, I explain this next part right."

"Say whatever comes to mind. All of your feelings and thoughts will be validated here," Lucinda comforts.

"Carmen explained how Moya Bailey shaped our language regarding the oppression we continue to face."

"Misogynoir! That term helped shape my activism."

"Right! It helped put so many of my experiences in perspective." I clear my throat. "So when Carmen finished explaining that, along with black woman entrepreneurship, Erika explained how veganism is in line with that and that the café should be vegan. And... I don't know. When she said, the same system that stole our ancestor's breastmilk to feed the slaveowner's babies is the same system that mass breeds cows to steal their milk to feed humans, something... something just clicked."

Lucinda puts her hand on her hip and smiles playfully. "Girl, are you paraphrasing?" We laugh together.

"You know I am," I say, holding back tears. "I've never seen my best friend so passionate about something before. She said so much, and I wished I had video recorded it so I could play it back and catch the other things she said."

"Well, you can always ask her again. And you have the women of Grox to ask."

"I know." I smile and look at my fingers. They are shaking, but I can't tell which of my feelings are making them shake. I look back up at Lucinda, who is writing in her notebook. She pauses and takes a sip of her tea. Mint, lemon, and ginger. The notes float through the air, and it is the first thing I've smelt since I sat down. My nerves must be blocking my senses, but being vulnerable has somehow unblocked everything. Everything. I can hear the pen scratching the paper as Lucinda writes. "I guess I'm trying to say that Erika decided she cannot support such a system. And neither can I."

Lucinda's eyes grow, and she drops her pen. The clacks as the pen hits the floor ring in my ears. I bend down and hand it back to her, and she immediately starts scribbling. "Wow, I was not expecting that."

"I wasn't either."

"This brings us to the second part of my question. Have you made any lifestyle changes?"

"I...," I squirm. "Everything I like to eat isn't vegan," I say. "It's so hard."

"But it isn't as hard as you think," Lucinda replies. "I see you in the cafeteria often. I see you grab that cheesy bread whenever you get soup. Why? When literally every other bread choice doesn't contain any animals."

I look up at her. "You can eat the other bread?"

She nods her head. "I think that knowing what you are consuming is very important. You can have more things than you think."

"I should probably read labels more," I say.

"No worries. What to eat is the easy part." Lucinda fingers through the sheets in a folder and hands me one titled The Vegan Food Pyramid. It is shaped like the pyramid I learned about in school, but now has items like tofu, seitan, vital wheat gluten, nutritional yeast, and kombucha. She hands me another sheet. A list of all the vegan foods on campus and dishes that can be made vegan with slight modifications.

"I can work with this," I say, flipping the sheet to the back to see more food choices on campus.

"You can," Lucinda confirms. "Now, the hard part will be learning about the industries and systems that intertwine in your life and how you sometimes can't do anything about it. That helplessness is going to sting!"

We wrap up, and I thank her for the opportunity to interview with the Grox. We hug, and I wave goodbye as I head to my next house: The Goddesses.

Jackie, the vice president of the Goddesses chapter, opens the door and welcomes me in. The Goddesses collectively decided it wouldn't be fair if I interviewed with Kiana, given how close we are now. She leads me to the same room Kiana interviewed me in last time, albeit different because of changes in the decoration. They must have taken my comments last semester to heart. The fancy art, the vases, they have all been replaced. Most of the gold has been stripped out of the house, and only slivers of it remain.

"Would you like something to drink? Coffee, tea, water?"

"Tea, please."

"Okay, be right back!"

I look around the room. The paintings are now art pieces by local indie artists. And not just any indie artists, black women indie artists. There is a bookshelf full of literature by womanist scholars. I glance over the titles, recognizing some books that Kiana loaned me. Jackie saunters back into the room, holding a tea set, the same fancy tea set from last time.

"Here's your tea. So you're ready for the interview?" she says in a high-pitched voice.

"Yes, I am."

We go through all the questions, mostly the same ones from last time. I answer each question with certainty and honesty. I feel more confident this time and have a different purpose. Last time, I just wanted to be a part of a sorority. This time, I want to be a Goddess.

She praises my answers. "You are Goddess material."

"Thanks," I say, awaiting the questions still to come.

"How was your break?"

"It was okay! I saw Erika, my best friend. She is actually rushing Grox. I can't believe we are going to be in different sororities. But enough about me. How was yours?"

"It was fine. I went to Hawaii with my family. Trying to get out of this chilly weather." She grabs a few sheets of paper from her folder and glances over them. She nods her head. "So, I know that you have been hanging out with us a lot, especially with Kiana, and we've been coming to your marches, adding that feminine touch to them."

"Yes, I love this group of women. Thanks for giving me a new strategy. I think it is more effective."

"Great! Do you feel like a new person?"

"Yes! I've grown so much as a person, as a woman, as a black woman. I am so grateful that I met all of you!"

"Can you name something specific you've learned about?"

"I learned more about my identity as a black woman."

"Did you know anything about your identity before? Did your mother teach you or demonstrate to you black womanhood?"

My legs start to wiggle. I open my mouth, but words won't come out. I look down at my shaking hands.

"It's okay. Take your time." Jackie says, trying to encourage me. She places her hand on my knee. Empathy covers her face. My nerves ease up a bit, and I let out a sigh.

"So, I grew up in the suburbs, one of the few to do so in my family. I was raised to be a respectable black woman, and I still embody that. In college, I'm learning that some of the values I was brought up with aren't the same as my current values. I'm having difficulty embracing my values because I don't want to lose the respectable black woman label."

"We have quite a few women like you in our sorority. Women who want to redefine what is respectable to them."

"You do?"

"Yep, some are further along in their journey, and others are only beginning, just like you. They've been helping each other become their true, authentic selves. I think that it will benefit you to join them."

"That will be awesome."

"Being respectable doesn't mean being submissive to the men in the black community. It doesn't have to mean looking the other way while harm is being done to the women in your life. It doesn't have to mean standing up for black men who constantly play victim to white men."

"Okay," I say, raising my eyebrow.

"It could simply mean being educated, dressing nicely, sitting in your femininity, voicing your concerns smartly, and not doing anything embarrassing."

"I can get behind a couple of those things."

"Okay, and what about my second question? Your mother? Did she show you black womanhood through her actions?"

"This is a tough one for me."

"If you're uncomfortable answering it, you don't have to. I know how personal it is."

"No, I've been reflecting on this a lot, and I think it will help me if I talk to someone about it."

"If you think it helps, go for it."

I take a deep sigh. "I do not have a close relationship with my mother. We've never really talked. I always call my best friend if I have problems or need advice. I know she loves me. She just doesn't know how to communicate with me. She prides herself in having only guy friends, and I think that is part of the problem. During winter break, I came to terms with her being black male-identified and black male-centered. Like every action she takes, she asks herself whether black men will like it. Even the purse she bought me. She only bought it because it was mentioned favorably by a black man."

"That had to be hard, especially as a young girl. Did you grow up in a black male-centered household?"

"Yeah, pretty much, and it was difficult because everything revolved around men."

"You used the term black male-identified. What do you mean by that?"

"I learned that term from Kiana. Mama identifies more with men, especially black men, than black women. It was difficult for her to see anything from my perspective. It was difficult for her to see any of the wrongdoings of the males in my family, especially if the victim was a woman."

"Mmm, I've had my share of experience with women like your mother. They ignore issues that black women face at the hands of black men. Other women grew up like this in the sorority. Do you find any connection between her and your first house, Qousa?"

"The women at the Qousa house remind me so much of her."

"For sure. As you can see, they only join in on marches and protest that affects the entire," she air quotes, "black community." She scoots in her chair. "They are very male-centered. Do you think that's what attracted you to them the first time? Being similar to your mother? Feeling like home?"

"Haha, pretty much." Nervous laughter escapes my mouth. "I was even more attracted to them once I learned about the Kousa men."

"That explains a lot." She finishes writing on the sheet of paper on her lap and gets up from the chair. "I'll be right back. I seem to be missing a few sheets. It shouldn't take long. We have snacks in the closet. Feel free to walk around."

"Okay."

She exits the room, filing through the papers she is cradling. I get up from my seat to observe the art pieces closely. I love the theme that the art pieces showcase. Mostly pampered black women, subtle feminine power. I look at the pictures of the chapter. They have a tiny group compared to the other sororities. Next to the photographs is a map, marking all of the Goddesses chapters across the United States. I study the map briefly to see what major cities have chapters. I would love to graduate and move to a big city close to a Goddesses chapter.

I start to make my way over to the literature section before my stomach starts rumbling. Damn, that's right. I've only eaten ice cream today. *Where did she say the snacks were?* I look around the room to see if I spot any when my eyes land on a wooden door. *Oh yeah, the closet.* I open the closet door to find not snacks but rocks and a lot of cultural stuff. Forgetting about my hunger, I go inside and look at the various rocks, which I now realize are crystals.

I cannot take my eyes off a section of beautiful amethyst crystals. Next to them sits a beautiful white crystal, which is labeled azeztulite. It reminds me of a snowball but with an irregular shape. As I reach for the azeztulite, I look at the top shelf to see a colorful wooden mask staring back at me. The details of the mask start to get darker and darker. I suddenly realize that it isn't the mask getting darker but the door closing and blocking the light coming in. I hear a soft click, confirming the door has been shut.

I make my way in the dark to the door, trying not to knock over anything in the room. I get to the door and search for the knob. I twist it, but it isn't working. I pull on the knob. The door doesn't budge. My heart starts to race. Sweat beads form on my forehead and fall down my face. I try to open the door again but with no success. I raise both arms in the air and make fists as I realize it is time to start banging on the door. I strike both arms forward, awaiting the loud thuds they would make as they come into contact with the door. But that never happens. My arms, suddenly weak, do not have the power I need. My fists make light taps on the door as I fall back gently, laying my head on the floor, closing my eyes, tears mixing with sweat as they drip off my cheeks.

I feel a bright light shining down on me. I open my eyes slowly, like I've just been awoken by the morning sun. I see a single, bright light bulb on the ceiling. I look around the room. Extremely small, with only a little wiggle room. Empty, except for a shelf a few inches above me and a mirror right in front of me. I stare into the mirror, and who is looking back startles me. The reflection is indeed me but not present me. I look at my tiny frame. I feel the braids and the rugged ridges of the colorful beads adorning them. I look down at my little hands. I have to be about 5 years old.

I feel quick pressure on the side of my head and then pain. A green apple, already bitten, rolls in front of me. I pick it up, recognizing it as the source of my pain. I turn my attention to the doorway, where a shadowy figure emerges. "I told you that you can play the game for 45 minutes," a deep, booming voice shouts at me. "Looks like you played for 47 minutes! You think you slick, huh!"

"I'm sorry," I pleaded. "The timer didn't go off."

"What the fuck did I tell you about talking back to me!" He comes into the small room and slaps me as hard as possible. I fall back onto the floor. Shaking, I lift my head and look at him. He hovers over me, and I recognize some features of his face, although much younger.

"Ja...Jason?" I say quietly.

"What!" he screams. I didn't say anything else. I hear footsteps behind him, and I pray that someone is coming to save me. A little girl, same stature as me, stands in the doorway, clothes dirty and ripped, holding a teddy bear. "What the hell are you doing up here?" Jason grabs her shirt and drags her out. He looks at me and yells, "You're in here, indefinitely!" before slamming the door behind him. Still lying on the cold floor, staring into the darkness, I close my eyes.

"Destiny, Destiny!" I hear a high-pitched voice call out. I open my eyes to see Jackie shaking me, her face flushed. "Oh my god! Are you okay?"

"I think so..." I answer slowly.

"OMG. I'm so sorry. I got distracted by that new discipline porn video going around."

"Discipline porn video?"

"Yeah, those videos of black parents abusing their kids disguised as punishment. This one seemed to have happened at a family gathering. A young black girl, who's now missing, got beat by her mother and uncle for having sex with a pedophile! Shit like that just works my nerves!"

"Wait, wait... that sounds like... is the little girl named Rachel?" I muster out, voice still weak. My mind is still in a blur.

"Yes, you know her?"

"Yeah, that's my little cousin! Did you say she's missing?"

"Police say that she's a runaway. I hope she's okay."

"How did I miss this? What else do you know?"

"She's been missing for a few days now. Her mother started worrying this morning and went on social media for help. Now, this video has been released. The police say that she may have run away to get away from the abuse. They are now actively looking for her so that they can hand her to the state."

"This is terrible."

"Yes, so terrible. The mother and the uncle have been arrested for the actions shown on the video."

"Wow!"

"All of these comments online refer to it as 'good parenting.' No offense, but I hope they never get out of jail. Why? So they can get out and abuse more black women and girls? What they did to that little girl was horrible. I can't even imagine what they do when people aren't watching. I hope they find her and she goes to a better home."

I look down at my hands. "Yes, they are pretty extreme. I couldn't even watch."

"You were there?"

"Yes..." I say hesitantly. She looked at me, waiting for an explanation. "I panicked. I had to go to another room. I couldn't take it. And I think I just found out why."

"What do you mean?"

"A little bit before you woke me up, I remembered something terrible from my childhood."

"Oh, no!"

"I remember the abuse that I went through as a child at the hands of a family friend. It was so vivid. I was five years old, being babysat by my mom's friend. Or, at least, she was supposed to be babysitting. She often passed us off to her brother, Jason, who supposedly loves kids." Tears start rolling down my cheek. "He was an abusive fuck! And the memory was so surreal. It was like I was there, five-year-old me, trying to survive contact with that piece of shit!"

"Oh, my! Come here. This is terrible." She tries to help me up, but I collapse back down to the floor. She reaches to help me again, but I put up my hand. I think I just need a moment.

"I can't believe I'm just now remembering this asshole. I knew something was up with Jason when I saw him at the party."

"Suppressed memories are a pain. You panic in certain situations, and you don't know why. And when the memories return, you find yourself questioning whether or not they're real. You don't know if you're being delusional and your mind is making this up. Or if it really did happen, and the pain was so excruciating that your mind suppressed it to protect you."

"You know so much about this."

"I've been through it. That's mainly why I volunteer with an organization for abused kids. My memories were suppressed for so long, and when I finally remembered, I broke down. Memory after memory keeps returning to me, and they still come to this day. You should see my doctor. She's not a Goddess, but she helped me. She's very good at what she does, and she's nearby." She hugs me as I sit, crying my eyes out.

She attempts to help me up, and I can finally come to my feet. I follow her as she leaves the closet. She exits, but I feel a vibration in my purse just before I reach the door. I take out my phone. A text from Lucinda.

Hey! Just saw that you left your ice cream.

Wanted to give you a heads-up about the brownie.

It's special!

Like drug special.

Those weren't even a part of the buffet.

You really need to read labels more!

Shit!

It all makes sense now.

I hope you aren't tripping too hard.

Because half a brownie?

Girl?!

I'm fine.

I'm glad, actually.

I saw what I needed to see.

I put my phone away, and another memory flashes in my mind. *Grab the white quartz.* I look back at the azeztulite I was about to grab before everything went dark. Was this the quartz that Aunt Vanessa was talking about? I seize it, feeling the sharp edges. Am I supposed to feel something spiritual? Because I don't. I look underneath the rock and read the words printed. **DON'T JOIN THIS ONE!**

Drama

I draw the curtains to let some sunlight in. I open the massive window to test the temperature. Ah, it's pretty warm, just like it has been these past couple of weeks. Maybe I'll wear one of the long sundresses I bought over the weekend.

Like I do every morning, I stream one of my favorite podcasts, a local one operated by two of my sorority sisters. They give me a quote for the day, weather updates, progress reports, and discussion topics, and they always end in meditation.

After the meditation, I strip out of my night clothes, grab my towel, and head for the shower. I see someone down the hall heading to the same shower.

"Well, good morning!" Deidra says to me, full of joy.

"Good morning!"

"Are you about to use this shower?"

"Yeah, it'll be swift. I have an appointment with my doctor today. So, I'm just going to shower quickly and head there."

"Oh, girl, I can wait."

"Thanks!"

"No problem. So, are you liking it here so far?"

"Oh, I love it. This place is amazing! It's so peaceful."

"Yep, one of the best qualities about living here. Enjoy your shower!"

"Thanks."

On my way to my doctor, I take a few selfies with the blossoming flowers on campus. I breathe in the fresh air as I leave campus to visit the office buildings the next block over. I love the spring.

At the office, I sign in and wait patiently for the doctor to call my name. I read some of the pamphlets while I wait. One titled, **Finding Your Voice**, really resonates with me. I tuck it in my purse for later use. Maybe I'll go to one of their meet-ups.

"Destiny," a warm voice calls out. Dr. Amora Solace is smiling, waving me to come in. I hurry over to hug her. It annoys her when I bend down to give her a proper hug, but she always smiles and returns the hug. The curls on her head have been dyed red in a cool swirl pattern that you can only see from the top. The red dye matches her signature red lipstick. She serves as my inspiration professionally and for hair and makeup.

"Okay, Ms. Lowry. What's new?" she asks while sitting down in her chair. She pours me a cup of tea like she does every appointment. She always has a new blend, too. This time, a lovely aromatic mix of peach and pistachio.

"Well, remember the sorority that I got accepted into?"

"The Grox, right? It's the same one my twin sister is in."

"Yes! So, I finally moved into the house!"

"Oh, that's wonderful. I'm glad that you'll have less stress now!"

"It's serene. My room is small, but I don't have to share it with anyone, so it's not a big deal. All that matters is that I'm there and have my own private space."

"I am so glad to hear that. Are you growing closer to the women there?"

"So close. We know so much about each other now. They told me that I'll find out more about the national group and their cause on the road trip we're taking this summer."

"A road trip is good."

"All the new recruits go on a summer road trip to meet the sisters on the other campuses."

"Fun, fun, fun! How are the other relationships in your life?"

"I mean, nothing much has changed. Marcel and I are still off and on, but it's been pretty good lately. He's getting used to my hair now, so that's a plus. I talk to my family a little more now."

"All of those are good. Remember, little changes are just as valid as big ones," Dr. Solace says. I look down at my feet and scoot them around a bit. "What's wrong?" she asks warmly, concerned.

"She brought up that she lost her virginity to the man she married again."

"Your mother? How did she bring it up?"

"Abruptly, like it had nothing to do with our conversation. Remember last time I told you that she was talking to her young virgin coworker who explained to Mama that all men want her now because she isn't all used up like the other women out here? Yeah, she brought that up again. And then Mama told me who she lost her virginity to: my dad. Since then, she's casually brought it up in our conversations."

"Yes, I remember. What did your mother say this time?"

"She basically said that being a virgin is so important and valuable. That she didn't choose to have sex until she found the man that she wanted to marry."

"How did that make you feel?"

"I don't know. I feel like she's trying to tell me to hold on to my virginity, but little does she know, I lost it a few boys ago. I don't know why she's telling me this now. I'm in college."

"Do you think it has anything to do with your relationship with Marcel?"

"Maybe. This is my first serious boyfriend. Maybe she's not familiar with casual sex. I mean, she's only ever had sex with one person, so..."

"I see. So, you don't think your mother is familiar with casual sex because she only has had one partner?"

"Yes, she doesn't know anything about it! I feel like she will judge me if I tell her."

"She'll judge you?"

"She will. She raised me to be the respectable girl, and I'm afraid of how she'll look at me if I ever tell her."

"I see." Dr. Solace scribbles some notes on her paper.

"We just have different views when it comes to all of that. I'm learning more about the dangers of respectability politics through Grox, and like I said before, my values are changing."

"That's understandable. It's normal for your values to change as you grow and learn more about yourself."

I finish the rest of my tea and quickly pour more into my cup. The aroma of the tea is heavenly. I take a moment to take in the fragrance before sipping, letting the warm liquid run across my tongue, activating my taste buds. I take a few sips while considering what I want to say.

Dr. Solace is writing in her notebook. I admire the photos of her college graduation behind her. Her family surrounds her in the photos as her dark skin glistens in the sun. Her smile says that she knows what she wants to do next. The smile that I want to have one day. Next to her graduation photos are the certificates she earned in psychotherapy. Maybe this is the brain work that I want to do.

"So," I say, still calculating what to say next. "Another memory came back."

"Do you want to tell me about it?"

"I was five years old again. I was trying to get the video game to work. Unsuccessful, I took out the cartridge and went searching for Jason. The basement door was open, and I could slightly hear his voice. So I go down the steps to see if he could blow on the cartridge to fix it." I take a pause and sip some more tea. I look at the clock to see how much time we have left for the session. More than enough time. Tears start rolling down my cheek, and I question whether or not I want to say anything about the memory right now.

"It's okay. Take your time," Dr. Solace encourages me. She hands me a tissue.

"So, I go downstairs and pause in my tracks. I see Jason standing in front of some cages, which housed several little girls." I break down sobbing. "And that's all I remember."

"It's going to be alright." Dr. Solace sits next to me, comforting me and bringing me more tissues.

"I want to know whether or not he's still doing this. But I'm afraid. What if I'm misremembering? How will I tell my family?"

Dr. Solace comforts me more. I'm glad I found a caring doctor who helps me with my memories. For the rest of the session, we discuss the memory, what it means to me, and what I want to do about it once I'm ready. She tells me about her twin, Dr. Aurora Solace, a Grox sister who does hypnotherapy. She says that hypnotherapy can help with the trauma of the memories. I leave the office feeling stronger than I did before and a lot more confident about my memory.

Walking down the sidewalk from the office building, I notice some flowers I didn't see coming in. Kousa flowers. The flowers that Cel always gives to me. He's given me a variety of colors, but never this color. They are a beautiful orange with faded green tips. I have a few hours before my class, so I pick some to surprise him.

I pass the Kousa house, whose architecture is as beautiful as the Qousa house. Cel's house, which he is renting, is next to the Kousa house. Whenever I asked him why he didn't live at the fraternity house, Cel would say that he needed his own space and didn't like the rules of the house.

I walk past the Kousa house, slowly taking in the beauty. I reflect on when I was a Qousa woman, coming to this house to chill and talk. I often wonder about the events they do now. Cel keeps me updated on all of the Kousa events, some I'm even invited to, but I don't know anything that the Qousa women are doing nowadays except the few things that Jennifer tells me about. I wonder how my life would be if I was still a Qousa woman. I quickly shake the thought. No, I'm happy and grateful to be a Grox woman.

I arrive at Marcel's house, peeking at the different colored Kousa flowers in the front yard. I look down at the flowers I hold and think how good they will look on his window sill. I look back up to see if his window sill is empty. I notice two things.

The first is a family of green, spiky cacti sitting on the sill, catching all the sun rays on this beautiful day. The second is bare, pale skin rubbing against the window, blonde hair swinging side to side. *Trixie?* I see brown fingers going through her hair. Big, strong brown hands caressing her backside. My heart is racing. I run to the door, scrambling around my purse for the extra key. I find it and burst through the door. Trixie is looking at me, mouth in a smirk. Still caressing her, Mike grabs the nearest piece of fabric, a throw, and begins to cover himself. I cover my mouth. "I... I..." I begin, trying to find the words of an apology.

"I found a new position," Marcel says, walking in, having not spotted me yet. I squint at him. He's looking down intently at his tablet. I look at his glistening abs, then down to his bone-hard, condom-covered, thick dick. "Yes, so the way I see it, two of us will be getting penetrated, and the other..." He finally looks up from his tablet. "Ba... Baby? What are you doing here?"

"Really, that's all you got to say to me? I came here to give you these flowers." I throw the flowers at him. "I came here because I was thinking about you. But now I discover that you're not only cheating, but you're cheating on me with two people. What the fuck?"

"Baby, it's not what it looks like. I can explain."

"How the hell do you explain this, Marcel Moore?"

"Just come into my room. I will explain. Just calm down."

I follow him to his room, wanting answers. I close the door behind me while he sits on his bed. "What do you have to say to me?" I ask him. He motions for me to sit on the bed next to him. "No, I'm fine standing. What do you have to say to me?"

"I'm sorry."

"I ain't."

"Baby, don't be like that. Let me explain."

"I should have listened to the Goddesses when they tried to tell me you weren't it. Grox said you were toxic, too." I start shaking my head, thinking about how they warned me about him. "I ignored them whenever they told me because I loved you." I pace back and forth. "I hope you know that this is the end of the relationship."

"So, you going to give up on us?"

I scrunch my face. "Give up on us? You're the one who gave up on us by running around on me. It's over! I'm just here in this room because I want to know why."

"I already told you why. You weren't listening."

"You told me why you were cheating on me? How? How when I literally just caught you a few minutes ago? How the hell does that work, Marcel?"

"Remember, I told you I didn't like short hair on girls."

"That's bullshit! You don't like my short hair, so you decide to cheat? And I was supposed to somehow know this?"

"Babe, you just changed so much. I took a chance on you when we first met. I don't usually date brown-skinned girls, but then I saw you and decided to take the risk."

"Take the risk of dating a brown-skinned girl!"

"Yes, I overlooked that because of your pretty face and hair. When I tried to tell you I didn't like your hair, you gave me all attitude. I couldn't tell you anything! You were being brainwashed so much by those Goddesses! And now you don't eat the same things because of those gross women."

"Grox, asshole! Grox!"

"This is just as much your fault as it is mine. I think once you quit your sorority, we'll be fine. They're messing up our relationship!"

I look at him in disbelief. How can I just now see how self-centered this fool is? I let out a sigh. "Everyone was right about you." I open the door to leave. I pass Trixie, sitting naked on the couch, armed with a strap-on dildo, looking at Marcel's tablet.

"Marc! Hurry up. I want to try this new position," she whines. She looks at me and rolls her eyes. It takes everything in my power not to say or do anything to this lil girl. I ignore her and keep on moving. Mike gets up and holds the door open for me.

"I'm sorry for all of this we were—" he starts explaining.

I put up my hand, stopping him mid-speech. "Save it." I walk out the door and beeline towards campus, never looking back.

I tell the Grox women about my breakup with Marcel when I return to the house later that evening. There is no berating, just comfort and support. They even plan a girls' night.

"Everything is going to be fine. You deserve better anyway," Deidra says while sitting in my beanbag chair.

"I know. I'm just very heartbroken right now. I mean, how could Marcel do this to me." I put on my work shirt and stare in the mirror. I look at my low, red eyes, wishing they would disappear before my shift starts.

"You did nothing wrong. Marcel took you for granted. Some people just look for ways to mess things up."

I wipe my eyes and grab my badge and bag. "Thanks for everything! I need to go off to work, I'm already late. Don't want the boss yelling at me. Thank God it's a short shift. All I want to do is lay down in my bed."

I leave the house and speed walk to the dining hall. Healthy Starts is the first plant-based eatery in the dining hall, and it opened at the beginning of the semester, thanks to Grox. It has a rotation of roasted veggies, fresh greens, grains, and sauces. The versatility has been a great help in getting my lifestyle to match my values.

Tonight, I'm working half of Gary's shift. When I open the dining hall door, I see Gary still serving hot dinner plates to the students and the staff. I catch his eye, and he offers me a friendly smile before waving me over. I meet him behind the serving window to wash my hands and put on gloves.

"I'm so sorry for being so late. Today has been tough for me and…" I start rambling.

"Ah, don't worry about it. I can see it all in your face. What happened?" He asks.

"My boyfriend," is the only thing I could muster. My body begins to warm up. I wipe away a single tear. "I don't really want to bring it up, and I definitely don't want to be thinking about it at work."

He nods. "You know I can work the rest of my shift if you're not up for it."

"That's sweet. But I need to work and take my mind off Marcel for a little bit."

"I understand." He begins to unglove. "Have a great shift, and I hope the students aren't as picky today."

"Haha, thanks."

The traffic in the cafeteria slows. Tonight won't be as busy as all of the other nights. I check the food to make sure we have enough of everything for the group of students I see coming my way. They're all good. However, we are low on bread rolls. I call back to the kitchen to get more. I hear the door behind me swing open, and I turn around with my hands out, expecting to grab a tray of rolls. What I get instead is my boss, Jeanette.

"You were a little late today. That's very unlike you," Jeanette says.

"Yes, I'm so sorry. It won't happen again."

"Is everything alright? You don't look too well."

"Yeah." My voice cracks just thinking about Marcel again.

"We'll talk after the shift, alright?"

"Okay," I say, voice still cracking.

She returns to the back, most likely going to her office. I turn my attention to the students standing before me, waiting to get served. I spend my entire night serving food and calling in special orders.

Even when it isn't active, I keep my mind busy by doing small tasks and ensuring the station looks presentable. When Marcel pops up in my head, I turn my attention to another task that needs to be done. I remember what mindful meditation teaches me: keeping my mind focused on the now.

After closing, I spend a few minutes wiping down everything. There isn't a speck to be seen after I finish. I go to Jeanette's office.

Knock, knock, knock.

"Ms. Jeanette?"

"Yes, come on in," she says, her voice firm.

There are posters of zombies from one edge of the wall to the other. The retro room has lava lamps and a shaggy carpet.

"You wanted to see me?"

"You were pretty late, and I just wanted to see if everything was alright with you. If something is going on and you need to take time off, I will completely understand."

"No, I don't think it's that serious. I should be over it," I say, thinking about Marcel. Tears start forming in my eyes. "I'm going through a breakup."

She puts down her pen and steps away from her desk. "Aw, is this your first heartbreak?"

"Yes," I say, choking back tears.

"I remember my first heartbreak. It'll be alright."

"Really? How did you overcome it?"

"Poetry. I wrote all of my feelings down in a poem."

"Poetry?"

"Yep. Say we're having a poetry slam tonight. You should join. The poetry there ranges from heartbreak to freedom to zombies. You can probably guess that the last topic is mostly my poems."

I chuckle. "That's amazing."

"I'm performing a poem tonight, although it's not my usual sci-fi poem. I've been inspired through my talks with the Goddesses. Showing me who the real enemy is. Would you like to come?"

I cringe at the mention of the Goddesses. But I want to hear what Jeanette has to say. "I would love to!"

We clock out and head to her truck, which still has the zombie aesthetic. She offers to drive me to the poetry slam and back to my sorority house. I hop inside the spacious beast of a truck. The interior is just as zombied out as the exterior. The gear is in the shape of a gun. Brains line the roof. The steering wheel is in the form of a...

"Is that a UFO?" I ask, pointing to her steering wheel.

"Why yes, it is."

"It's so different from the rest of your truck."

"I know. I love zombies, but aliens are a very close second." She points to her glove department, which has an alien head for a latch. "I'm slowly incorporating more alien trinkets."

"Cool."

The place that hosts the poetry jam has a nice ambiance. The lights are low, and although there is a vast audience, the site is relatively quiet. Jeanette and I nab two seats in the front.

The first woman's poem is about the loss of her aunt. She speaks passionately about her and the relationship she had with her. She left everyone in the audience teary-eyed. The second poet talks about heartbreak. I listen closely, relating to each and every word of her poem. The poem invokes thoughts of Marcel, but I do not cry. Instead, I focus on healing myself, as the poem suggests. Jeanette looks at me, checking to see if I'm alright. I nod my head, telling her that I am just fine.

Jeanette places her hand on my arm. "I'll be back," she says to me. "I need to prepare to go on stage."

"Okay, good luck!"

Jeanette goes to the back, passing the performer about to take the stage. The performer is an older woman, heavy set, with a buzzcut and tattoos up and down her arms. The audience roars as she grabs the mic. "Alright, settle down," she starts, "y'all know we ain't supposed to be making all this noise." The audience snaps. "So, this poem is about what I went through in my earlier days before I was introduced to poetry." The poet, Sam, captures our attention with the details of her early life, from being trafficked to being introduced to heroin by her ex. How can a human being go through so much in such a short period? When she finishes, the audience gives her a standing ovation. She bows and leaves the stage, passing the mic to Jeanette.

"Hello, everyone," Jeanette says.

"Hey," the audience responds.

"So, I know you all are used to my sci-fi poems, but tonight, I'm doing something different. This poem is inspired by my early adulthood and recent events that have been going on in my life. It is titled **No More**."

Hot glue, rod, poster board

Another king shot by those uni-
formed pigs in a Ford

Blood paints the black tar, giving me
more unfortunate material

Sick of being treated like an extrater-
restrial

Writing words in red, enraged, engraved

Trying to catch the moment before
it fades

Titties bouncing, we strut, we chant,
we raise our fist

No one else can do it like how we do
this

Standing alongside those who happen to look like me

We understand that you can't fight,
homie

Since we've been born

We've walked the streets, torn

Parallel universe, day and night

Entering in and out, a dream reality
to a fright

Praise for fighting the battles of the
man

Venom for being just who I am

I hold hands with my sistas as we
march the streets

The two worlds, intersecting, on repeat

A queen sits on her throne, never
phased

Hey ma, lemme holla at you. Nah?
You ugly anyways

Natural hair is always a good fit

You need to do something to that
nappy shit

You are powerful, you are strong

Fix that attitude. Y'all always look for
the negative and wrong

Look at how much they do for us

Yeah, but I'd rather have one who
doesn't put up a fuss

Hot glue, rod, poster board

I no longer do labor that I can't afford

Looking back, I cannot deny

Those two separate worlds were a lie

One in the same, different actions at
arm's length

Used and abused my kindness and
strength

Tired of putting out, waiting for my
turn

Fighting for you, getting hatred in
return

I finally got the strength to pull the
cord

On that hot glue, rod, and poster
board

Besties

The vibrations on my desk break my focus as I study for my upcoming test. My phone, which I put at the other end to avoid distractions, is lighting up, indicating an incoming call. I rush past my phone to look out the window. A hot pink convertible is pulling up, top-down, old R&B music coming from the stereo. I run out of my room and down the stairs, almost tripping. I run outside just in time to see a slender woman pulling a suitcase from the trunk. Her long, dark hair covers her face, but I'd know her from anywhere.

"Erika!" I shout, running towards her.

"Destiny!" She gives up on the suitcase and starts running towards me. We collide into a hug, the force almost knocking us to the ground. I can't believe my eyes.

"It's been so long, girl," I say, embracing her.

"I know, I know! I wish I could have come earlier in the semester, but I had so much going on."

"I understand completely."

I walk towards her trunk to help her pull out her suitcase. We walk back into the house, and I introduce her to my sorority sisters.

"We've heard so much about you," Deidra says, giving Erika a hug. "Nice to finally put a face to the name."

"Oh, we do sound alike," Erika says, laughing. I've been telling Erika how much she sounds like Deidra and vice versa. "It's finally nice to meet you."

I take her bag to my room and head back down to the dining room, where the Grox women have set up a catered lunch. While eating, we talk about the events that the Grox women have put on her campus and the events on my campus. We laugh at the fact that the sororities are so different on the campuses. On Erika's campus, the Grox focuses more on the intersection of race and species, while on my campus, we focus more on sex and species. Lucinda and Erika clicked just like I thought they would.

After lunch, Erika and I head to my room for a BFF chat. I give her a short tour of my room, showing her where she can place her stuff for the weekend. I make room for her in my wardrobe and empty one of my drawers. We talk as she hangs her clothes in my wardrobe.

"Always overpacking," I say, laughing, observing all the outfits she brought for this short three-day weekend.

"You know me. I have to have a variety of outfits to choose from."

"You don't have to tell me. Haha, at every sleepover, you always had the biggest bag."

We both laugh.

"You made all of this space for me? You didn't have to do that. I'm only staying one weekend."

"I know. I was just so excited to see you again!" I reach for some of her clothes to help her put them up and notice that some of them still have price tags on them. "You bought new clothes?"

"Yes, it is so cold up north right now. I didn't have anything to wear for the beautiful weather here. So, you know me, I had to buy some outfits to make a proper choice."

After hanging up her clothes, she moves to the drawer and the desktop space I cleared. She opens her bag and starts placing her makeup on the desk. Vegan and cruelty-free labels on all of the products she pulls out. She was always a good makeup artist. Her face is beat for the Goddesses today. Beautiful gold and pink eyeshadow with matching lips and the usual contouring and highlighting that she does. Her artistry always impresses me. Such details are in how she paints the color on her face and her precision while holding the brush.

She moves to the drawer, where she places essentials, including a bottle of multivitamins and maca. She goes to the bathroom to find a place for the rest of her shower items and comes back to the room smiling.

"All done! What's the plan?" she says in her soothing, soft voice.

"I was thinking of just doing a movie night. I didn't know how tired you'd be after that long drive, so I didn't want to exhaust you with a party or anything."

"Sounds awesome! What kind of snacks do we have?"

"I have popcorn and chocolate-covered nuts."

"Ah, we have the best traditions!"

After making the popcorn, we click through the television to see what's available to stream this month and land on a comedy. We really need something to laugh about at this point in our lives.

"So, how was school this week," I ask her.

"Lots of studying and activism!" she says. "My family finally told me not to come home this week unless I get rid of my girlfriend."

My eyes widen, and my jaw drops. "So where are you going to go? You can stay with me if you like."

"I'm volunteering with the Grox at a sanctuary up north. I guess I'll stay at the apartment connected to the café for the summer." She glances at me with puppy dog eyes. "Help me renovate it?"

"For sure! Honestly, I think you need a break from the toxicity anyway." She looks at me, and I shrug. "Taking care of your siblings and working to pay the bills is just too much. Your mama and her boyfriend got it. And if they can't accept you for who you are, they don't deserve your labor."

Erika nods and grabs more popcorn. She gets up and pulls one of the makeup wipes from the dispenser on the desk. The dispenser, a glass tulip with hints of green and pink, tilts but doesn't fall over. But my best friend's reaction to it almost falling over actually knocks a folder to the ground. And as if destined, a sheet of paper slides out of the folder and in front of her feet. Erika picks up the paper and screams, running toward me.

"Oh my god! I can't believe you kept this," she says, waving the paper before me.

"Well," I start. I take the paper and look at it intently. "It is my perfect MASH. Or what used to be my perfect MASH. I found it the other day and went through my fortune with my sisters. They gave me pretty good insight."

"I want to hear," Erika says, face nearly naked after wiping it with the cloth. "What did they say?"

I trace my finger along that old swirl I drew on that sheet in high school. "Where should we begin?"

Erika lays on the floor and takes the paper from me. "Let's start with MASH. It was predicted that you would have a mansion."

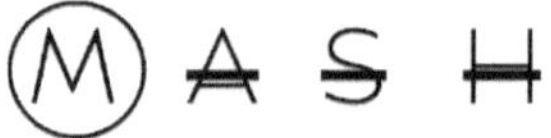

I lay back, staring at the ceiling, reflecting on when the letter M was circled. I remember me, a teenager, being so happy, dreaming about the different rooms my future mansion would have: a grand staircase, the theater with a popcorn maker, the bowling alley, the tea room, the gym with a connected sauna, the tennis courts, the large infinity pool with a view that was to die for.

"I think that the money will be better spent on a community garden or a sanctuary," I say, watching the ceiling fan go round and round. "A large megamansion just seems like such a waste now."

"Unless multiple families are living there," Erika says. "I love the setup of my sorority house. We have our own bedrooms and cook together in the kitchen every day. I have the support of a community every time I return home."

"Ugh," I say, exaggerating my face in disgust. "I can't be around people at home twenty-four-seven."

"Girl, you're doing it right now. And you have your own bedroom! You're so not around people twenty-four-seven," Erika says, rolling her eyes.

"I know," I say, rolling my eyes back. "But I don't want this after college. It's good now because I'm learning and getting to know my sisters. But in the future, I will need my own space."

"Gotcha." Erika grabs the paper. "On to the next one. Spouse! Oooohhhh! I remember Devondre." She blinks her eyes lovingly and makes kissy faces at me. I throw a pillow at her.

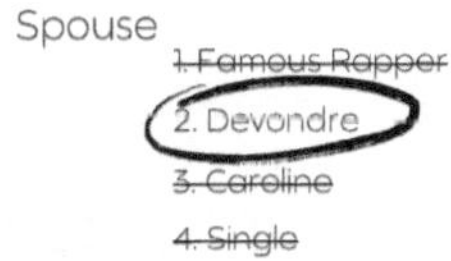

"Why was I so excited about marrying that loser?"

"Because he was popular," Erika answers.

"He was such a shit."

"I didn't like that he only referred to women as bitches. Not women, not girls, not even females. He didn't even try to conceal his sexism."

"I know, I know." My hands cover my face as I shake my head. "I want to slide down a wall whenever I think about my past crushes."

"You leveled up a little with Marcel."

"Ugh, I don't even want to think about him."

"How are you holding up? Do you still see him around?"

"I not only see Marcel all the time, but I also see Trixie and Mike regularly because of our shared night class. It's so annoying. And they're blaming me for what happened!"

"They're blaming you for the cheating! How the hell does that work?"

"No, not for the cheating. For getting removed from Qousa and Kousa."

Erika's eyes widen, and her pace of popcorn eating quickens. "Wow, they got removed?"

"I didn't tell you?" I take a deep breath, anticipating the lecture that is about to follow. I've been trying to avoid telling Erika about their removal since it happened.

"What did they do? Are they now excommunicated as well?"

"Yes. At least my former sisters look at or have small conversations with me, even if it's on accident. With Marcel, Trixie, and Mike, they're not even acknowledged. It's as if they're invisible."

My best friend sits up, obviously enjoying the tea. "Oh my god, oh my god. Why did they remove them?"

"Okay, so I might have had something to do with it."

"Destiny!" She puts down the popcorn and claps her hands. She stares at me. If I don't tell this girl what happened right now, she will shake it out of me.

"So, I told some of the Qousa women the reason for my breakup with Marcel."

"So, they got removed because of the cheating?"

"No, they got removed because of sodomy."

My friend cocks her head, her face puzzled. "What?"

"Both of the houses have rules against lewd acts, apparently. I wouldn't have said anything, but they hurt me greatly."

"So you got them removed from their groups?"

"They deserved it."

"But that's so homophobic!"

"It's not like I'm homophobic."

"But you used both houses' homophobia to get your ex and his lovers removed."

I cross my arms and shake my head. I look back down at the game sheet. One of the names crossed out is Caroline, a beautiful, popular girl I went to school with, but a name placed on the list as a joke. A homophobic one. "Unlearning this shit is so hard," I whine.

"It absolutely is not," Erika says.

Tears stream down my face. "I was surrounded by it."

"I know, but you have to take accountability for your actions at some point. And learn from them."

"They didn't give a fuck about what they were doing and who they were hurting. So I don't give a fuck about them!"

"Ouch." She gently places her hand on my knee. She can tell that I'm getting flustered. "So what have they said to you?"

"At first, they would say how horrible of a person I am and shit like that. But now they just give me nasty looks whenever they see me."

"What do you say back?"

"Nothing, I just smile."

We sit in complete silence for a few moments. Erika takes my hand and looks at me. She still knows me after months of not physically seeing each other. Tears fall from my eyes. "I was just so hurt!" I start. "I was impulsive and set on hurting them just like they hurt me."

"I understand."

"No, you don't," I yell.

"I've never been in that situation, so I can't say how I would have reacted. But I understand your need for vengeance. It's crucial to examine your emotions and why you reacted the way you reacted." She dries my eyes and hugs me. "But when you take a shot at someone, you also need to examine if you are taking a shot at them or the oppressed community they are a part of."

I instantly feel better about the situation. Erika is right, like always.

I break from our hug and hold her hand while looking into her eyes. I nod my head, and she nods back. I stand up and let her know that I'll be back. I go to the kitchen to grab more popcorn and chocolate nuts, our third big bowl of the mix. I hope we don't wake up to stomachaches. I return with the bowl and ask her what's next.

"Hold on," she says, holding up her finger. "You have single crossed out, and I remember both of us being excited about that. About not being alone forever."

"Nothing much to add," I say. "I'm single now but have my best friend and sisters. I haven't felt more socially connected than I do now."

"Right on," Erika says. "The next item is the number of kids. Are you still good with two?"

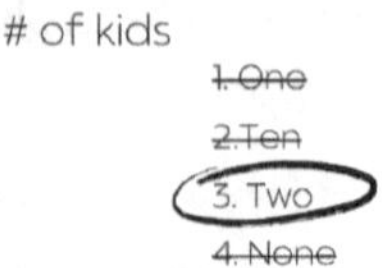

"Yes, I am."

"I'm in a pretty hard place regarding kids right now," Erika says. "My girl-friend and I have obviously talked about kids. IVF is expensive. Adoption has all kinds of ethical issues. I just don't know what the future holds for us in that respect." She tears up, wiping her face with the used makeup wipe. I take her hand in mine.

"We'll figure something out. I'll help you look into it when the time comes."

"Thank you," she says, choking on tears. "Let's move on; I don't want to discuss this right now." She hands me the paper, some words smeared from her tears.

"Transport," I finally make out. "Since being on campus, I've enjoyed being able to walk or take public transit everywhere."

Erika sniffles. "I remember us being relieved when 'bus' was crossed out and almost threw a party when Mercedes-Benz got circled."

"I had the color of the paint picked out and thought of features like heated seats and a drop-top. I had my mind set on getting that car."

"All that just for it to lose value as soon as you drive it off the lot."

"I feel more satisfied reading my book on the light rail."

"Same." Erika grabs my paper, her face dry, a smile painted on. "Career. You got scientist. Still happy with that choice?"

Career
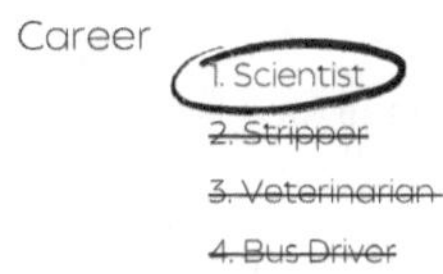

"Of course."

"I can't believe we made fun of strippers and bus drivers," she says, looking at the other choices in the category.

"I now thank my bus driver for providing such a service to the city." I grab one of the flyers for an upcoming panel I'm hosting for missing black women and hand it to Erika. "Sex workers are greatly targeted for human trafficking. So most of my advocacy is for them."

"So much growth in such a short period," Erika says, flipping the flyer over to read the back. "You should host one of these panels at my university. And I can do the same for you. I would love a majority black audience to talk about speciesism and race."

"That sounds great!" I say. "Let me know when your chapter is available, and I'll let you know when my chapter can make it up there. We can definitely get this organized."

"Sounds like a plan." Erika puts down the flyer and picks up the sheet that I now call my worst nightmare MASH. "So, Surgery."

Surgery
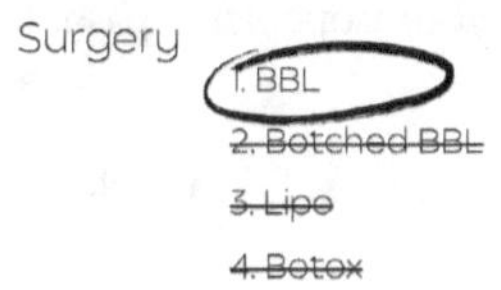

"We were so obsessed with having the perfect body."

"The perfect shape."

"As if that shape will bring about a new life."

"Why were we, as high schoolers, thinking about preventing wrinkles?"

"No clue, but I am embarrassed to say that I started researching flights to Miami and doctors as soon as BBL was circled."

"Ugh, social media."

"Right, I'm barely on it anymore."

Erika claps her hand. "Good for you. I haven't been on it for a while. Only to upload makeup videos."

I sit up and look at my friend. "I'm just going to ask."

Erika sits up and meets my eyes. "What?"

"You still contour your nose. How is that in line with anything we practice with Grox."

Erika pouts. "It's not." She sighs and looks down. "Nose size was something my mom was insecure about. She didn't like how wide and flat her nose was and praised me for having my dad's nose. My nose got a little wider in middle school. I guess she passed down her insecurities."

"For what it's worth, your nose is fine."

"Thank you!" Erika is holding back tears. "I guess that's something else for me to work on. Accepting my nose for the shape it is."

"The ideal being is who you're trying to be via makeup," a soft voice from the doorway states.

Erika and I whip our heads around to find Deidra peeking her head through the door.

"Sorry," Deidra says, waving her hands. "I didn't mean to startle you," she shrugs, "or eavesdrop."

"What's up?" I ask.

"Is it okay if i grab some of your popcorn? I passed it in the kitchen, and my body started craving it."

"Go for it," Erika responds. "But before you leave, can you expand on the ideal being?"

"Sure." Deidra sits down next to us and points to the bowl of popcorn. "Do you mind?"

Erika and I shake our heads. Deidra pops a flake covered in melted chocolate in her mouth. She pops another one and says, "This is really good."

"It is one of our favorite popcorn recipes," Erika says.

"I can see why." Deidra motions to Erika to give her the MASH sheet, and Erika complies. Her eyes move down from left to right as she takes in the words on the page. She then gives Erika the sheet back and stretches into a lying position. "The ideal being is the one who prospers the most under the institutions and ideologies of society."

"And these institutions and ideologies are influenced by systems of oppression," I say, remembering our previous discussions in the house.

"Correct. Humans begin to internalize feelings of superiority or inferiority depending on the messaging they get from society. They also place these feelings on other beings. So, instead of combatting the systems of oppression that inform society, humans try to get as close to the ideal being as possible."

"To escape the treatment of the oppressed group they're in," I add.

"But what if they cannot change to be closer to the ideal being?" Erika asks.

"Then they might try to combat it," Deidra answers. "But more than likely, they will start spewing the ideology to get some acceptance."

"And hope that spewing the ideology provides some cover for them," I say.

"Nice!" Deidra says, drawing out the word enthusiastically. "I need to look into that perspective. Providing cover?"

"Yep," I say, grinning from ear to ear. "It's something I've been researching myself."

"That's great," Deidra says. "I can't wait to see what it turns into." She gets up and wipes her hands with a paper towel. "I'll leave you two to it. I'm going to head out with Lucinda, but not before grabbing some more of that delicious popcorn from the kitchen." She winks and glides out of the room.

"I can see why she reminds you of me," Erika giggles. She pokes me in the side, "Unlike that Kiana you kept comparing me to."

We burst out laughing.

"Hey," I say. "How was I supposed to know Kiana was super toxic?"

"Girl, there were red flags everywhere!"

"I mean, I see them now. But at the time, I thought she was just focused on fighting for black women."

"While the whole time, her plan for liberation was to become the oppressor." She rolls her eyes. "Next category!" She hands me the paper.

"Pet," I say. I hold up a finger before Erika can respond. I grab a pen and cross out the word pet. Next to it, I write animal companion. "Animal companion," I say.

"Good catch," Erika says. "But these options are so telling."

I cringe. "Yes, they are. I only wanted a horse so I could tame it and ride it."

"Didn't you want to join a black equestrian club?"

I cringe even harder. "Yep, whose motto was *Tame the Wild*."

"Ugh," Erika says, scrunching her face. She looks back down at the sheet and laughs. "We put this on here as a joke, right? We didn't actually know what a Dik Dik was, did we?"

"Girl, no," I say, joining Erika's laughter. "We just heard it in ecology and thought it was the funniest thing ever."

"They really need to change that name." Erika looks at the sheet once more. "I'm good with just adopting from an animal shelter. So many innocent beings need homes."

"I'm going to do the same." I grab the paper from her. "Next category is place. The suburb is circled. I think we already accepted that we need somewhere walkable to live."

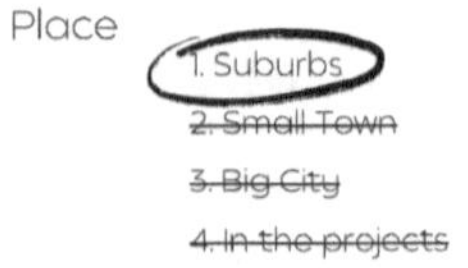

"No more commuting long distances and taking a car to do everyday tasks." She grabs the paper to look at the other options under the category. "We just could not stop making fun of poor people, couldn't we?" she asks.

"I've never lived in the projects, but I was deathly scared of getting that option."

"It's the media," Erika says. "Look at the next category, hobby." She flips the page over to show me shopping is selected. "They need our hobby to be shopping so that we can keep a job to support our hobby of shopping. It is neverending."

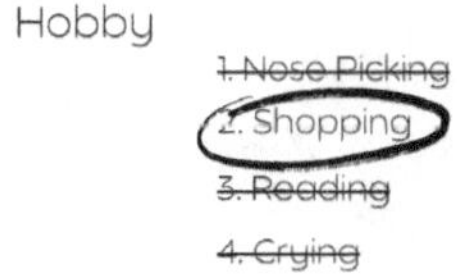

I squint my eyes at the last category, which is vice. The word greed is circled. I point to it. "And we thought it was okay to be greedy because the world forces us to. If we are greedy, we are more likely to hoard, which will keep resources away from others, providing a permanent underclass."

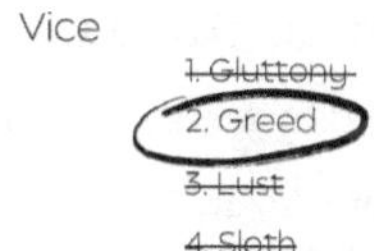

Erika tosses the paper to the floor and sits next to me. "In hindsight, I think that was your worst MASH. I much prefer the one where you were a lustful, single photographer living in a shack in space with a botched lip injection and a pet rock."

We burst out laughing, rolling on the floor, holding our bellies.

"Now that one had more flavor," I say. I take what used to be my aspirational MASH, fold it into a little football triangle, and flick it perfectly into the trash can next to my desk.

Our World

I look at the pictures my parents took when they first dropped me off at the doorsteps of the Asher dorm and compare them to the new images they took of me in front of the Grox house. Oh, how things have changed.

Being back at home for a month and helping Erika renovate is the self-care I needed. We developed a business plan for our new vegan café, and it should be ready to go by the time we get back from our road trip.

My parents are stubborn, but they are learning, and I see a little growth. Maybe my destiny is different from Kiana's, after all.

I've been helping Laila with her ballet steps and reading to her every night before bed. I'm determined to never let her feel the hurt I've felt growing up. She got into the ballet school next to my university, and I am so excited to drop her off when I return to campus in the fall.

I wait on the porch of my home with a hardshell roller bag. A black van pulls up. I text both of my parents to tell them that I'm off. Mama is the first to respond.

Okay, be safe. Love you!

Then my dad.

Have fun, princess!

But not too much!

I hug Laila and tell her that I will be back soon. I go into the house, walk past the babysitter, and poke my head through the opening of the living room. PJ is sitting on the couch, eyes glued to the video playing on his phone. I hear the manipulative words of AuthenticCap, trying to sell him a new course that supposedly helps him land foreign, submissive bitches. His words, not mine.

"Bye, big head," I yell. "Dad and Mama will be home tomorrow. Be good for the babysitter and take care of Laila."

"I will, long neck." He chuckles and goes back to brainwashing himself.

"Don't let AuthenticCap trick you into a life of misery. He is on the internet begging for money for a reason."

PJ is taken aback. "He's not begging. It's called selling."

I shrug my shoulders. PJ is going to be a little more work than my parents. The wrong messages are coming across him, mostly from his little friends and internet personalities. He highly values their opinions, and getting him to see a different perspective is challenging. The Grox women suggest digital literacy classes for him. Hopefully, it will be a success.

I return outside just in time to see Lucinda hopping out of the driver's seat. She pops the trunk. "I'm so glad you came!" she says.

"I needed a break away from this place. And to get closer to my sisters, of course."

"I promise it's worth it."

Erika hops out of the back seat to hug me, a tall black woman following behind her.

"This is my girlfriend, Kacey!" Erika says.

"Oh, hi, Kacey. I've heard so much about you!"

"I've heard so much about you, too!" she replies in a high-pitched voice.

We all gather in the car and start our journey. Kiana still hasn't told me where we're going yet. Erika can't tell me much. Her girlfriend hasn't told her anything, so she is as clueless as I am. These Grox women really know how to keep a secret.

Lucinda has our trip well organized. We drive and sightsee during the day, and in the evening, we book a hotel or crash at a Grox house, depending on the city we are in. Meeting with Grox chapters on different campuses is very eye-opening. Each chapter has a different intersection on its campus. Whether that's racism, capitalism, sexism, colorism, food insecurity, environmentalism, ableism, or homophobia— there are always new lessons to learn.

We stop by a gas station to grab some snacks. "So, what city are we visiting next," I ask Lucinda as I get back in the van.

"It's a surprise!" she replies.

Kacey and Lucinda both turn around and smile at me and Erika.

"What," we both whine at the same time.

Erika pulls up a map app on her phone to see what city we're heading towards.

"Aht, aht, no cheating," Kacey says. She reaches her arm back, opening and closing her hand. "Give me your phones."

Erika and I look at each other. "Okay," we say in unison.

We sit back in our seats, eating our chips and looking out the window. We watch as we go from the big city to smaller and smaller unfamiliar towns.

"Let's play a game!" Lucinda suggests.

"How about I spy? It's a good car game." Kacey says.

"Okay, sounds good. Erika, Destiny, are you playing?"

"Erika always wins at this game!" I say, looking at Erika, who is smirking back at me.

"I'm just a detail-oriented person," Erika says. "I'll start!" She looks out the window and then out of the windshield. "Okay, I spy, with my little eye, a refrigerator!"

We all search for the refrigerator. My first thought is to look for a billboard.

"Found it!" Kacey yells, pointing to an old white man wearing jean overalls, loading a stainless steel refrigerator into a moving truck. "Okay, my turn! I spy, with my little eye, red heels."

"Got it!" Erika shouts. I didn't even get a second to look. Erika points to a fairly tall woman wearing an all-red ensemble consisting of a belted long-sleeve blouse and a short skirt. The woman has big, curly red hair. I feel a wave of nostalgia sweep over me as I reminisce about the times Erika and I sat in my mom's backseat playing the game. "My turn again." Erika laughs. "Looks like I'm going to be going every other turn."

"Don't get too full of yourself now," I say

She looks at me, still smirking. "I spy, with my little eye, a bald man!"

I look, desperately searching for this bald guy.

"Hurry up! We're about to pass him!"

"Oh, right here!" Lucinda says, pointing out her window. A bald man with a long blonde beard and piercing blue eyes passes my window, holding a hammer in one hand and a for sale sign in the other.

"I'm so bad at this game," I say. "Lucinda found him, and she's driving."

"He just so happens to be going past my window," Lucinda explains. "My turn. I spy, with my little eye, a ladder."

"Found it!" Erika says quickly.

"Uh, again!" I say.

"Yep." Erika points to a ladder leaning on the side of a house. A woman with a big afro stands on the middle beam with a paintbrush. She and her entourage, who all have natural hair, are painting what looks like a mural. "My turn, again. I spy with my little eye something pink and white."

I am determined to get this one. I frantically search for the item. There is no way this game ends with me not scoring. I look through the windshield, my eyes searching the field. I then land upon a big, pretty pink and white bow. "Oh, I found it!" I say. I point to the bow with several women in front of it. A new shop, *Latasha's Hair & Nails*, is opening up. A woman with beautifully done bantu knots is holding scissors and cutting the ribbon as we drive by.

"Okay, I guess I get to pick," I say, finally proud that I found one of the items. I look around the small town, reading a few signs, until I see this beautiful building with remarkable architecture. The building has gorgeous white columns and a green dome on top. A gold spire twists out of the dome like a staircase, ending at a narrow, sharp point at the top. "I spy, with my little eye, something gold and sharp."

"Found it!" Lucinda says quickly.

"Already?" I ask.

She points to the stunning building. "Of course," she says. "That's our destination." She pulls up in the front. We all hop out, tossing our food bags in the recycling bin. We bypass the ramp and walk the many steps up to the building instead.

"Wow, it's like a mini White House," I say.

"That's the same thing I was thinking," Erika replies. "What is this place."

"You'll see," Lucinda and Kacey simultaneously say.

They open the doors for us. The place is crowded, and a sign, **Town Hall Meeting**, greets us at the entrance. We go to the four seats closest to us and listen to the woman presenting. The woman, who has her hair up in a ponytail, is wearing a canary yellow dress, which pairs perfectly with her dark skin.

"So, in conclusion," the woman says, "our reach with our messaging is already up from last quarter."

The audience claps as the woman walks off stage and sits in a chair. Another woman, older with gray hair and beautiful mahogany skin, approaches the podium.

"Thank you, Ms. Clark, for that wonderful news," she says sweetly. She opens a folder. "Now, I will reread the measures we must vote on. Remember, you have three days to vote. We're voting on a measure for birth control to be free and available to everyone." The audience erupts in loud applause. "We're voting on funding research for vertical gardening. We're also voting for candidates," she says, pointing to the group of diverse people sitting on stage behind her, "to lead our city to greatness."

I take my eyes off the woman on stage. Marcel was right about another thing: this isn't a sorority, and it's not all black. As I peer over the audience, I feel someone looking at me from the right. I turn, locking eyes with the only woman I wanted to see here. She waves at me, and I wave back.

"Is that..." Erika trails off.

"Aunt Vanessa," I say, still waving and probably smiling goofily.

"Now, most of these are expected to pass and are just formalities," the woman on stage continues. "We live in the USA, after all. Don't want to be accused of being a sovereign city." The crowd chuckles. "Nevertheless, the future looks bright as we expand this community. These recent graduates are the biggest class to date. Thanks to you, they all have places to stay and a place to learn, grow, and do good."

Erika and I look at each other, eyes wide. Lucinda grabs both of our hands, "Come on. I want to show you around the town."

"But, what about the people here?" I ask.

"Yes, do we get to meet them?" Erika chimed in.

Kacey holds the door open for us to exit and says, "We'll meet them and many others later at the social gathering. That is where all the littles across the country meet and learn more about the town." We follow Kiana and Kacey around the city. They show places from sanctuaries and vegan holistic centers to local television networks and dentist offices, all owned and operated by Grox. We even peek inside an art and history museum which tells the stories of activists worldwide.

The city has its own distinct architecture. Accessibility is built into the design. It is so clean here, and the people are friendly and community-focused. The fear of technology is absent as most jobs are automated. People work less, have time for leisure, and are more taken care of. I feel completely safe.

Between getting to know some residents and learning how to get my little sister, Laila, to this magical place, I forget to ask one crucial question. I walk toward Lucinda, who is reading a billboard advertising a workshop on the meeting of racism, sexism, and speciesism. **Let's talk about the common denominator**, the subtitle of the sign reads.

"That workshop sounds interesting," I say, stepping beside her.

"I'm the lead panelist."

"Congrats! You have so much knowledge, and I am glad you're sharing it with others."

She nods her head. "I hope we can get to a point where activists can stop measuring oppression. Because that leads them to only fight for the group they think is most oppressed and downplaying others. Which gets us nowhere."

"We need to fight the root, right?"

She sighs. "We have black men who want to be liberated but also want dominance over women. Adults, treated as commodities at their workplace, come home and treat their children as possessions. People's morality pauses when it comes to nonhuman animals. Healthy, intelligent extroverts want to condemn the opposite to a life of hell. And a whole bunch of other shit. Honestly, I'm so tired."

"Thinking about all of that sounds tiring," I say.

She chuckles, "You know, I almost joined the Goddesses?"

"Nuh-uh," I shout, then instantly cover my mouth. "Tell me you're kidding."

"Nope."

She smiles and motions me to follow her. We arrive at a patch of land with a small playground and seating. Pocket parks are what they call them. We find a bench facing the lake.

"So, how... I mean," I stumble over my words. "You've really shocked me."

"Once upon a time, I thought it would be easier." Lucinda's voice breaks as she shakes her head. "And some aspects were." Lucinda wipes away tears. "Misplaced hatred was easy. It was easy to make the men in my community the target because of everything they do to us."

"You thought it would justify doing it right back, just like the Goddesses," I say.

"Exactly. They make me the target, so why should I feel bad about making them the target? But I quickly realized that I was doing nothing but aiding white supremacy. Trying to further oppress the oppressed does nada for my liberation."

Her hands are trembling. I put my arm around her and hold her hands until they steady. Her warm body comforts me enough to grasp her tighter. I can feel all of the tension releasing from both of us.

"But that femininity killed me," Lucinda continues. "I felt like I was performing all of the time. Trying to fit into this small ass box. Learning ballet and all of these classical dances. Girl, all I wanted to do was twerk."

We both throw our heads back and let out roaring laughter.

"I think that would have killed me, too," I say through my laughter.

"It was also hard to learn new information that would drastically change how I live my life. When I first met Grox, I tried to empty my mind of what they presented so I could continue to live life as I was. When I couldn't ignore their facts, I tried to make excuses, play oppression Olympics, the works. But I couldn't ignore it, and I am so glad I am now a Grox woman. I've grown so much."

"I'm glad you are, too," I say. "You've taught me so much and aided my growth."

We continue to cuddle on the bench, looking at the lake in front of us. Ducks honk and swim happily across the water. Behind them, a pair of swans embrace each other. Further in the distance, skyscrapers touch the clouds. A land that is not a part of this place, judging by the plastic surgery advertisement that hangs on the building.

I imagine being able to walk to places by myself. Enjoying my own company and the company of my sisters without worry. I envision Laila bypassing the emotional turmoil of unlearning by getting to grow up here.

"So," I begin, "what is the name of this city?"

A big smile comes across Lucinda's face. She points to a sign behind us, far in the distance, but I can barely read it.

"It's an amazing community, isn't it? I'll live here after this last semester of studying abroad, and I can't wait." Lucinda grabs her phone from her purse. She opens a map app and zooms in. The map doesn't have any names and is mostly terrain. "Now, you probably won't be able to search it on your maps as it isn't updated yet. But don't worry, you'll get all the information you need on getting here at the social tonight. But to answer your question, the city's name is Starfish."

"Starfish," I repeat.

Epilogue

Trixie hugs Destiny longer than she needs to.

"Girl, it's not like we are going to be separated forever," Destiny says. "Just meet me at the ice cream booth in thirty minutes."

"Okay," Trixie says, sniffling. Hopefully, Destiny can see how sad Trixie is and decides against splitting off. But she doesn't.

Trixie watches Destiny saunter down a dirt path until tall students block her view. Trixie looks at her map and decides to return to the Kousa table to chat with Marcel for a little bit. Or who she affectionately now calls Marc.

Trixie pouts her lips, watching Marc as he is in a deep conversation with a beautiful, thick black woman. Is he cheating on Destiny? Trixie thinks to herself. *Is he cheating on me?* She takes it upon herself to protect her best friend and herself by confronting Marc about his wrongdoings.

"Who is this?" Trixie asks sternly.

"Hey," Marc says. His friendly smile tells Trixie that his conversation with this woman is strictly platonic. "This is Jenn."

Trixie turns to Jenn and smiles, forgetting to say anything. She looks down at Jenn's large posterior and imagines squeezing it. She wonders how firm it is. She wonders if it is smooth. She wonders how it will taste.

"Umm," Marc says. "Jenn, this is Trixie. My girlfriend's roommate."

"Nice to meet you, Trixie," Jenn says. Jenn shakes Trixie's hand, then turns to Marc and asks, "Is your girlfriend also white?"

"Nah, she's black," Marc says. "You'll be proud of me. She's not what I typically date. She is going to be a Qousa woman."

"Nice! Hopefully, Mike can take a few cues from you," Jenn says, winking at the man standing next to Marc, whom Trixie just now noticed. "Maybe she'll be my little."

"I'm also rushing Qousa," Trixie butts in.

"Aight, I see you, white girl," Jenn says.

"Thanks," Trixie says. "Marc, can I talk to you for a minute?"

"New nickname?" Jenn asks.

"Nah," Marc says. "I'll be back."

Marc and Trixie walk a few feet away, mean-mugging the Goddesses as they pass their table. Marc violently turns around when they are at a safe distance.

"What the hell are you doing?" he whispers. His eyebrows furrow, and he is biting his bottom lip.

"I thought that we could spend some time together since I was finally able to ditch Destiny," Trixie says, rolling her eyes. "That girl is so clingy."

"This is a down-low thing," Marc says. "We can't be out here in public like this."

Marc storms back to the Kousa table, leaving Trixie to soak in his words.

Trixie decides that Marc really didn't mean what he said. She brushes it off and decides to explore some of the clubs at the Activities Fair. A table with large balloon cocks and pussy pillows catches her eye.

Trixie beelines to the table, digs in her pocket, and slaps a five-dollar bill down. "What is this club? I need to join it now!"

The woman behind the booth laughs. "It's free," the woman says. "Put your money away."

Trixie rolls her eyes while putting the five-dollar bill back in her pocket. The woman behind the booth obviously doesn't understand her sense of humor.

"This is a sex-positive club that..." the woman drags on and on about sex.

Trixie looks at the table and spots a VHS. "What's that?"

"Oh, it is a movie about pegging," the woman answers. The woman giggles. "I brought it myself to put on the table since I'm the only one manning it today. Or should I say womanning it?"

The woman laughs. Trixie doesn't.

The woman gathers herself. "Anyway, I'm trying to build up the courage to present the idea of showing this movie to my club."

"I'll do it," Trixie says.

"Do what? Help me build up courage?"

"No," Trixie says. "I'll present the movie. Trixie grabs the movie and reads the title, **Bend Over Boyfriend**. "I'll just need to take this for research purposes."

Trixie starts to walk off, but the woman grabs Trixie's arm.

"You can't take that," the woman says. "It is my only copy, and it was tough to find."

"Fine," Trixie says, placing the VHS back on the table.

Trixie grabs one of the pens to take down information about the VHS tape. Her map is the perfect thing to write it on. She decides that the title is way too long, and she isn't going to write all of that. **BOB**, she writes, placing a star next to it. Vague, but only one person needs to know what it means: Trixie. She writes down a couple of notable names and draws a line underneath.

She's about to write down a few names she wants to watch this video with but pauses for privacy's sake. The booth woman's eyes have been glued to Trixie's map since she started writing.

"Do you mind if I take this pen," Trixie asks.

"It's all yours," the woman says. "Take this pamphlet as well."

Trixie grabs the pamphlet and smiles at the woman. The paper is thick, firm, and smooth. Perfect for writing on top of. She walks away, placing her map on top of the pamphlet. She writes down her first name: Marc. The obvious choice. She then writes down two names that surprise her: Mike and Jenn. *Maybe I am a little bisexual*, she thinks to herself.

She holds her map out and looks at it excitedly. She is proud of her plans for the future. She brings the map to her face, looking at the names again. She makes a mental note to slow down when writing in the future because she can barely make out these names. Then again, only one person needs to know what is written: Trixie.

She kisses the map and skips until she comes to another table.

She doesn't introduce herself to anyone at the table. Instead, she eavesdrops on the conversation.

"Stars represent a lot," the tall woman with the curly updo states. "We are actually trying to redo our logo to include a starfish instead."

"Why a starfish?" Trixie asks.

The woman spins her head around to look at Trixie. "Hi," the woman says. "I'm Deidra."

"Nice to meet you Deidra. I am Trixie."

"So, a starfish," Deidra says, making eye contact with each woman surrounding the table. "A starfish is an awesome being with the power to regenerate."

The women's mouths drop in awe. Trixie is also in awe but expresses her astonishment slightly more animatedly. She bulges her head forward, widens her eyes, opens her mouth, and expands her arms as far as possible. She then remembers that she is holding her map, and her map has a list that she doesn't want anyone to see yet. So, she retracts her arms but keeps her head in the same position.

Deidra nods at the women's expressions satisfyingly. She continues to talk about the starfish. "So, when a starfish loses a limb, they can grow it back. Sometimes, they can regrow their entire bodies."

The women look at each other in shock.

"Wow," one woman says. "I learned about regenerative creatures in school but never knew they could regrow their entire bodies."

"That's awesome," Trixie says.

"It is," Deidra says with a smile. "So once they regrow this limb that they lost, it is completely different from the rest of the body."

"Ooh, Ooh," Trixie says, raising her hand and jumping up and down. "I learned this from my pet lizard. My brother told me that their tails grow back. We disagreed, so we made a bet. Little scientist me," Trixie says, patting her chest proudly, "decides to cut off my lizard's tail. And what do you know? It grew back, but it looked like he stole a tail from another lizard."

Silence.

"I always joked with my little brother," Trixie continues, "that he lost the bet because he couldn't prove that the tail actually belonged to our pet lizard."

Still silence, and Deidra looks visibly disgusted.

Trixie shrugs her shoulders. *No one ever gets her humor.*

"Anyway," Deidra continues. "That different little limb is what we focus on. You can unlearn something, put the more ethical actions in its place, and still be you."

"Nice," Trixie says.

"So we have these beautiful, complex, sentient beings called starfish, which happens to be the current shape of our logo. By the end of next year, our logo will be a starfish and have all of the symbolization of our current logo."

"Yeah, logos are supposed to be animals anyway. Why just have a plain-ass star?" Trixie asks.

Deidra rolls her eyes. She reaches behind the table and pulls up a poster, unveiling the new logo. Or at least a working one. A drawing of a starfish surrounded by swirls is on the poster's left. The cursive words next to the starfish read, **STARFISH, THE SHAPE OF DREAMS AND GUIDANCE WITH THE ABILITY TO START ANEW.**

The women, including Trixie, clap as Deidra holds the poster in the air.

Trixie walks off to meet back up with Destiny, but she returns to the starfish table to grab a pamphlet.

"G. R. O. X," Trixie spells out. She has no clue what this is. *If I can't pronounce it, then I can't consume it,* she thinks to herself, a common phrase she uses. She goes back and forth between putting the pamphlet back on the table or keeping it. She ultimately decides to keep it. She walks a couple of feet from the table and looks for the ice cream booth. She can still hear Deidra's voice—though soft— behind her.

"Don't forget to rush our sorority this fall!" Deidra says. "And you can sign up for our newsletter to stay up to date on deadlines, projects, events... books."

About the Author

Doeliza is a novelist from St. Louis, Missouri, who has traveled and lived in several countries. A self-declared lifelong learner, she likes to share her knowledge and experience through her art. The Shape of New Beginnings is her debut novel.

Her website is www.doeliza.com

Hey,

Thanks for reading! Please consider leaving a review. I am excited to see your feedback.

Until next time,

Doeliza

www.ingramcontent.com/pod-product-compliance
Lightning Source LLC
Chambersburg PA
CBHW061801190726
48289CB00007B/2025